City N

A novel

Olga Korol

CROWN|PUBLISHER

First Edition

Publisher's note: *City N* is a work of fiction. Names, characters, places, and incidents are the product of the author's imagination, and any resemblance to actual persons, living or dead, business establishments, events, or locales is entirely coincidental.

Library of Congress Cataloging-in-Publication Data

Korol, Olga.
City N : a novel / Olga Korol. – 1st ed.
p.   cm.

ISBN 978-0-9893124-1-7 (paperback)
ISBN 978-0-9893124-2-4 (hardcover)
ISBN 978-0-9893124-0-0 (eBook)

1. Family – Grandparent and Child – Brothers – Fiction. 2. Russia – Leningrad / Saint Petersburg – Siberia – Fiction. 3. Social Life and Custom – 20th century – Humor – Fiction. I. Title.

Artist of cover painting © by Anatoly Kostovsky
Cover & book design by Jiri Petrek

Published by Crown Publisher
For information regarding special discounts for bulk purchase, please contact Crown Publisher at www.crownpublisher.com or books@crownpublisher.com

www.KorolOlga.com
www.CityNnovel.com

Printed in the United States of America

From the author:
If you ask me: "Is this tale truthful?" I will say: "Yes."
If you ask me: "Is this tale fictional?" I will say: "Yes."
You decide...

City N

Prologue

In a small auxiliary room of the People's Commissariat for Internal Affairs, located in a semi-basement, three agents headed by an unshaven man were sitting on the floor around a wooden beer crate and gambling at cards. Sitting among clouds of cigarette smoke with concentrated faces, they exchanged words every now and again. Sipping hot tea from the mugs standing on the floor at their feet, next to their revolvers, they seemed to have forgotten about everything in the world, savoring their game. Forgotten that it was now midnight in Leningrad*, and that their wives and children could be awake and worrying, awaiting their speedy return from dangerous night service, delighting in their valor and their devotion to the motherland.

For them, only one thing was important on that rainy night in the fall of 1937: whose yet unknown fate it was laying there on the misshapen wooden boards of the crate, lost in a game of cards. And it would have been impossible

---

* In 1991 city was renamed to Saint Petersburg

to imagine a more exciting game, one that would simultaneously kill time and squarely carry out their commander's order regarding the arrest and resettlement of new, free laborers needed by the enormous nation.

First, the players selected three districts in the city, and after the first hand was dealt, everyone knew that the lot had fallen on Vasilevsky Island. Then, streets were used as bets, and each of the three participants amused himself with the hope of making his chosen street the subject of tonight's raid. By two o'clock in the morning, they already knew the house number, and when the cards were dealt for the last time, it was time for the most soulful event. The players named their favorite numbers, usually personally significant ones, such as the birthdays of children, wives, and mothers. These digits would become someone's fate, indicating the apartment number.

No one heard a black, brilliantly polished car drive into the courtyard of a five-story building in Vasilevsky at three o'clock at night. A tarpaulin-covered truck followed the car. The very next moment, three men walked up to the second floor noisily and stopped in front of a door painted dark green, leading to apartment #5. The unshaven man in front, dressed in a heavy leather coat, rang the doorbell. The doorbell would not stop ringing until a sleepy man appeared on the doorstep, wearing pajamas and a burgundy robe thrown casually over his shoulders. He said something indignantly and then stepped back in confusion, pressed inside by the unknown men entering the apartment.

The unshaven man entered first in a businesslike fashion and announced proudly that the family had been chosen for the great honor of joining numerous other citizens of the great nation for resettlement in Siberia. After giving the residents thirty minutes to gather their belongings, two of the men sat down on the sofa in the living room, watching their reaction. As for the unshaven man, he walked out on the staircase landing and lit up a cigarette.

Horrified by what had transpired, the inhabitants of the apartment, Clement and Claudia Voronov, and their children – six-year old daughter Anya and fourteen-year old son Alexander – began to dash back and forth, exchanging glances and looking to each other for assistance.

Afterwards, everything resembled a nightmare, or perhaps a novel penned by a writer's ruthless hand. Anya was crying, trying to pack her things into a small brown travel bag at her mother's request. When she was done, she stood in the living room, leaning against a round dining table, looking over the uninvited night guests, who were lounging indifferently on the sofa. Not understanding a thing but ready to leave, she was holding the travel bag in one hand and hugging a violin – a Christmas gift from her parents. Claudia, shedding silent tears, was throwing warm clothes, photographs, and anything else that could be useful on the long road into a large suitcase.

Alexander pulled his father by the hand into his bedroom and begged him hysterically to do something, threatening that he would not go anywhere and refusing to participate in the packing. Clement, for his part, was pleading with his son to be sensible, accept the mysterious events of fate, and help his mother in this difficult time.

The teenager walked unhurriedly to the dresser. He opened a wooden box standing on it, took out a pocket watch on a long chain that he had gotten last Christmas, and hid it in his pocket. Then he approached his mother and gave her a firm hug. Unable to foresee her son's intentions, Claudia pushed him aside with a casual motion and asked him to hurry and help his sister. Then, glancing round as if recalling something very important, she rushed suddenly into the hall. She placed a chair in a corner beneath a small icon-lamp hanging from the ceiling, got up on it, and began to pull on the lamp with all her strength, tearing out the nail attaching the lamp to the ceiling. The oil from the lamp spilled and splashed around, leaving greasy stains on the wall, on the floor, and on her trembling hands. The packing time expired, and they were ordered to move out.

A finely written sheet of paper with a round seal appeared on the oval table in the front hall. The men pointed to the official document and demanded that Clement come and sign it immediately to signify his consent to voluntary resettlement to Siberia and the transfer of all his property and his apartment to the state.

"Look at these bourgeois living in a three-room apartment when the working man has nowhere to lay his head," strangers were saying to each other.

Glancing furtively at Claudia, Clement silently picked up the pen, sighed heavily, and signed without reading.

On the landing, the unshaven man was still smoking, apparently without taking a large part in the proceedings. And when Anya, who was walking in front, passed by him, he gestured suddenly at her violin in a friendly fashion and said:

"Look at that, so little and you can already play. Can I have a look?" When the trusting girl handed him the instrument, the unshaven man lifted it up and fitted it carefully to his shoulder. He plucked the strings, emitting a flat sound, and then took a sudden swing and slammed the violin on the staircase with all his might. And when the violin, broken in half, froze in his hands, he leaned over the railing, tossed the smashed instrument down, and said:

"You won't be needing the violin anymore. You must grow up a real member of the Komsomol, and members of the Komsomol only play brass and drums."

Anya began to cry. As for Alexander, he slipped ahead and pushed the unshaven man in the chest with all his strength, using both hands. And when the latter swayed and crouched, trying to stay on his feet, the teenager darted down the staircase, leaping over several steps. The unshaven man pulled out his revolver, aiming at the fugitive, while Clement grabbed his arm and begged him not to shoot. With the revolver raised high above his head, muttering that he would "catch him and shoot him like a dog," the unshaven man gave chase, throwing off his long coat as he ran.

At five in the morning in the railway station, the settlers were being loaded into freight cars, with small signs on each car indicating the destination: the Urals, Kazakhstan, and Siberia. Those who had come to say goodbye thronged behind the guards' shoulders, shouting the names of their relatives and throwing them bundles of food and clothing. Wailing could be heard here and there. Dank Leningrad weather wept for the departing settlers with an unceasing drizzle of rain and snow, adding even more tragic color to the proceedings.

Alexander's face flashed in the crowd; he kept dashing back and forth between the last four cars until he finally saw Anya's face, and then his parents. He got as close to them as he could, shouting his sister's name, trying to get them to notice him in the noise and confusion.

The loading continued, and Alexander shouted in vain, watching his family walk up the wooden ramp and vanish from view. Then he rushed towards a guard and begged him for permission to board the train, shouting loudly that he, too, had been chosen for the "holy mission" of resettlement to Siberia. Taken aback, the guard stared at the teenager, unsure of how to reply. The crowd around them quieted down in anticipation of the consequences. The settlers heard his shouts and turned their heads towards him, stopping in their tracks for a moment to try and get a better look at the madman who wanted to board the train of his own free will.

"Please let me!" Alexander pleaded.

"Maybe next time, kid. There are no free spots," the guard called out half-jokingly, pushing the boy back with the butt of his rifle.

The boy had time to grasp a tall, thin settler by the arm and ask him to tell his parents that he was alive, and that he would definitely find them. The heavy wooden door closed. A guard bolted it shut, attached a small red flag to the barrel of his rifle, and raised it as a sign of readiness. And when similar red flags appeared in silence by all the cars, the train started.

Inside the freight car, which had been adapted to carry people, there was barely room to stand. Those who had been fortunate enough to find spots on the wooden bunks lay there with their entire families, afraid to move. The Voronov family settled on their large suitcase on the floor. Claudia sat hugging Anya, her face buried in the girl's shoulder. Clement stood nearby, leaning against the wall of the car, swaying in rhythm with the train as it picked up speed. He pricked up his ears when he heard someone calling his name. Soon, a male voice repeated his name, and Clement saw a tall man making his way through the people sitting on the floor, repeating:

"Comrade Voronov, I have news for you…"

Swaying and leaning his entire body forward, Clement asked:

"News? Would you be so kind, from whom?"

"Your son, Alexander. He is alive, and he asked me to tell you that he will definitely find you." Claudia burst into tears when she heard the news, while Clement sat down next to her, repeating:

"You see, he is alive, he is alive, he is free... he is free, he came to see us off, he..." Without finishing, Clement covered his face with his hands.

The settlers talked quietly, trying to get to know each other and realizing the full seriousness of the two-week journey. After the train was sorted in Moscow and the cars were separated according to destination, train wheels began knocking hurriedly throughout the enormous country in various directions, measuring off thousands upon thousands of kilometers, delivering their passengers towards their new "joyous future..."

Alexander wandered the streets restlessly all day and was completely drenched. For the first time, he felt resentment and hatred towards his home city, trying to find some sort of explanation for what had happened.

In the evening, he appeared on his street and, out of habit, forgetting momentarily about what had transpired, ran up lightly to the second floor. He stopped and froze in front of the door of his home, which had been sealed by the authorities, bearing the inscription: "Property of the NKVD." The door of the flat across the hall opened, and an old lady called to him, peeking carefully from side to side:

"Come in, Alexander, warm yourself up."

She led him into the kitchen, drew the curtains shut, and began to lament:

"I always loved your parents, but I greatly pity Anya."

"Why are you lamenting as if they are dead? They're alive, after all," the teenager said, trying to calm both her and himself.

After giving him a drink of hot tea and some food, the old woman offered him to stay the night, but only until the morning. She lived with her granddaughter Alona, his classmate. The only thing he knew about them was that Alona's parents had died during the establishment of Soviet power somewhere in the south of Russia. Also that she was the pride of their school, an honored student and a devoted member of the Komsomol*. For this reason, he and Alona never spoke and even avoided each other. The girl came into the kitchen, gave him a haughty glance, and said:

"See, Voronov? The truth will always come to light."

"What truth are you talking about, Alona?" Alexander asked, taken aback.

"Your father used to serve in the White Army, while mine gave his life for the Red."

"Alona, for God's sake," the old woman implored.

"How can you talk about some kind of God, Grandma? You should be an atheist, like me," she said proudly, tossing her long braid over her shoulder. "And he's got no business being here. You can't band together with enemies of the people. Here you are, giving him tea, and he is not even in the Komsomol."

Alexander was staring at her as if he were seeing her for the first time, while she sat down at the table across from him and continued:

"They will catch you anyway. Tomorrow, the entire school will be talking about you, traitor. Playing your little

---

* An organization for young people from age of 14 in the Soviet Union

violin." She got up abruptly and, casting a contemptuous glance at Alexander, left the kitchen with the words: "Oh, Grandma, Grandma!" and slammed the door of her room defiantly.

The old woman calmed him down and asked him not to pay attention to what her granddaughter had said; complaining that she was too trusting and believed everything they taught her over at that Komsomol. She offered him to sleep in her room on the couch, but Alexander refused, saying that he could sleep on the floor in the kitchen, or, better yet, by the front door. The mistress of the house did not object; she brought him a quilted blanket and wished him good night.

He settled in by the door in the front hall. For some reason, he thought that Alona could leave the apartment at night and report him.

Alexander lay on one side of the blanket and covered himself with the other, trying to stay warm somehow. There was a draft blowing from under the door. He lay there, staring into the darkness, until several trucks drove into the courtyard at around ten o'clock in the evening. Brakes screeching, they stopped by his entrance. Dashing to the kitchen window and seeing, in the glow of a streetlight, the group of people that had been in his apartment the previous night; he froze, not knowing what to do. Hearing a noise, Alona appeared in the kitchen, looked outside, and said:

"See? Now we are going to have trouble thanks to you. Oh, Grandma, Grandma!" she exclaimed, glancing at the pale Alexander.

They heard the men walk inside in their heavy boots and stop at their landing. Alona stood holding her breath, listening tensely to what was happening behind the door.

"You are lucky, Voronov. They aren't here for us," she said after a brief pause.

Scuffling, the stamping of boots and the sound of moving furniture came from behind the door.

Walking up to the door on tiptoes and peeking through the peephole, Alona stepped back suddenly and whispered:

"I think you'd like to see this."

Alexander leaned to the small hole in the door and saw quite a sight... The all too familiar unshaven man was walking out of his former apartment, carefully holding a large mirror in front of him. People walked in and left carrying furniture, kitchen utensils, and everything else that Alexander could have considered memories of his past. By twelve, the apartment was empty, and the three fully loaded trucks drove out of the courtyard.

When everything around him sank back into silence, Alexander crossed the landing quietly and, pushing on the unlocked door, walked into the apartment. Empty, lit by streetlights alone, it seemed even more spacious to him now. Entering his former living room, he sat down on the floor by the tiled furnace, its surface covered by multi-colored pieces of tile and crowned with two molded angels beneath the ceiling. His former abode consisted of three bedrooms, a living room, a front hall, and a spacious kitchen where the family would often sit late into the night. Overcome with exhaustion, having cried out all his tears during the day, he sat down and leaned his cheek against the rough surface of the furnace. He was even thinking he felt incredible warmth streaming from it. He sat like that for a long time, his head thrown back, until he fell asleep.

He woke up from the sound of a hammer. Alexander gazed in surprise at the familiar bearded janitor, who was nailing something to the door of his parents' former bed-room.

"Sorry, buddy," the janitor said to him. "That's my job, move people in... move people out... You know you shouldn't be here."

"Whom are you moving in?" the boy inquired.

"Workers. There, the first apartment's ready," the janitor said, pointing at the small square board nailed to the door, bearing the number one.

Alexander wandered aimlessly through the streets for almost two months, spending the nights in basements and attics. Once, on a rainy November noon, as he sat on the granite steps of the Fontanka river embankment, he saw a young man dressed in clothing typically worn by revolu-tionaries. High boots with breeches tucked inside them, a belt with a shiny star over his clothes, and a hat with earflaps on his head, with a smaller star. Stopping at the top step, the young man began to cough heavily; then, after a pause, he walked quickly down, leaned over to scoop the water from the river with both hands, and began to drink. Then, turning to the watching Alexander, he asked:

"Waiting for someone?"

Alexander shook his head.

The stranger's face became inspired, and color appeared on his cheeks; he walked up to Alexander, sitting by the wall, and introduced himself unexpectedly:

"Grigoriy," the stranger said, extending his hand. "Grigoriy Petrovich," he repeated firmly.

Raising himself a little, Alexander shook the icy hand hesitantly, realizing the full absurdity of the situation.

Grigoriy was tormented by thirst, and, sitting down once again on the lower step and scooping the water with his hands, he continued to drink.

"I saw a drowned man float by in this river yesterday," Alexander warned him.

Throwing back his head, Grigoriy burst out in laughter.

"I could drink straight from the hands of a drowned man, and I know that nothing would happen to me." He began coughing again, and it was difficult for him to stop. The next moment, he turned and walked back up the steps, saying:

"You can come with me if you want."

Alexander followed him obediently, so sweet and welcoming was this invitation.

The eighteen-year old fighter for truth, Grigoriy Petrovich Kvas, was the first tenant in an apartment that had just been prepared for settlement on the Petrograd side.

The room he occupied looked rather spacious when half-empty, with a thick mattress lying in the corner, a small writing desk, and numerous newspapers scattered all over the place. The dwelling was crowned with a high ceiling with molded images of three cupids around a crystal chandelier. An enormous window looking out on the courtyard filled the room with light.

Soon they were sitting on the mattress, stretching out their legs on the parquet floor, trying to warm up as they drank tea from aluminum mugs and ate small pieces of rye bread with thin strips of cheese on top.

Reared on big ideas, Grigoriy came to Leningrad from a distant city in the Urals in order to take part, as he put it, in the "Creation of History." He firmly believed that the revolution of 1917 and the subsequent civil war were absolutely necessary. They were necessary because they had given him enough hope to learn, work, and be a free citizen, a master of his nation. "We are good people," he said proudly. "We took from the rich and gave to the poor.

Take this fact, for example: this apartment used to belong to one family, and now four families will live here. We know how to share and how to apportion." Alexander listened to his new companion silently, hopelessly condemned, for the moment, to his company alone.

As for Grigoriy, he was a walking embodiment of the ideals of his government, and he knew all the party statutes by heart. Every day he repeated that he would soon get a new job in the department to combat homelessness, a position of great importance and responsibility.

"So that's why you took me in?" Alexander asked.

"That's why," Grigoriy replied happily. "You have to start somewhere. So you'll be the first of my homeless."

That night, tormented by his cough, Grigoriy could not sleep. The next day, he looked pale and tired; the color visible in his cheeks the previous day disappeared and was replaced by dark circles under his eyes.

"I warned you not to drink the water from the river," Alexander said, concerned. A week later, Grigoriy's condition worsened sharply, and he admitted that he suffered from tuberculosis. When asked about his relatives, he said that he had no close family except for the party.

"Ah!" he said pensively one day. "I won't be around to see true socialism, but you; you can carry on my work."

"I cannot," Alexander said.

Having gained considerable sympathy for this youthful representative of the new regime and feeling that the sympathy was mutual, Alexander did not wish to conceal the truth and told him about what happened two months ago. After listening to him, Grigoriy was taken aback:

"So I took in an enemy of the people?" he said questioningly.

"Do you want me to leave?" Alexander asked.

"No, I want you to stay, I... I don't want to be alone."

His strength was leaving him rapidly, and Alexander, forgetting about personal worries for the moment, made every effort to help somehow. He would sit with Grigoriy at night, covering him with a warm blanket. He would give him hot tea, and he even learned to make buckwheat soup, soaking pieces of crackers in it and spoon-feeding it to the sick man patiently. They barely spoke, but once Grigoriy asked him worriedly all of a sudden:

"Alexander, what are you going to do?"

"I don't know. Honestly, I don't know."

"They're going to catch you, I know it. And when that happens, you'll be sent to a penal colony or worse... You can't end your life as a stray dog. Promise me something," Grigoriy said insistently, motioning for him to sit closer, and then spoke to him for a long time about something... until he fell back on his pillow in exhaustion, repeating over and over:

"You have to do what I asked, you must. Promise me. I beg you, you must do it." Finally, Alexander nodded in obedience.

Four days later, Grigoriy was no more. He lay on the mattress wearing a clean shirt and his shoes polished to a shine by Alexander. He lay there, a young man who did not get a chance to fulfill his hopes. Alexander summoned the janitor, who arrived, called a special service, and stood leaning against the window in anticipation of their arrival. He was holding the dead man's papers in his hands, looking at them from every possible angle and asking:

"What does it say? Haven't learned to read yet?"

"It says," the teenager said in a trembling voice, "it says: Alexander Clementievich Voronov, and the year and place of birth."

"Young, oh how young. I see you are new here. What's your name?"

"Grigoriy," he replied in a hollow voice.

"And what's his relationship to you?"

"He was a relative, he came to visit me."

Soon, two servicemen appeared. They loaded the body on a stretcher with indifference, took the dead man's birth certificate from the janitor's hands, and headed out. The teenager started to cry.

"Where will you bury him?" he asked.

"In a good spot, on Smolensky," came the reply.

"He was a devoted member of the Komsomol," the teenager said, weeping. "And I'd really like to ask you to give him a monument with a star."

"That's popular now, stars instead of crosses. Very well, star it is," the response came from somewhere on the staircase landing, through the open apartment door.

City N

An enormous sun rose, like a beast, over Siberia. Its color was more reminiscent of sunset than sunrise. Rolling out slowly from beyond the Sayansky Mountains, it climbed higher and higher, and, for a moment, it seemed as though it had dominion over all: both the boundless taiga and City N, scattered carelessly across two banks of a river, with crooked, dusty streets, uneven sidewalks, and wooden houses fused into the ground.

Sleepy people emerged mechanically from their dwellings and, covering their faces with their palms, looked at this orange beast and kept saying that today would be a very hot day, just as it should be in mid-June in Siberia.

There came a moment when the sun was literally flooding everything with its light; merging with the sky, it froze at the zenith, an unmoving point, gazing from on high at the military unit and its entire arsenal, rusting in the soaking rain and snow. Its guns and tanks were not destined to make a single shot. Spreading its rays lazily, the sun glided among the buildings, illuminating the city's only bank and the railway station – a window into the greater world –

crawling into every yard, seeping into every house, warming all life big and small in City N, a place unmarked on any map.

Such was the work of the sun: "Shine always! Shine everywhere!" As per the slogan put up above the local government house. So it shone, spilling tons of warmth onto the downcast shoulders and heads of passers-by, scattering the reflections of its sunbeams with particular love on the wooden floor of house #17 on Third Proletarian Street, the occasional residence of the brothers Sanya and Fedya Vetkin.

Slogans about the beautiful, bright future were hung everywhere. Over the recreation centers, at the intersections, and even over the tuberculosis hospital there hung an enormous poster with the words: "Man is the forger of his own happiness." At the railway station, a sign shouted at the visitors: "Be faithful to Lenin's work! Finish the five-year plan of 1976 ahead of schedule!" Trains full of young people recruited to build new thoroughfares sped through the railway station. Songs, laughter, and the sounds of accordions rang out through the open windows of the train cars, lingering in the air and shattering over the clanging wheels of the departing train. "If so many young people are headed to build this 'bright future,'" mused the inhabitants of City N, "it means that all those comrades, the party leaders are running things well."

All of this filled the lives of Sanya, Fedya, and all the other exiled and resettled citizens of City N. Parades and slogans, public festivities on the Ut River during the week before Lent. Public discussions if someone were to go on a drinking binge, fail to appear for work, or, worse yet, leave his wife and children. Such a scoundrel would first be summoned to a general meeting with discussions and explanations, and if that did not help, threats and dismissal from work would follow. "The family is the basic cell of the state!" was the slogan of the meeting.

And of course, there was the biggest truth, which every citizen had to remember, even if woken in the middle of the night: "Learning is light, ignorance is darkness!" So everyday life passed in the pursuit of this mysterious light through various schoolbook truths, learned by rote:

"Russia is the strongest and most just nation in the world, for everyone in it is equal. The first man in space was Russian. Capitalism has failed to justify itself in Western nations, particularly in America, where man can shamelessly exploit another man's labor." The foreign order had a simple definition: "rotten capitalism."

It would seem that, surrounded by all these slogans and propaganda, the younger generation would grow into loyal defenders of the homeland or first-rate producers who worked two full shifts a day. But, in reality, the inhabitants of City N could be divided into several categories: businesslike, honest, and a third one...

The businesslike people were those who listened carefully to the authorities and attended all the public meetings as dutifully as if they were going to confession, but, under the guise of truth, even as they flaunted their active involvement, they made off from their workplaces with what they could. The confectioner would steal chocolate. The baking factory employees would steal flour and sugar. Products from the beer brewery could be traded for other goods or sold on the black market. They stole, sold, and bartered, risking prison.

The honest people were those who genuinely believed in building "a brighter future." They knew all the agitprop songs by heart and walked at the front of every parade, carrying the pictures of party leaders high above their heads like the relics of saints. Such people would not accept a piece of bread stolen from the state even if they were dying of hunger. These honest people therefore became the primary engine and conscience of the great nation.

As for the third category, it consisted of people – and there remained fewer and fewer of them – who, in the depth of their hearts longed for their real homes and lands, and the eternal question: "Why?" plowed through their weary minds. They mingled with society, participating with detachment in all that was going on, but in their souls they never made peace with someone's order that had changed their lives forever.

The Vetkin family belonged to this third category. They occupied half of house #17 on Third Proletarian Street, numbering five people. The lawful residents of the thirty-five square meter space consisted of Claudia, her daughter Anna, and Anna's sick husband Ivan, a disabled Patriotic War veteran, the father of teenage brothers Sanya and Fedya Vetkin.

Anna worked dutifully as a doctor at the local clinic and practically supported the entire family. Once, the chief of the clinic called her into his office and, offering her a seat, wondered:

"Citizen Vetkina, why haven't you joined the party yet? Your salary would increase, and your character reference would be better as well."

"Please, Comrade," she said, shy as a freshman. "I am not worthy of such a pious organization, plus my children are growing up. I don't have any time for social work."

"How can you not have time for the most important things? Find time!" the chief demanded.

Months flew by, but she still could not find the time, so

Doctor Vetkina was transferred from a resident position to field physician. And the journeys she had to make were long and distant to faraway settlements in the north of the region, leaving her sons, her sick husband, and her mother for long months. Every now and again, when she would come back for a couple of weeks, she would say to Claudia:

"Oh Mama, what will happen to the kids? Maybe I should have joined that bandit organization after all."

"We should be thankful, they could have disqualified you entirely," the father would comment, joining the conversation.

He suffered from constant headaches after numerous injuries on the battlefield, and since his disability payments were meager, he also moonlighted sometimes, however he could. The brothers did not understand much, explaining to themselves that it was just their mother's job, to help people, since she had to disappear for long months in distant settlements to immunize and treat patients.

And when it came time for Sanya and, soon after, Fedya, to attend first grade, they were deemed, as children from a destitute family, unable to remain in the care of their grandmother Claudia and their physically disabled father, and assigned by the humane government to an orphanage named after Lenin as visiting students. They were given the right to live and study there, at the expense of the state, for the six long winter months, and then to return in the spring to Proletarian Street and attend the school daily, using public transportation.

This situation led to general resentment from the children who were doomed to spend all of their time on this state-owned territory. The territory was located on a mountain, surrounded by a rather tall fence, which separated it from the outside world and from the unpleasant proximity of two hospitals – one for infectious illnesses and one for skin diseases – as well as the city clinic and the morgue.

A two-story wooden school, painted dark brown, towered above the uneven fence. The road, creeping over a bridge and up the mountain, split in two when it reached this tall fence. The left branch curved in an arc towards the city cemetery, while the right turned into the Moscow highway, along which, people said, it was possible to walk all the way to Moscow. Only this journey would take a year and six months, and no one ever wondered where such a precise time was obtained.

Next to the school was a pair of two-story brick dormitories, one for younger children, inhabited by those attending grades one through five, and one for older children, for grades six through the final grade, ten. Obviously, the heart of both buildings was the dining hall. It was a separate one-story building, also made of wood, plain and not attracting much attention, but it became a most important object in the lives of the young occupants of this space. On the front door of the dining hall was a slogan, well known to each student: "He, who does not work, does not eat!"

The principal made a habit of appearing suddenly in the doorway, jabbing his index finger at the words, and asking the students:

"You! Did you work today?"

"I did," came the timid response.

"What did you do?" the principal demanded, making a show of it.

"I got a B," said the sniveling voice from below.

"Then come in! And you, did you work today?" the principal continued. And even on winter days, he would not tire of standing in the doors and teaching the students about the reality of life with object lessons. Every now and again, someone would hesitate to reply and be deprived of the state-assigned rations.

A water pump stood not far from the dining hall, in case the city water was shut off, and further on, there was a storehouse with clothes and food. And, were it not for an apple orchard that added some color and freshness in the spring and summer, and were it not for the golden balls of African flowers scattered on flowerbeds, then the orphanage would have seemed more like a final resting place than a beginning of bustling life.

The city where Sanya and Fedya Vetkin were born and lived sprawled on the two banks of the Ut River. Beginning its journey as a small stream somewhere in the Sayansky Mountains, the river became deep and capricious as it flowed through City N. Small ships and fishermen's boats sailed on it. Every spring, when the ice broke up, a fierce battle ensued between the river and the bridge. The river kept threatening to destroy the old, creaky bridge, but the bridge resisted and kept on standing. A wooden construction, like most things in town, it rested on eight stone piles shaped like Egyptian pyramids. It was rather broad and had sidewalks on each side.

The brothers were standing in the middle of the bridge, leaning over the railing and exposing their suntanned faces to the gusts of wind that cooled them pleasantly as the June heat poured down from the sky. Fedya, a fair-haired twelve-year old youth, smiling and restless, and Sanya, pensive and attentive, a year older than his brother and therefore his exact opposite.

They silently watched the fishermen in their high rubber boots, knee-deep in the icy water. The fishermen communicated through signs, trying not to scare off their quarry. Grasping the railing with both hands and leaning back,

Fedya broke the silence:

"Sanya, do you know why Grandma Claudia runs to church on Sundays?"

"They sing there."

"Do they have a choir there or something?"

"No, their God lives there, so they sing to Him."

"Do you think she'd take us with her if we asked? We'd sing too," Fedya continued, not giving it a rest.

Sanya's eyes went wide and he blinked for a long time.

"What are you talking about? We're not allowed to go."

"Why not? We're only going to sing."

"We'll get expelled from the Pioneers and maybe even kicked out of school."

Jumping off the railing lightly, Fedya continued:

"I'm not a pioneer, or have you forgotten? They expelled me already." He stood there, scratching the back of his head playfully and pretending that he was trying to remember: "Oh yeah, why did they expel me? Do you remember, by any chance?"

Without taking his eyes off the rapid waters of the river, Sanya recalled what happened. Of course he remembered how, half a year ago, during the second period, there came three sharp rings, indicating an extraordinary event at the school. As if on cue, all the classes interrupted their studies and assembled in the urgent lineup in the long schoolhouse corridor. Beneath a huge portrait of Lenin hanging on the wall, there stood Fedya, his head bowed low. The principal looked strictly over the assembly with his dissimilar eyes, and, when all students had frozen in their spots, he said:

"Today we have gathered to expel Fyodor Vetkin from the pioneers for shamelessly inventing nicknames for our invaluable teachers, and these nicknames were, in turn, repeated by the entire school."

Sanya raised his eyes with difficulty and looked at his brother. The latter was practically bent in half as he stood, his thin shoulder blades sticking out like wings behind him. Grandfather Lenin was looking down from above on his descendant Fedya, who had breached his trust, and it seemed that Lenin's eyes had grown even narrower. The principal asked Fedya to return his red necktie and his pin, a symbol of belonging to the organization. Removing his red necktie, Fedya said, barely audibly, that he could not return the pin because he lost it. Yes... it was a horrible day...

Now, in the middle of the bridge, Sanya was staring intently at his brother. In the reflection on the water, Fedya looked fragile and light and it seemed, as if he could flap his tailfin like a fish and swim away at any moment. His face, at the same time open and sly, could disarm anyone. They had never discussed that "black lineup" before, but today they wanted to talk about it.

"Fedya, so you gave the principal the nickname 'Goblin,' well now everyone is calling him that."

"Well yeah, who else could he be if not a goblin? His right and left eyes are different, he screams constantly and his hair is always messed up, typical inhabitant of a haunted forest."

"I don't remember what you called the math teacher."

"I didn't call her anything," Fedya said. "She's nice, and she never gets mad. But the Russian teacher got her comeuppance, 'Madam Wrong!'"

The brothers burst out in laughter, so accurate was Fedya's assessment of her character. He had even called one teacher: "The American."

"But why 'American?'" Sanya inquired.

"Because she acts like a foreign visitor."

"Do you even remember where America is?" Sanya wondered.

"Over there?" Without thinking, his brother waved his hand along the river in the direction of the current. "All rivers flow to America," he said confidently.

"All roads lead to Rome? Is that what you wanted to say?" Sanya recalled from a history lesson.

"See?" Fedya smiled slyly. "If all roads can lead to Rome, why can't all rivers flow to America?"

Sanya knew that it was useless to argue with his brother and occasionally admired Fedya's self-confidence. Even Sanya could not always figure out if he was joking or telling the truth.

Here, in the middle of the bridge, one had an excellent view of the rocky Ascension Mountain, its peak propping up the heavens. But if one were to ask the local residents why the mountain had that name, they would find it difficult to explain who ascended on this mountain. Ascended to where? And why?

On the right riverbank, one could see the city bank, the confectionary plant, and the mica plant, as well as another very important site: the beer brewery.

On the left, there was a view of that none too dear to their hearts abode, the orphanage named after Lenin, crowning the mountain triumphantly, and also of the military unit with an enormous flag of the Soviet Union waving above it. At the foot of the mountain, a bright blue glum stand caught the eye, indicating the bus stop, and next to it was a small kiosk, also blue, which always sold hot pies regardless of the weather. Across from the kiosk was the city barbershop, brightly lit despite the sunny day.

"They must be having some important client," Fedya commented.

"Do you know that the barber, Vitek served for the Germans in the war?"

"I heard," Sanya said, "but perhaps it's not true."

"You saw him. Huge as a bear, wears the same shirt all the time, and doesn't always speak Russian."

"The shirt doesn't mean anything," Sanya kept defending him.

"He's a traitor. I bet you he's a traitor," Fedya would not let up. "Let's go, let's go and ask him." He pulled his brother by the hand.

"Okay, let's go," Sanya said nervously, knowing that Fedya was capable of anything. "But if he says he is not a traitor, then…"

"Then what?" Fedya stopped.

"Then you have to carry out the trash ten times instead of me and wash the floor three times, agreed?" Sanya extended his hand to his brother to signify an accord.

"As if I'm that dumb." Fedya turned around and began to walk in the opposite direction.

The brothers lived in anticipation of summer adventures, planning to go with their mother for the first time to a distant settlement of the North, where she had to work until August. They loafed around the city from morning till night, relishing life without school responsibilities, returning home in the evenings and telling Grandma Claudia about their day.

The family occupied three small rooms in a single-story wooden house partitioned into two halves. The second half was occupied by their neighbor Lena, who lived there with her three adult children and her hunchbacked husband – a taciturn and stern man.

Their neighbor in the next house over was a very loud and restless woman named Grusha. From early in the morning, her ringing voice could be heard from beyond the fence, singing the song from her favorite movie: "The heart grows light from a merry song..." and the smell of genuine Ukrainian borscht would saturate the air.

In the Vetkins' home, many things were not openly discussed, and on the rare occasions that they were, the boys were given a strict order never to speak of it to anyone. They were also instructed never to talk to strangers, and this secrecy almost turned into tragedy for their neighbor Grusha, who suffered from heart disease.

One day at noon, when the brothers were playing *lapta** with the neighborhood boys, a tall, thin man appeared out of nowhere, came up to them, and asked quietly:

"Where do the Vetkins live?"

The Vetkin brothers looked at each other and shrugged their shoulders. They did not like this guy, who was glancing round suspiciously. The other kids also looked around in confusion, wondering if this was some sort of new game, sort of like "broken telephone." The stranger tried to smile and repeated:

"You don't know where they live? I have a letter for them, here." The man took a folded envelope out of his pocket and showed it to the boys.

"There's nothing written on it," Fedya said.

"It's written here," the man pointed to his head.

"Toss it in the mailbox," Sanya suggested.

"Which one?" the stranger sighed in relief.

"The blue one over there," Fedya said, getting ahead of his brother, and pointed to the mailbox belonging to their neighbor Grusha.

---

* A Russian bat and ball folk game first known to be played in 14th century

Swaying in the wind like a blade of grass, the man tossed the letter in the blue box, turned, and walked away. Grusha, who was digging around in her yard, noticed the man by the mailbox and walked out on the street. They saw her open the envelope quickly, begin to read, and then scream in desperation:

"My dear, my dear... how could you leave me all by myself...?"

She screamed so loudly that the neighbors heard her and ran out on the street. Sanya saw how the stranger, who had already moved away a considerable distance, heard her piercing shout, turned around, and stopped on the road. Grusha fell to her knees, crying and wailing:

"Basta-a-ards, goddamn bastards..."

Grandma Claudia and their mother rushed to her aid, lifted her by the arms, and led her inside the house. Seeing nothing, the desperate woman moaned and lamented like at a funeral, clutching the envelope in one hand and the letter in the other. "Her husband is in prison, he must have died," the neighbors said to each other. The brothers slinked inside the house and saw how the woman was seated on a stool in the kitchen. The smell of valerian, spilled on the floor, cloaked everyone who had gathered in its calming aroma. Grusha dropped the letter, and it twirled to the floor, landing by the feet of the neighbor Lena.

"Read it, read it..." came impatient shouts from the neighbors, who were dying from curiosity. Lena picked up the letter and began to read it:

"My dear wife, I am writing you my first and last letter. I am sick with tuberculosis, and there is no hope of salvation. It is spring now, and when my friend is released and gives you this letter, it will be summer. Please take him

in and treat him well, and he will tell you many things."
Grusha stopped crying suddenly and, raising her swollen
face, glanced at everyone else in confusion.

"What's the old buzzard going on about?" she said.
"Last month he wrote that he is alive and well, and now
he's dying. Seems awful quick."

"Read on, read on..." the neighbors pleaded, wanting to
know everything.

"See how life turns out? My fifteen-year incarceration
turned out to be a life sentence. All this time I never
stopped thinking about you, our daughter, and the grandsons, whom I have not been able to raise."

Grusha got up again, her face distorted by anger.

"Dear God!" she cried out. "He doesn't have tuberculosis. He's simply lost his wits. He thinks, it's fifteen years
instead of five, and he calls our granddaughters grandsons.
Just you come back, old fart, I'll show you how to die."

She ran to the stove and, grabbing a broom, propping up
her side with one arm, began to swing the broom menacingly like a sword. The neighbors retreated just in case,
ready to leave the scene at any moment.

The people protested, imploring Grusha to be quiet,
sitting her back down on a chair, and offering her another
dose of valerian. Lena continued:

"I close my eyes and I see the Summer Garden, the Neva
River, and us, young and carefree."

At that moment, Sanya glanced at Grandma Claudia.
She stood leaning against the wall, staring dully and
indifferently into the distance. His mother hurried to Lena
and took the letter from her hands, saying:

"Your husband is alive, Grusha, it's all a mix-up. He's
not gone mad, and he'll come back soon. Let's go, Mama,"
and she hugged Claudia and they walked out.

The crowd began chattering in bewilderment and disappointment about the unfinished letter.

"Now there's news for you," people said resentfully. "We didn't even know her husband was also doing time. They said he went away to earn some money…"

All night, an icon-lamp burned in the Vetkins' house, and three slender church candles illuminated the curves of an icon with golden light, casting uneven shadows into the corners. There were no tears or lamentations. The boys were sitting tensely in their rooms, trying to get their heads around what happened. Unable to bear this uncertain state, Fedya headed to the small living room where Grandma Claudia was sitting with his parents. He sat down on a bench next to his father and started chattering:

"That man, he was so scary and thin…"

"What man, Fedya?" asked his father.

"The man, he brought the letter and asked about the Vetkins. But I did not speak to him, he is a stranger after all, I did not tell him where we live."

"You did everything right, Fedya," Claudia said tenderly.

"Then why are you all so sad?"

The father asked the son to go back to his room. Upon returning, Fedya would not let up, asking his brother:

"Sanya, the man who wrote the letter, who do you think he is?"

"Auntie Grusha's husband."

"Are you sure?"

"Of course, you saw how she cried."

"Then why is Grandma Claudia so sad?" Fedya kept pestering.

"Because she feels sorry for that guy, he's our neighbor after all."

Finally, exhausted from all the questions and answers, Fedya fell asleep, while Sanya opened the door wider, lay down on the floor, and began to listen carefully to every word of his grandfather's letter as his mother read it.

"My dearest, I know that you believe in my innocence. I never did any of the things of which I was accused, and I only confessed so they would not disturb you. I implore you, do not judge me! These past seven years without the right of communication were like a blade of a knife, and there was only one thing they could not take away, something that consoled me immensely – my memories. Despite all the difficulties, how happy we were!

"Do you remember the 'flower roulette'? I brought you three chamomile bouquets, and you had to pick the only one that had the wedding ring in it. I was so afraid to lose you that, I admit, I was a little naughty: I bought three rings and placed one in each bouquet. You said: 'You aren't worried at all, as if you don't care whether I choose the right one or not.' Yes, I was not worried. I knew you would choose the right one. Forgive me for this only secret I had from you. And one more thing! I believe that our son Alexander is alive, and that the news about his death from tuberculosis was untrue... And if it is? Good God! What a silly coincidence. Forgive me, for if you forgive me, the Lord will forgive me as well. Eternally yours, true to my family and to my fatherland."

Sanya lay on the floor, burying his tear-stained face in his hands. He knew that after the war, the family began an extensive search for Uncle Alexander, left in Leningrad for unknown reasons. Letters with inquiries were sent everywhere, and the search dragged on for many years. But one day in the late sixties, a letter arrived from the Red Cross with a brief note on the death of Alexander Voronov from tuberculosis and the place of his burial.

After receiving the news, Claudia wept incessantly, while Grandfather Clement fell into utter desperation. His first arrest was for refusing to use the passport of the Soviet Union, but he was soon released. The grandfather continued to openly express his views criticizing the politics of the country, sending numerous letters to the General Committee of the Communist Party with requests to help his family return to Leningrad. Claudia begged him to submit, but after receiving the news about his son, he could not submit; it was a genuine, senseless rebellion, destroying the imaginary peace the family had worked years to create. Soon, the grandfather was arrested again, and this time he did not return. Following the arrest, came the horrible notification that citizen Voronov stood accused of undermining the government and had been punished by fifteen years imprisonment in the northern mines, without the right of communication.

Although Sanya was only six years old at the time, he remembered his grandfather always being well-groomed and kind. He would often seat Sanya on his knees, place his heavy accordion on the boy's thin legs, stretch out the bellows, and order him to start playing. Unable to bear the weight of the accordion on his child's legs, he would beg his grandfather to play instead. And his grandfather would play, closing his eyes and leaning his head back, he would play with his fingers barely touching the enticing, shiny buttons, leaving ethereal, distressing melodies in the boy's memory. That was how he remembered him: dashing, kind, and just. And now he felt immense love for that man and could not believe that he was already gone. No longer walking, no longer speaking, no longer playing the accordion or placing his hand on Sanya's head, saying:

"A decent man must remain a decent man in any situation, Sanya."

Sanya's soul was troubled. He suddenly felt sorry for Grandma Claudia, and his parents, and his grandfather, and his hunchbacked neighbor, and all the known and unknown inhabitants of City N. That night, he first asked himself the question:

"If my country is the strongest and the most just, why was my grandfather arrested?" But time went on, as it was supposed to do, and no one spoke of the letter again, and only once did Claudia say, sighing:

"He is better now. He is up in the sky."

Sanya tried many times to imagine his grandfather living in the sky, but he could never do it. He even invented a theory that his grandfather was an angel, invisible to people's eyes, with large transparent wings, like a dragonfly, who appeared only when no one was looking at him. As for Fedya, he simplified his brother's theory considerably, still thinking naively that the subject of the conversation was his neighbor:

"What heaven?" his brother insisted. "They say this neighbor was a big drunk. He could barely walk on the ground, so he would surely have fallen from the sky."

This was Fedya, straightforward and naive. But as for Sanya, he wanted to believe Claudia's words.

Birth of an Artist

From an early age, Sanya began to show ability and interest in drawing, studying the objects around him for long periods of time and trying to portray them on paper with a pencil. He also liked to copy postcards, book illustrations, and occasionally draw caricatures and holiday greetings for the school paper. Fedya was annoyed at his brother's interest in drawing, because Sanya would frequently brush him aside, saying:

"Can't you see a man is creating? Don't bother me."

"Can't you see a man wants to play? Let's go kick a ball," Fedya would demand, prodding him in the back.

"You're about to get it!" Sanya would shout disappointedly, jumping up and trying to catch Fedya as he disappeared quickly behind the door. Running out into the yard, Sanya would see his brother's face, shining with joy and with an unspoken expression: "See? I won again!" The anger and disappointment would disappear immediately, and the desire to draw would disappear along with them. And this would go on endlessly...

The parents encouraged their son's abilities and treated

them as something natural and ordinary, or at least harmless. Thus, very modestly, without getting in anyone's way, Sanya's artistic talent took root. But, one day, Grandma Claudia bought him a box of real oil paints, three brushes of different sizes, and a bottle of paint thinner.

Somewhat lost, unsure of where to begin, Sanya wanted to try the new, as yet unknown, technique as soon as possible, and he was aware that the most appropriate place for this was canvas. Fedya suggested insistently that he paint on the furnace a scene from his favorite fairy tale "Yemelya the Fool," which the newly minted painter dared not do. Soon, a more suitable place was found in his parents' room. Their fairly large bed with an iron headboard stood next to a wall painted a light green color. Above the bed hung a massive frame containing numerous photographs of unknown relatives, just as everywhere else in the house. Without thinking of the consequences, the boys removed the frame from the wall, and two birds sitting on a cedar branch, pecking at nuts from a pinecone, appeared in its stead. Fedya rejoiced, as he liked anything that reeked of secrecy. For the first time, he did not shove or interfere with his brother, and only hurried him along, saying:

"Hurry, hurry, or you'll run out of time," – realizing that by concealing this incident from the adults, he would always be able to blackmail the poor artist into giving him sweets or anything else he desired. As for the artist, he only thought of how oil paint was not some lowly pencil, which did not require much in terms of initiation. His first work in oil paint was finished fairly quickly.

"Hey-ho!" Fedya admired in earnest, as if truly seeing his brother's talent for the first time. The heavy frame returned to its former spot with two large pieces of plasticine stuck to the back so as to increase the gap with the wall and give the painting a chance to dry.

"It reeks of paint, come to think," Fedya noted.

"So I'll paint the legs of this chair, and everyone will think it's the chair."

Sanya had barely finished speaking when multi-colored butterflies began to circle the legs of a wooden chair covered in clothes. After writing a sign, "careful: wet paint," and leaving it in a prominent place, the boys retired to their room. The artist was still under the influence of the new experience, whereas his brother behaved like a genuine conspirator. He was whistling, winking at the artist, and did not even realize that he would soon become a victim of the artist's talent.

"Kids, why does it smell like paint so strongly?" Grandma Claudia asked, appearing in the door.

Slinking outside, Fedya engaged in sweet explanations that it was only the chair legs. Seeing her grandson's artistry, Claudia clasped her hands in surprise, only what could she do when she had given him the paint herself? The parents returned and began to complain in chorus about the paint odor. The boys quieted down and listened to Claudia's optimistic voice, repeating Fedya's story word for word.

"At least it's just the chair," the father grumbled discontentedly.

The next morning over breakfast, the father, suffering from headache, asked suddenly:

"So where did you buy this paint?"

"At the stationer's by the bridge," Claudia replied, oblivious to the coming storm.

"What sort of paint is this, then, something foreign?" he wouldn't let up.

"Oil!" Fedya exclaimed proudly, showing off his knowledge. Sanya was sitting very still, while his father continued:

"Sanya, you only drew six butterflies on the chair, but it smells like someone painted the entire floor."

Fedya began to fidget in his chair, as if trying to convey that "if someone were to offer him a kilogram of candy or something like that, he'd explain everything real well." Except that no one was offering him candy. The storm clouds thickened.

"Show me the box of paints," his mom asked quietly.

In a stilted gait, swallowing a piece of sandwich that had become stuck in his throat, Sanya shuffled off to his room. He returned with the box, placed it on the table, and stood there, hanging his head guiltily. Taking out the tubes one after the other, his father asked angrily:

"There's barely anything left in here, did you use all this up on six butterflies?"

Seeing that no one was about to bribe him, Fedya rushed to his brother's defense, making it up as he went along:

"He... he drew them many times. He couldn't get them right. It was the first time in his life that he was painting, after all... So, then... he... he painted over them and painted them again, and again, and again..." The parents grew upset. Claudia disappeared from the kitchen, not wanting to hear the children nagged.

"Tell me the truth, Alexander, I give you two minutes," the father summed up, looking at his son's lowered head, and everyone understood that he was not joking, that in his extremely rare moments of wrath he could be unpredictable. Fedya grew worried. The first minute was not yet up, and yet it seemed to him the second was all but over. Unable to bear it, he got up decisively, gestured for the parents to follow him into the room, and, entering first, pointed at the wall.

"Over there," the boy exhaled, climbing up on the bed and removing the frame from the wall.

And then something completely unexpected happened, like the flip of a coin. As you flip the coin and watch it drop, you try to guess which side it will fall on, which choice will lead to victory. At that moment, in their parents' cramped room, the coin fell on the right side, because the mom smiled suddenly, while the father, seeing her reaction, said:

"Son, why are you hiding such beautiful birds from us?"

The frame with the photographs was moved to a different spot, and the birds no longer needed to hide. Henceforth, Sanya was allowed to express his talent everywhere and on any surface, provided that he aired out the rooms properly and transferred movable objects to the yard for drying. Moreover, it was decided to buy him new paints once every three months. And for Fedya, due to a lack of any sort of talent, a kilogram of sweets would be purchased. Calling himself a foreign word – "manager" – that he heard during an English lesson, Fedya flew around the house in search of new places for his brother to showcase his talent. Soon, the house was difficult to recognize. Everything that could be painted had been painted. Sunflowers adorned the front door. Scenes from fairy tales were on the furnace. Chairs, benches, table legs, bedside tables, doors, and even water buckets – everything that caught their eye had altered its former dismal appearance.

"You'll be going to the neighbors soon," Grandma Claudia joked.

He was not to go to the neighbors, however, because September came and brought back a time of scholastic obligations. The leaden autumn sky blanketed the earth, obscuring sun and warmth for many long months. Siberian falls, one of the most confusing times of year, when the endless taiga and the woods transform into colors that leave no soul unmoved. But, in this admiration, a fear of unknown origins is born, weighing on the heart and forcing everyone to ask himself the question: "How will I make it till spring?"

The air fills with freshness that seems to emanate from the earth, float down from the mountains, crawling out of the taiga. The fall comes like a thief, suddenly, in the night. Only yesterday it was a warm summer day, and today everyone understands that it had been the last day of summer. Nature begins a new temporal cycle and demands: "Are you ready for winter? Have you prepared firewood? Have you bought coal? Have you mended the warm *valenki*? Have you cooked preserves, pickled mushrooms? Stored up on potatoes, cabbage, and everything else you need to survive? For if you have not, there is much cause for sorrow. Since childhood, everyone knows the fable of the grasshopper spending the summer singing and, before he knew it, found himself face to face with winter."

During one such fall day, Fedya was preparing for school early in the morning and could not find his shoes. After a quick search, they were found, and on them...

"This is awful!" Fedya exclaimed, seeing his only pair of shoes mercilessly painted over with daisies.

Casting angry glances at Sanya, the adults pleaded with Fedya to put on his shoes and go to school. Fedya despised his brother, promising to throw away all his paints.

---

* A traditional Russian winter footwear, made of wool felt

He had almost agreed but then, before walking out the door, he threw off the shoes and shouted: "I'm no girl to walk around the city in daisy shoes!"

As for Sanya, he enjoyed his nighttime prank, and the daisies looked almost real. Left with no choice, Fedya put on his shoes again. He ran to the bus stop, barely feeling his legs under him. It seemed to him that the entire planet – billions of living, sentient beings – was staring at his shoes. Sanya was keeping his distance from his brother just in case, and when the bus approached, the boys ran for different doors.

The bus traversed its daily route unhurriedly and finally passed over the bridge and stopped by the blue kiosk at the foot of the mountain. Fedya ran uphill on the wooden sidewalk so quickly that his brother could barely keep up. And if the principal had seen just then how enthusiastically a student was returning to fulfill his school obligations, he would surely have noted Fedya's efforts and rewarded him with praise. But instead, everything happened much more mundanely. Running through the enormous creaking gates onto the territory of the orphanage, Fedya disappeared in the apple orchard. Weaving from tree to tree like a rabbit, he was heading for the schoolhouse, leaving behind his brother, who was shocked by this reaction. Sanya thought that Fedya would jump for joy upon seeing his footwear transformed into something extraordinary. The only thing the young artist regretted was that he hadn't painted airplanes or cars. And why daisies? He didn't understand it himself.

The school was waking up; one after the other and the windows were illuminated with bright light. Sanya saw Fedya jump from behind the last tree and dash for the schoolhouse door. Sometime later, he saw his brother by the door of the gymnasium. The latter stood leaning against a wall, wearing his socks and no shoes. Soon thereafter, Fedya slinked by him with his head downcast, heading for class. Following him with his eyes, Sanya exclaimed in horror:

"This is a nightmare, what have I done?"

Fedya was wearing someone's stolen gym sneakers. Sanya spent the next six lessons on pins and needles waiting for recesses, trying unsuccessfully to establish contact with his brother. As he strolled through the hallway during the final recess, Sanya heard the loud chatter of some girls crowding by the window like a flock of disheveled magpies. Slowing down, the boy became all ears, but the only thing he heard was:

"This is the latest fashion, and you can only buy it in the capital…" came a voice sounding like Mashka, a gossip from his class.

Buy what? In what capital? He did not understand, but the thought of whatever it was kept haunting him.

After school, Sanya waited for his brother in the agreed-upon spot, at the bottom of the staircase, but the latter did not show. The already familiar group of girls was walking down the stairs, headed by Mashka. She walked proudly in the middle and spoke loudly, while Fedya's shoes adorned her thin legs.

"What are you staring at, you moron? That's the fashion right now, got it?" the girl said contemptuously as she passed him.

"Oh," Sanya sighed quietly, "if only she knew who started this fashion, she'd never have put them on."

Finally, Fedya appeared, sneaking cautiously around a corner.

"Let's go, then," he said, looking left and right.

On the way home, Fedya stomped on puddles defiantly in Mashka's gym sneakers with only one shoelace. He had always dreamed of being an invisible man, but not to this extent. All day he had to glide like a shadow between desks and flowerpots. Wait behind doors, holding his breath, and hide under the staircases. He did not even suspect that Mashka had no intention of looking for her missing sneakers, but rather, upon finding the daisy-painted shoes in her closet, took them for a gift of fate and claimed them quickly as her own.

Refusing to wait for the bus, Fedya continued on his way, making a special effort to step in puddles.

"Please don't do it, you'll catch cold," Sanya pleaded.

"And who's to blame?" his brother said meanly. "You shouldn't have destroyed my only pair of shoes. And if I get sick now, it'll be your fault," an offended Fedya grumbled, contemplating his revenge.

The boys rounded the old bank and emerged on Lenin Street, the main street in town stretching from the bridge all the way to the train station. They passed Lenin Square, the location of the eternal memorial flame and the cinema. A large, wet, and saggy poster was tacked to a board, displaying the name of the latest film: "Amphibian Man."

The previous week, all the older grades went to the theater to see the movie, marching in formation down the streets and singing.

Trying to start a conversation with his brother, Sanya asked without thinking:

"Would you want to live under the water, like Amphibian Man?"

"Would you like to walk through the whole city wearing soaking wet sneakers with one shoelace?" came the hostile response.

"Why aren't you happy? This is good news – you'll get sick and won't have to go to school."

Fedya raised his eyebrows, and an undisguised joy flashed in his eyes. How did he not think of it himself? After all, he could not stand school and kept repeating: "Why would I need school? Let them teach me something I don't know."

At his twelve years of age, he thought that he knew enough to make it in this difficult life.

"I'll race you! First one to the house is the winner!" Sanya commanded.

Sanya did not have to repeat himself, because Fedya loved to compete and, of course, to win. He was already flying like the wind, as if released from a cage, leaving his brother far behind. His cheeks were blushing happily as he waited for Sanya by the gate of his home, shouting:

"We wear sneakers with one shoelace and we win anyway!"

Hearing his shout, Claudia went to meet him with concerned interest, wondering about the sneakers.

"Oh, Sanya, Sanya. As if you could not find a better place to paint," she kept repeating after seeing her grandson.

During the evening meal, the main topic of discussion was Fedya's shoes. It was resolved to trade Mashka's sneakers back for the shoes, which Fedya refused categorically and almost began to cry:

"I don't want to wear them after Mashka. Please don't make a fool out of me. The whole school will make fun of me."

After dinner, a box of shoes was brought from storage, but the selection was not impressive. Everyone had only a single pair of shoes for each season of the year. Sanya's father ordered him to give his own shoes to his brother and take the father's old boots. Sanya's complaints that the boots were three sizes too big fell on deaf ears.

A jubilant Fedya made a show of trying on Sanya's shoes, saying:

"A little big, but I'll grow into them."

That night, perhaps agitated, perhaps hurt, Sanya could not fall asleep for a long time. The wind sighed and groaned outside the window, rustling through the few remaining leaves. The window shutters in Grandma Claudia's room moaned pitifully in the wind. Sanya's father had been planning to fix them for several years now, but kept forgetting. Fedya slept restlessly, having tied his "new" shoes by the laces to the metal leg of his bed.

Forcing himself asleep, Sanya thought of his grandfather for some reason, and whenever he thought of him, a trembling pain would always appear somewhere inside, in his stomach. He thought of how good and peaceful it was to be alive, to be here. The boy tried to imagine Kolyma, the corrective labor camp, his grandfather's final resting place. He tried to imagine how such a place might look. "It's somewhere very far, in the North, at the very border dividing the earth and the sky. And it's probably even colder there than it is here," he thought.

All through previous years, Grandma Claudia wrote her husband incessantly and sent him packages, but nothing came in return. Perhaps, someone else was receiving all the packages and letters. "Without the right of communication. Without the right of communication," the words twirled in Sanya's head like the final leaves, carried off by the wind. With these thoughts, rolling into a ball beneath his comforter, Sanya fell asleep.

Revenge or Monday's a Tough Day

Every week at the orphanage named after Lenin, Monday was a humdrum bath day. Immediately after breakfast, a long chain of students lined up by the younger kids' dormitory. Here, a cantankerous laundrywoman handed each child, one after the other, a towel, underwear, socks, and their daily uniform wrapped in a gray sack permeated with the smell of cheap laundry soap.

Despite the fact that, during spring and fall, the Vetkin brothers were visiting students, they were bound by the same rules as the children living here permanently.

The students were picked up by a bus that barely drove, gifted to the orphanage many years ago by its patron organization – the Auto Depot. The old, white, rickety bus smelled of gasoline and dust. Driving its route all day, the bus delivered the students to and from the city bathhouse. The children dashed into its open, and only, door, and rushed to occupy the best seats in there, preferably by the window.

Fedya did not sit next to his brother, as per usual, but suddenly plopped down on the seat next to Mashka.

"Fedya and Mashka, sitting in a tree..." the girls began to squeal.

"Shut your mouth, you fools," Fedya said, smiling contentedly.

Casting a questioning glance, in case the younger Vetkin did this accidentally, Mashka moved closer to the window just in case. She sat with her thin legs tucked under the seat, wearing shoes with daisies that had been half washed off by the rain and the fall mud. Failing to understand what was going on; Sanya kept spinning his head, trying to hear what the two conspirators were whispering.

The housemistress commanded them to sing, and Songbird, a thin girl with large green eyes and a ringing, perhaps even beautiful, voice, began to sing:

"When you smile it brightens up the day, when you smile it brings a rainbow through the rain. Share your smile with others on your way, and you'll see your smile time and time again."

And then it began... the girls picked up the song, trying to outshout Songbird.

But Sanya had other concerns besides smiling. He was pressing his gray sack of clothes against his knees silently. Every now and again he would peer into the profile of the admirable girl leading the singing, who was sitting just ahead across the aisle. At that moment, for some reason, he suddenly felt a great affinity for her and wanted to draw her.

They reached the bathhouse quickly, and Sanya pulled his brother by the arm and inquired as to what he was talking about with Mashka.

"About boots," Fedya replied, smiling slyly and hiding something in his pocket as he ran ahead. The students separated into two groups as they walked, boys to the left and girls to the right, and the housemistresses hurried after their charges.

The bathhouse, a low brick building located right on the riverbank, was closed every Monday to everyone but the orphanage kids, giving them the opportunity to wash off a week's worth of dirt. In the bathing room, everyone tried to grab an aluminum basin as quickly as possible, as well as a piece of utility soap and a loofah. The noise was unimaginable, and the children dashed chaotically with their basins through clouds of steam like small, harmless apparitions. The hot water from the rusty faucets was nearly boiling, while the cold seemed like it could turn into ice any moment. There were not enough faucets, and the students lined up, prodding each other impatiently, saying: "hurry up, hurry up, or you'll freeze." Filling their basins with water, the children settled on the cement benches, two to a bench.

The Vetkin brothers, even though this was strictly forbidden, liked to sit in the steam room next to the door leading to the women's section, which was locked from both sides, just in case. The steam room was nothing like the bathing room, the atmosphere here was completely different. It still held some of the heat from the previous day, and one could detect the scent of birch, oak, and fir sauna switches. The boys figured out long ago that the headmistress would not dare enter the room in her dry clothes to check, so they used the steam room, giving it a foreign name: "lux."

Sanya could barely stand the smell of utility soap, especially for washing the head, and he tried to use it without breathing. Fedya, knowing his brother's weakness, managed to obtain a small plastic bottle ironically filled with "Daisy" shampoo from his fellow conspirator Mashka.

Begging his brother to share and unable to control himself, Sanya poured almost the entire contents of the bottle onto the palm of his hand. He was sitting on the third, top bench, savoring the pleasant scent of the shampoo, and his head resembled a snow-white mohair hat.

"Fedya, change the water," he asked, trying unsuccessfully to wash the foam off his face.

"Ten basins won't be enough for this. Why don't you go under the shower?" Fedya suggested sweetly. Of course, under normal circumstances, Sanya would have easily cracked his brother's crafty plan, but his circumstances were far from normal.

"Let's go under the shower, only quickly," he pleaded, grabbing his brother by the hand and feeling his way down from the top bench.

Fedya took him out of the steam room and led him to the door leading to the women's section. Opening the door, he let his brother pass obediently through it, and locked it behind him. His fellow conspirator Mashka had previously unlatched the door from her side and was expecting her victim. Without any shyness, she grabbed Sanya by the hand and dragged him under the shower.

"Don't pull so hard, Fedya, I'm going to fall," he pleaded, unable to see anything.

But Mashka kept pulling him along, motioning for the rest of the girls to be quiet by pressing her finger to her lips. Silence rang in Sanya's ears; ascribing it to shampoo blocking his hearing, he only dreamed of escaping his unpleasant condition as soon as possible.

As if on cue, the girls poured the water out of their basins, covered their stomachs, and froze in anticipation of Mashka's signal. Sanya, not suspecting a thing, washed off his head, regained his sight, and suddenly saw a gang of girls amid the clouds of steam. Smiling foolishly and thinking that he was imagining all this, he shook his head from side to side, trying to banish the nightmarish vision.

Mashka gave the signal by banging on her basin with her fist and... all the girls started screaming as hard as they could. Sanya, also screaming in terror, dashed to the door and found it to be locked from the other side. He grabbed a basin lying on the floor, spun around, taking turns covering his back and his front, and started kicking the door and shouting:

"Fedya-a-a-a, open up..."

The housemistress, Galina Petrovna, came running at his shouts. Seeing him dashing back and forth by the door, she ordered the girls to turn around and be quiet. They obeyed grudgingly, moving the basins from their stomachs to their behinds. Galina Petrovna, all wet, with drops of sweat and steam on her face, kept knocking on the door until it was opened.

Seeing red from shame and anger, and capable of anything, Sanya dashed off in search of his brother, clutching the basin in his hands. The culprit, meanwhile, having put on dry, clean clothes, was sitting in the foyer in a deep chair covered with artificial red leather. Sitting there, expecting to hear the news.

Hurling the basin to the floor, Sanya ran into the changing-room, cursing at his brother and wishing him illness or even death; anything, to never see him again or live under one roof with him. Paying no attention to the whispering boys, Sanya dressed himself instantly and jumped out of the changing-room like a guided missile. Seeing Fedya sitting in the chair, he ran up to him without delay and punched him in the face as hard as he could. It was the first time in his life that he had hit a person, hit his brother.

Covering his face with his hands, Fedya began to moan, and Sanya pulled him down to the floor by the legs, climbed on top of him, and continued to beat him.

The boys crowded around them, observing with interest and not even trying to separate them. Still wet from the washing room, Galina Petrovna appeared, grabbed the teenagers with her powerful hands, and pulled them apart, yelling:

"Stop this at once! You – senior Vetkin, go and put your dirty clothes in this sack. And you – junior Vetkin, go wet a towel in cold water and hold it to your face." Fedya's eye was red and swollen. The other children could not understand why the usually close brothers were fighting all of a sudden. Oh, if only they knew that all the blame lay in the daisy-painted boots on the feet of Mashka the conspirator.

There was no singing on the return trip, and everyone was talking about what had happened. The brothers were sitting in opposite ends of the bus, and no matter where Sanya looked he saw the smirking mugs of the students. He caught the voice of Romka, a mean, overgrown student from his class. Romka was pleading with Fedya to send him to the women's section next time. "It's my life's dream!" Romka was exclaiming.

As soon as the bus drove onto the school grounds and came to a stop, Sanya dashed towards the exit, paying no attention to Galina Petrovna's calls. He did not remember how he ran or rode home. Without answering any of Grandma Claudia's questions, he dove into his bed and covered his head with the blanket. He decided not to engage in conversation with anyone in the family and remain silent all week. Or, better yet, declare a hunger strike.

"Perhaps then, perhaps then mom and dad will punish that dunce Fedya. What a disgrace! And what about the

Songbird girl? She... she saw me naked. No, I won't go to school anymore," Sanya grumbled, wiping his tears all over his cheeks.

Soon, a tearful Fedya arrived with his eye swollen. Sitting on the low bench in the front hall with his head downcast, he was also silent. The father was about to punish his son for such stupid and uncaring behavior, but changed his mind after he saw his face. Claudia served dinner, but no one wanted to sit at the table. Sanya continued to lie in his bed, hiding his head under the pillow. The parents decided to wait until morning and retired to their room, discussing something quietly. Claudia still could not believe what she had heard, sat near Fedya and asked him if he had really done it. Seeing his slight nod of admission, she said:

"Go to sleep. An hour in the morning is worth two in the evening."

Fedya undressed obediently and lay down, casting a dismal glance at his brother's head, covered by the blanket.

The sound of the rain woke Sanya, and he stared into the darkness. This looked to be one of those lengthy rainfalls that poured for three or four days without pause. Then, the first snow would take the place of the rain, spinning and turning into water as it touched the copiously moistened earth. And, of course, the wind always joined this usual fall crowd. The window shutter emitted a pitiful creak, familiar to him for many years. Sometimes Sanya thought that his father was not repairing it on purpose, having grown accustomed to the sound and perhaps even enjoying it. At least it conveyed the state of the weather, if it was windy or not. Sanya also found something unique in this sound, something that said: "see, time passes and nothing changes." And this simple thought filled his heart with peace.

The light from a streetlamp made its way through the shutter and into the room. The lamp swayed in the wind, and the thin band of light would disappear one moment, plunging the room into darkness, and reappear the next, illuminating it. Contemplating what happened at the *banya** that day, he no longer felt the previous anger and hurt for some reason. Smiling, he pictured the silly girls with basins over their stomachs and himself, running helplessly by the door, naked. "Maybe I'm crazy," he said, "but I'm going to draw them and bring the picture to the school – let them be embarrassed instead of me."

Fedya slept restlessly, sighing and moaning in his sleep. Turning on the light and approaching his brother's bed, Sanya leaned over him and looked into his face. Seeing the enormous black eye, he suddenly took pity on his brother. "Why, it's actually pretty funny, to run naked around the *banya* surrounded by girls," he laughed. Jabbing his brother in the shoulder, he whispered:

"Fedya-a-a, get up…"

Opening his only working eye and seeing his brother standing over him, Fedya put his hands over his head and pleaded:

"Sanya, don't hit me anymore, I… I get it, please forgive me."

"I'm not going to hit you. Wake up," came the response.

Waking up fully, even more surprised Fedya whispered:

"Sanya, you've gone nuts."

"I haven't gone nuts."

"So what, you're not angry at me or something"? Fedya asked.

---

* A traditional Russian steam bath, sauna

"I was. And now I'm not. I have a plan."

To the sound of the rain and someone's light snoring coming from the depths of the house, the boys agreed not to reveal to the adults that they had made peace. And, next morning, Fedya was moaning about his headache and nausea, while Sanya kept laying motionlessly with the blanket over his head, staging a scene of utter despair.

"Poor Sanya," his father's voice came, barely audible, "he's completely depressed."

"Are we going to leave the two of them at home alone? They'll kill each other," the mother's voice chimed in.

"It's all right, it's all right," Grandma Claudia intervened. "The time of war has passed, and peacetime will soon begin."

Walking out into the garden, she opened the window shutters one by one, letting dim daylight into the room. Soon, the house emptied, and only the clock's confident ticking reached the boys' ears. Ah! It was an unforgettable day. Jumping out of the bed, Sanya began drawing with a pencil, taking his time and concentrating as he made various sketches, while Fedya headed to the kitchen in search of sweets.

"At last!" he declared with a joyous look. "Finally I can eat what I want for breakfast instead of what they make me."

With these words, he set the foodstuffs before his brother, extracted some "Red October" cookies from their package, and handed them helpfully to the artist, who was busy with important work.

"Do you even know what this means, 'Red October?'" Sanya wondered.

"It's a month, just like December and the others," Fedya smiled, and Sanya gave him a studying look. Yes, he really had the most enchanting smile in the world, and even the black eye did not rob him of his charisma.

"Sit still and stop chewing, I'm going to sketch you. Haven't you studied this in school by now? The Great October Revolution happened in October. That means a take-over," Sanya spoke, quickly shifting his attention between Fedya's face and the paper.

Fedya, however, showed with his entire being just how little he cared about who had taken over whom, and, stuffing his mouth with candy, out of nowhere he brought up their neighbor, Auntie Grusha:

"One time in the summer, when her granddaughters came to visit, I heard her keep asking them to finish their meals so that she wouldn't have to finish their leftovers. The granddaughters suggested: 'Grandma, why don't you just buy a pig?'

"Fedya, you're such a fool. I'm telling you about the revolution and you're telling me about some pig."

"Well the pig has some use, at least, and what good's the revolution?"

He sat on Sanya's bed, leaning against the warm chimney, blissful, without any responsibilities, perfectly content with himself and his life at that moment.

Finishing the sketch of his brother, Sanya carefully placed it in a folder and started on the next sketch, titling it: "Monday's a Tough Day."

"You forgot to draw their faces," Fedya noted, looking at the sketch.

"I didn't, that's the next step."

Fedya jabbed his finger at a girl standing a little apart from the group:

"That must be Mashka. Please draw her with a long nose and cross-eyed."

"No, that would make it a caricature and not a drawing. I really want to draw something special," the young artist argued.

"Special... Oh!" Fedya picked up optimistically, "Draw them naked and fat."

"I don't want to draw them naked. You'll see what I'm talking about when I finish."

Until the evening, they did whatever their hearts desired: played chess, battleship, and even managed a game of hide-and-seek.

The rain outside kept pouring without respite. The pedestrians walking on the sidewalk were wrapping themselves in their coats and clutching their umbrellas with all their strength, guarding them from gusts of wind.

Returning home and finding her grandchildren still in bed, Grandma Claudia went to her room, lit the icon-lamp, got down on her knees before it, and began to pray for something fervently. Then she went into the garden to close the window shutters, pushing long metal bolts into round openings that led inside the house. Entering the house, the grandmother walked through all the rooms, placing a flat metal dowel into the hole in the tip of every bolt.

No one ever wondered about the purpose of these shutters. It was certainly not to defend against burglars. How hard would a burglar have to work to get inside the house, how much noise would he have to make removing the window, only to get slammed in the head with a log, or, worse yet, a frying pan? No, the shutters were not for this. There was just a tradition to close them at night and open them in the mornings. And if, in some house, the shutters were still closed come noon, this meant that some sort of calamity had occurred, preventing the owner from getting up at dawn and opening the shutters.

Upon returning home and finding the situation un-changed, the parents decided to give the brothers until the end of the week. The brothers waited for everyone in the house to fall asleep, whispered until morning, and then, after sleeping, pranced around the house like two young stallions. Glancing at the mirror and discovering that the bruise under his eye was fading, Fedya asked his brother for paint to spruce it up a little. And their carefree life continued in this manner until Saturday. And on Saturday, they emerged from the room together and announced that they had made peace, thus pleasing all the other family members. Afterwards, the brothers stood beneath the porch canopy for a long time with a ball in their hands, staring at the pouring rain.

"We're fools," Fedya cursed, upset. "We shouldn't have shown them that we made up yet."

"We would have had to do it sometime, or it would have looked suspicious."

Sanya had finished his drawing by then. He really managed to convey the drama and the humor of the inci-dent. He never brought it to school, of course, but only shared it with his brother and then hid it in his folder along with the other drawings that he kept in a wooden bedside table. Fedya finally understood what Sanya had meant and agreed that long noses and crossed eyes would have been completely inappropriate.

"How you can remember them all!" he marveled at his brother's talent, recognizing each girl. The only girl that Fedya could not find in the drawing was the one called Songbird.

Winter

Life is such that we are all visited by different emotions. They come suddenly, and sometimes, just as suddenly, they disappear. One day, not long after the fatal events at the *banya*, Sanya was visited by a new, very hard to understand yet warm emotion. And it happened during a real Siberian winter, when one would not even send a dog outside, and a man avoids leaving his dwelling unless strictly necessary.

With the start of winter, the Vetkin brothers stopped being visiting students and became just like all the children living at the orphanage permanently, given the right to three meals a day, bed linen, and even winter outdoor clothing. During the first week, they were happy at this annually scheduled change, but soon the discipline would burden them more and more and they would only dream of a speedy return of spring.

Every morning, even on Sundays, the day began with a wake-up call at six o'clock, followed by exercises. The students lined up in two rows in the long corridors of the two-story dormitory and waved their arms out of rhythm, doing their exercises as the housemistress shouted: "One! Two! Three!" Then they walked in formation to the washroom, permeated with the pungent odor of chlorine, waiting for their turn to wash their faces and brush their teeth with nasty strawberry-flavored powder. At six thirty, dressed in their school uniforms and wrapping themselves in their coats, the children ran in formation to the dining hall.

The breakfasts differed little from one another: usually it was some sort of porridge, two pieces of dark bread with a choice of chocolate or salt butter, and a glass of warm tea.

The breakfasts, lunches, and dinners did not differ much from each other, accompanied by the telling slogan posted on the wall of the dining room: "Breakfast – eat yourself! Lunch – share with your friend! Dinner – give to your enemy!"

After breakfast, no longer in formation but every which way, throwing on their coats and hats as they ran, the students dashed to the nearby schoolhouse. At seven, the bell rang, and the students sat at their desks, trying to wake up completely and concentrate. This carousel continued all day; after lunch, twenty minutes (it was impossible to bear more) of playing snowballs or walking around, then back to school, then homework, then dinner again, then reading a book together or watching a slide show, and then a bell indicating it was time to turn in.

In this way, the full support of the state became heavy bread for the Vetkin brothers. They slept on the same floor but in different rooms. They saw each other rarely; sometimes, during recess or between classes, they could only manage to wave to each other or shout something only the two of them could understand. And as he lived there, among the orphanage children, Sanya began to understand how lucky he and Fedya were to have parents, and a room on Third Proletarian Street, and even Grandma Claudia.

In the basement of the dormitory was a boiler room. On cold days especially, the principal would admonish the stoker:

"If you let the pipes freeze, I'll have you put on trial!"

The stoker, scared to death, covered in coal dust and resembling a black man, worked day and night, full tilt, tossing coal into the furnace. And heat flew down the pipes somewhere deep under the frozen ground, warming all the buildings on the territory of the orphanage.

One time, Sanya woke up an hour before the wake-up call. In the city, a wailing siren warned the residents not to leave their houses without need and not to send their children to city schools. It meant that the temperature had fallen below forty-five. The city siren was joined by another from the factories, announcing the cancellation of work.

Sticking his feet into his worn flannel slippers, Sanya left the room. Dim lamps were on all night, illuminating the dismal walls of the long corridor. At night, the doors to all the rooms remained open. Boundaries were erased under the roof of this house, and the word "mine" ceased to exist, replaced by the word "communal."

He went down the stone staircase to the washroom, tormented by thirst. On his way back, he saw a girl's fragile figure standing by the window next to his room. Coming closer, Sanya recognized the girl known as Songbird. She was standing barefoot on the cold floor, wearing short pajamas, her face turned towards the window. Perhaps she had been standing there for a long time, but he had not noticed. The girl was admiring the frosty ornaments on the glass. He heard the watchman, working also as the janitor, beginning to clear the paths between the two dormitories, the dining hall, and the school with his wooden shovel. Hearing Sanya's steps, Songbird turned her sleepy face, not at all surprised at his presence, and whispered:

"Frosty. Maybe they'll cancel our classes too."

"Maybe," Sanya repeated, pausing. He had no idea what to do in these circumstances. "Leave? Stay? What?" It seemed to him that his heart was beating so loud in his chest that the girl could also hear it.

For eight years now, studying in the same class with her, he did not know her name. Everyone, including the teachers, called her Songbird. He never paid any attention to her and noticed her for the first time, during the fatal trip to the *banya*, on the bus. Since that moment, he thought about her a lot for some reason. The watchman-janitor kept scraping his shovel all over Sanya's nerves right under the window, as if he could not find a better place. Sanya could see blurred light from the yellow streetlamps through the frosty glass, as well as the movement of large falling flakes of snow.

"My name is Alya," the girl said suddenly. "Is that what you wanted to ask?"

"My name is Sanya."

He thought that there was nothing sillier than introducing themselves after eight years of studying together, thirty minutes before the wake-up call.

"I know," she smiled, sitting down on the floor.

She leaned her back against a radiator, then drew away suddenly and whispered:

"Oy... oy... how hot, touch it, it's practically boiling."

He extended his hand and lightly touched the curved metal implement hanging on the wall. He felt ashamed all of a sudden, recalling the events in the *banya*. Looking at her from above and finding the courage to start a more romantic conversation, he asked:

"What's your favorite time of year?"

"Fall," the girl replied without thinking. "And yours?"

"Why fall?" he continued, without answering her question.

"Because fall!" she exclaimed firmly.

"I like winter," he said decisively.

"Who could like winter? Only crazy people. We sit here for five months, like in prison, listening to the janitor scrape his wooden shovel."

Biting his lip, he regretted that he did not choose summer or spring. But now he decided to earnestly defend his position, since he really did love winter. Sitting on the floor next to her, he said quietly:

"What about New Year's? Presents? The tree? Skates? Vacation?" he listed his arguments, counting them one by one on his fingers. "There is nothing interesting about fall, why love it? Nature is dying."

"It's not dying, it's resting," Alya whispered indignantly, "and what good is your New Year, if it's the same every year? The Goblin in his faded Grandfather Frost suit. What's the point of presents if I can say for sure, exactly how many oranges or cookies there will be inside? And what good is vacation if we don't get to go anywhere? And uncomfortable skates and silly snowballs, which the boys toss around like fools, this close to hitting your head?"

She stood up, pouting, and marched off to her room, leaving him to sit under the hot radiator. And thus their friendship turned into complete alienation, perhaps even into enmity. "What a fool I am! Why did I have to latch on to winter?" he thought, but it was too late. Alya disappeared in the doorway of her room.

Returning to his room, he sat on the edge of the bed waiting for the wake-up call. Tossing and turning, the children were waking up. There were six beds in the room, two by each wall and two in the middle. There was also a closet housing twelve aluminum coat hangers with school and everyday clothing, and one bedside table per two people.

He thought about Alya again, sensing that he did not want to think about her and yet could not stop. Her sweet face appeared before his eyes again, slightly pale but very beautiful. There was something angular and boy like about her, and also something mysterious, which he could not understand. "How did I not notice her before?" he wondered.

There was a sharp, nasty ring, striking fear into things living and otherwise, rousing the students to their morning exercises. Despite the relentless cold, classes were not cancelled. How unfair!

Cold blew through the classrooms, and steam escaped from their mouths. The stoker's backbreaking efforts were being frustrated by the school's enormous wooden windows with large gaps in the frames, which had been filled diligently with plasticine. Radiators kept bursting here and there. There was not enough heat, and the children were allowed to sit at their desks in their outdoor clothing, without even removing their hats. And if a casual visitor had looked through the doors of the school during recess, he would have been shocked by what he saw. "Don't stop! Run! Run!" came the voices of the teachers. Yes, it was the only way to stay warm. Out of control, the children dashed around all the floors with glee, taking advantage of this hitherto forbidden fruit.

Almost all the teachers at the school were wives of

military men who had come to serve at the base. Some left when their husbands' terms came to an end, new ones arrived. Usually, they were the wives of officers, lieutenants, and even colonels. Regular soldiers did not have time to marry before being called into service. The housemasters, however, were all locals. But who could understand their charges, the orphans, better than them, when their fates were intertwined for many years?

Days dragged on, differing little from one another, until right before the New Year's. For the Vetkin brothers, this long-awaited moment brought great joy. For the two weeks of vacation, they were allowed to return home, where they could talk and sleep their fill. The younger grades especially were waiting impatiently for when the New Year tree would be put up in the dining hall, rising almost to the ceiling.

The girls fussed around, preparing their New Year's costumes, and even many of the boys, forgetting their manly dignity, were trying to think of something fancy to wear. A week before New Year's, the homely dining hall underwent a triumphant change. The sounds of dance and laughter rang incessantly. Alya, in the snowflake costume she devised, performed the song of Cinderella:

"Whether you believe or doubt I did dream last night... That a prince came riding for me on a stallion white."

Her tender voice rang out, indeed resembling a small, graceful princess who had accidentally appeared in the wrong dimension.

After the meeting in the corridor, Sanya did not speak to her again. She also ignored him openly, and it came so naturally to her. During the New Year's festivities, Fedya would not leave his brother's side, his face shining with genuine happiness:

"Hooray! Tomorrow we go home at last!" he whispered in Sanya's ear. Watching Alya, Sanya did not see or hear anything else. More than anything in the world, he wanted to approach her and... And what would happen next, he did not know.

"Sanya, what are you looking at?" Fedya asked, waving his hand several times in front of his face, trying to get his attention.

"Stop already," Sanya asked, grabbing his hand. "I'm just watching Goblin – look what a boring Grandfather Frost he makes."

Indeed, the principal looked pitiful. His false beard and moustache kept sliding off to one side, then the other. The children followed in his footsteps, forgetting for a moment that in front of them was the fierce principal, and, abandoning all sense of self-preservation, begged for a present: a long-awaited transparent bag of sweets.

Soon, all the songs were sung, and the gifts and prizes distributed. The happy students in their light suits rushed to the dormitories through the forty-degree frost, clutching the transparent bags in their hands. The brothers ran on the crunching snow, breathing in the needling, piercing air.

"Sanya!" Fedya shouted. "Aren't you happy? We're going home tomorrow!"

"Don't shout, I'm not at the North Pole, I can hear you."

"Are you in love or something?" Fedya asked, opening the dormitory door abruptly.

"Where'd you get that idea?"

"I am talking to you, and you can't hear me. I read that all lovers are deaf and blind."

"Where did you read that? You don't like to read."

"I don't, but I read it. Do you like that Butterfly or, what's her face, Snowflake, or something?"

There was no sense in hiding it: the perceptive Fedya saw right through him. The brothers retreated to Fedya's room and, closing the door behind them, began to whisper. Sanya told him everything, like in confession.

"I also like her singing. Here's what you do," Fedya advised. "Write her a note, for example: 'let's meet at five in the morning by the radiator and talk.'"

"How are we going to find out when it's five? We don't have watches. We'd have to run downstairs to the clock all night so as not to sleep through it. That won't work," the ardent lover objected.

"Yes," Fedya agreed, "that won't do." Thinking a while, he suggested: "Maybe you should write her a poem about love; they recommend it in books as well."

Realizing that his brother knew nothing about matters of love, Sanya waved his hand, walked out of the room, and was heading back to his own.

Fedya jumped out after him, shouting:

"Hey, you forgot your present."

"You can eat it," his brother said without turning around. Fedya froze in confusion, with present in hand.

"Ah, can't cure love, gotta do something," he said in disappointment.

"Love? What love?" he heard suddenly behind his back.

Turning around, he saw the smiling face of under-achiever and grade repeater Romka.

"Who's in love? With whom?" he asked curiously.

"Quiet, you..." Fedya hissed, looking at his departing brother. Romka stood in the middle of the corridor, cupped his hands together, and bellowed suddenly:

"Vetkin's in lo-o-o-ve!"

The words came like a gunshot in the back; stopping, Sanya said disappointedly:

"I can't tell you anything, can I Fedya?"

The next moment, turning around, he saw a strange scene. Romka was retreating, defending himself with his hands, while the small Fedya was advancing on him in rage, waving the transparent gift bag in his opponent's face and striking his arms. Unable to bear the uneven struggle, the bag burst and its entire contents – two oranges, cookies, candies, and a rooster-shaped lollipop on a wooden stick – went flying on the floor. Cursing, Romka went on the offensive, grabbing Fedya's arm and twisting it behind his back so hard that the latter fell to his knees, howling. Sanya dashed to his brother's aid, and, several minutes later, they were sitting triumphantly on the back of the vanquished foe, lying face down on the floor. Trying to throw them off, Romka yelled for help.

"Oh my, look how strong we are, crying for help like that," Fedya mocked him, glancing at his brother guiltily.

Not wasting any time, the other children were happily picking up the sweets scattered on the floor. A little boy named Sema came up to the brothers and asked:

"Can you hit him for me? He stole four afternoon luncheons from me already."

"No, we can't," Fedya said sternly. "He's getting it for something else right now."

And then Galina Petrovna appeared again, in a movie-style entrance, shouting from far away:

"If it weren't for you Vetkins, I would be sitting here with nothing to do. Why are there sweets on the floor? You had too much?" she scolded. "Who started it?" the house-mistress demanded, staring at the teenagers lined up against the wall, as if for execution.

"He did," Romka jabbed his finger at Fedya.

"Me and him," Sanya admitted, stepping forward; he had seen Alya's face in the crowd and wanted to be done with the incident as soon as possible.

"What were you fighting over?" the headmistress demanded an explanation.

The next moment, the brothers looked at Romka and saw his smiling face, ready for confession. But Fedya beat him to the punch and said:

"Over the present. Look at his snout – he sure likes oranges and stealing luncheons from the weak kids."

Some of the students clapped their hands. Romka's eyes filled with rage, and, forgetting completely about the real cause of the fight, he pushed Fedya in the shoulder. Losing her patience, Galina Petrovna moved on to the conclusion of the episode and said:

"You, brothers. Tomorrow, before going home, you are washing the floor in the dining hall. And you," she turned to Romka, "are washing the floor in the bathroom."

In the evening, as he lay in his government-issued bed and listened to the children sigh as they fell asleep, Sanya thought about Fedya. He thought about how courageously Fedya had defended him that day from Romka. He also thought about Romka's life, boring and monotonous, two years of it spent in the same grade. Romka said it was his own choice, only because he wanted to be in the same class as his brother. Perhaps he was like this because he was an orphan, Sanya thought. Gradually, thoughts of Romka were displaced with thoughts of Alya. She, too, had no one and was an orphan, somewhat withdrawn but not mean. She had songs, concerts, competitions.

The next day, during recess, Sanya placed a book on Alya's desk, saying:

"I am returning your book."

Alya moved the textbook closer in confusion and began to leaf through it until she found a sheet of paper folded in four. "Forgive me, I lied. I also love fall," she read.

After the final lesson, Alya walked up to Sanya and returned the book, saying:

"You are mistaken, this isn't my book."

"Hey, I lost my book, perhaps it's mine?" came claimed Romka's voice. "Mine has a goat drawn on the last page."

"It's my book, there aren't any goats here," Sanya shouted, running out of the class, clutching the book in his hands, knowing that the long-awaited response was concealed inside. The same piece of paper was lying on the first page, and on the back of it was an inscription in beautiful letters: "I also lied. I love winter."

"And what am I supposed to think now? Perhaps she is mocking me," he thought.

Regretting that Fedya did not know anything about love, he nevertheless shared the story about the note with him during the dining hall cleaning.

"What do you think it means?"

"It means forget about her," Fedya exploded. "And why do you two care about all those seasons anyway? You should have asked her what she likes best: fish or candy. Or which astronauts she likes. Or where she'd want to go when she grows up: Africa or maybe America?"

"What do fish and astronauts have to do with anything? You have to understand it all happened by itself. Somehow, I couldn't talk to her about the *banya*, after all.
I wanted to be romantic."

The brothers fell silent, concentrating on their work. The New Year tree had been put away after the previous day's festivities. There were numerous needles, twigs, candy wrappers, and even broken tree decorations scattered on the floor. After finishing the job, Sanya asked Fedya to wait and, wishing to see Alya for at least a moment, ran to the dormitory.

And indeed, she was standing near his room, leaning with her back against the windowsill and gazing at the long corridor. Seeing the breathless Sanya, the girl smiled and said:

"I thought you were long since back on your Tenth Proletarian."

"Third," he corrected.

"Third or tenth, does it really matter?"

Having learned that he should be careful with her, Sanya did not argue.

"Do you want to come visit us for New Year's?" he said haltingly all of a sudden, stepping very close to her.

Alya raised her eyebrows and her green eyes became round, gazing at him in surprise. Her cheeks flushed, and she lowered her head without answering.

When he had disappeared, the girl leaned against the window and tried to melt the ice with her breath, making a small opening that allowed her to peek outside. She saw him run to the dining hall and then head towards the exit along with his brother.

Marching on the crunching snow in incredibly high spirits, Sanya was contemplating his unexpected invitation to Alya, without asking an adult beforehand. "What if they say no? It'll be a disgrace!" He decided not to say anything to anyone, leaving it a secret between him and Fedya.

Now he knew for sure that she was not angry at him, she just had that sort of personality, like a hedgehog, who only has needles for show. In reality, she also liked him a little.

After learning about Songbird's special invitation, Fedya wrinkled his brow, not bothering to conceal his disappointment. Frankly, he was bored of all the snowflakes, Romkas, and Mashkas. He wanted to spend time alone with his brother, as it always happened. Fedya decided not to express his opinion, hoping that nothing would happen and that things would sort themselves out somehow.

"Are you jealous or something?" Sanya asked, puzzled.

"I don't care," echoed the indifferent response.

"Yeah, I see you don't care, but it shouldn't be like that."

"Why shouldn't it?" Fedya said acridly.

"Oh, get lost..." Sanya interrupted, not wishing to continue the unpleasant conversation.

He knew that nothing would work without his brother's help. Deciding to give him some time to think, Sanya switched over to domestic life, which, after his return, he found to be full of pleasant moments. The knitted rugs on the wooden floorboards, the painfully near and dear creaking of the shutters, the lace on the embroidered cushions, the crackling of the coal in the stove, and even the tin box from which Grandma Claudia and his mother would frequently take needles and thread to mend clothes, and the heavy frames on the walls with photographs of unknown relatives: all of it filled his heart with joy.

At home, he would not part with pencil and paper, making sketches and drawings. After the incident with the boots, he was done with oil technique forever. There was not enough time at school, and he was embarrassed to be better at something than the others. Sanya did not understand how Alya had managed to soar above the other girls like that, distinguishing herself with independence and talent. She paid a high price for it: others girls did not like her, tried to spite her, and once even tried to throw her a "blanket party." They turned off the lights and tried to beat her, but no such luck – the quick and nimble Alya squatted and slipped through the enraged gang of girls, led by Mashka. The girls ended up pummeling each other in the dark, punishing none but themselves. But when Alya started to sing, a genuine truce would ensue, if only for a short time.

Sanya was dreaming hopelessly about her. Seeing his brother in complete detachment, Fedya came to hate the girl in the snowflake costume more and more. Two days before New Year's, Sanya could not bear it anymore and convinced his brother to come to the orphanage with him to visit Alya. Fedya was ready to go to the ends of the earth if need be, if only he could prevent that singing girl from appearing in their house.

A New Year tree was standing on Lenin Square, decorated with large, multi-colored lamps and a garland made and hung there by workers from the factories. People with nets and bags full of various merchandise ran not walked, through the streets, afraid to freeze. Children were playing snowballs somewhere and building a snow fort.

Reaching their stop, with difficulty – the bus engine stalled four times, unable to handle the cold – the brothers hopped out of their transport and began to run.

"Oh my, I can't feel my extremities. That's it, they'll have to be amputated," Fedya whined.

"Your hands or your feet?"

"Hands and feet, everywhere." Tears flowed down his cheeks, dripping on the collar of his coat and freezing.

"Are you crying or something?" Sanya asked with concern.

"Of course I am. My limbs are howling from the cold, and the tears are coming out all by themselves."

Running up to the dormitory, they stopped in the foyer to catch their breath and saw, to their great surprise, Galina Petrovna coming out to greet them.

"Hello!" the boys called out in unison, as if on cue.

"You two?" the housemistress said with disappointment. "You have to be home now I have no right to let you in. Warm up and march along home!" she commanded.

They had certainly not anticipated such a turn of events. To ride over two bridges in forty-degree frost only to say hello to Galina Petrovna. Fedya tossed off his *valenki* and, rubbing his numb toes, begged the housemistress to give them more time.

"Warm up, I'll wait," she said, leaning against the wall, folding her arms on her chest haughtily, as always, and staring right at them.

"No, she doesn't like us," Fedya whispered and then said sweetly:

"Galina Petrovna, let us stay here for a little bit, I'll wash the floor for you."

"In the bathroom!" her eyes glittered happily.

Fedya glanced at his brother imploringly.

"Actually, I think I'm warm already," he said, pulling his *valenki* back on.

Suddenly, two girls appeared out of nowhere, chattering like magpies in one voice that a radiator had burst on the back staircase.

The housemistress hurried off with a look of concern, giving orders to fetch the stoker as she walked, and then turned to the brothers and said:

"Now I definitely need someone to clean up."

"Hurry up and get dressed," Fedya urged, "I'm ready."

"I'm going, I'm going, I'm ready too," Sanya answered reluctantly.

"Hurry or she'll really bring us a mop. Why did I have to say that?"

"Fedya, maybe you can wait, and I'll look for Alya in the meantime?" the lover said pleadingly.

"And what do I get in return?"

"I'll take out the trash three times instead of you." Sanya looked at him like at a savior.

"No," his brother said sharply. "I don't need you to take the trash out. Let's go home." And after a moment's silence, he suggested:

"Here's what you can do: leave her a note."

"Where should I leave it, by the front door maybe?" Sanya said sarcastically.

"Not at the door," Fedya continued, failing to understand his brother's subtle joke, "leave it in her room under her pillow."

Indeed, Sanya marveled at his brother's simple and brilliant idea. Not wasting any time, he found a piece of a paper and a pencil and began to write something. After finishing, he quickly ran up to the second floor. Silence reigned in the corridor. The children were either sitting in games' rooms or had run off to the back staircase to watch the stoker stop the leak from the radiator. Entering Alya's empty room, Sanya became confused, dashing between the six beds and not knowing which one to choose. Steps and voices came from the corridor, and, shoving his note under the pillow of the most neatly made bed, he ran out of the room. Only at home, warming up by the stove, did Fedya ask him:

"What did you write to her?"

"I wrote our address, invited her to come over tomorrow and signed: 'Vetkin,'" he said pensively.

"So what now?" Fedya would not relent.

"Nothing. I'm not even sure I placed it under her pillow."

"What do you mean you aren't sure?"

"I'm not. I don't know where she sleeps – on the left, on the right, or in the middle."

"Sanya, imagine if Mashka comes tomorrow."

"Why Mashka?"

"Because they sleep in the same room," Fedya burst out laughing.

Sanya did not have to think long to imagine how there would be a knock on the door the next day, and Grandma Claudia would open the door and let that nasty schemer into the house. Sanya's mood was ruined, while Fedya, by contrast, could not stop laughing.

Indeed, the next day, there was a confident knock on the door, telling Claudia to hurry to the porch and open up. Hearing a familiar voice, the boys froze.

"Hello, do the Vetkins live here?" Mashka asked just in case.

"They do," Claudia said calmly, letting in the girl, who brushed the snow from her *valenki*, entered the house, and said loudly:

"Your Fedya invited me over. Oh, it's so pretty here. Did Fedya draw all this?" the girl said in sincere surprise, glancing round.

The brothers stared at each other in horror until, finally, Sanya said:

"Forgive me Fedya; your friend's here to see you." Now he was the one laughing.

Fedya dashed throughout the room, not knowing what to do. If it had been summer, he would have jumped out the window, but the windows had been firmly shut. Thrusting his hands in his pockets and putting on an indifferent look, he sighed deeply and strolled into the living room in a stately fashion. Claudia began to fuss around in the kitchen and soon jam, hot tea, and sweets appeared on the table. Several minutes later, Mashka was sitting there, languid from the warmth and from Fedya's chattering. He told her excitedly about trains, ants, snakes, and airplanes. The girl also chattered incessantly in response. Completely forgetting that he had not invited her, Fedya told her about astronauts and seagoing ships, pouring more tea in her empty cup in a masculine fashion. Twilight arrived at about two o'clock in the afternoon, and Mashka hurried back. Walking her out to the bus stop, Fedya returned happy.

"Sanya, she's not so bad, you know… she kissed me goodbye right here." He pressed his palm to his cheek.

Sanya listened to his brother's tender chirping, and thought how fortunate it was that Mashka did not understand anything.

"Maybe she can't sing as well as Songbird, but at least she can chatter like a machine gun."

"Fedya, you don't have to make excuses. If you like her, you should be friends with her."

"What's being friends have to do with anything?" Fedya said, offended. "I was actually saving your skin back there. She came to you without knowing it."

"No," Sanya insisted. "As soon as she read the note, she immediately thought of you."

"You think so? You think girls can like me?" Fedya said coquettishly.

"I don't know about all the girls, but she sure likes you."

"She likes our candy and cookies, and your painted chairs. 'Oh, it's just like a museum in here,'" Fedya mimicked her. "She probably hasn't even been to a museum and wouldn't last a minute there from boredom."

"Have you been to a museum?"

"I have."

"And when have you been, and to which museum?"

"To our Ethnographic Museum. They have mummies sitting there, warming their hands around an artificial campfire."

"Did you like it?" Sanya questioned him.

"Like? You have to be nuts to like it. We have our own museum with mummies, right next door. You can look all you want at how they drag the dead bodies to the morgue and back. You saw how much old clothing they have by the fence there, a whole pile."

More than anything, Sanya hated talking and hearing about the dead. The dormitory's proximity to the infectious disease hospital and the morgue on the other side of the fence was enough for him. Every year, as he headed to the orphanage for the winter session, he was afraid to be assigned to a bed in a room that looked out on the hospital grounds.

"Let's not talk about it."

"Aha, you're afraid, afraid," Fedya would not let up. "You know, Grandma Claudia says you should fear the living, not the dead."

Fedya did not care which way his room was facing. "Let it be the moon," he'd say. To him, for some reason, the moon was the epitome of human tribulations. Claudia's voice came from the front hall, asking Fedya to take out the trash.

Left alone with his thoughts, Sanya contemplated the conversation they just had. He could not understand himself why the sight of funerals, which occurred almost every day in City N, except for holidays and Sundays, gave rise to such fear and desperation in his soul. Over eight years, he should have easily gotten used to them, like Fedya and the other kids, but for some reason he could not. Every time the music of brass instruments from beyond the bridge tore through the silence of the school and all the students plastered their faces against the window, trying to see who was being buried this time, Sanya sat motionlessly behind his desk.

The procession moved uphill, and the body of the deceased, dressed in new clothes, often better than the ones worn during life, lay open to the elements in a coffin decorated with artificial flowers. The slow march floated past the windows of the school named after Lenin, carrying the long-suffering departed on his final journey.

Everything looked solemn, in accordance with accepted traditions. There was always an old woman walking in front, tossing fir branches on both sides of the road. The friends of the deceased walked behind the old woman in pairs, carrying large wreaths with final messages. Then a four-instrument brass orchestra came, playing the same sad melody out of rhythm. After the orchestra, like in a slow-motion movie, a car drove where the relatives of the deceased were sitting next to the body, weeping endlessly.

And even though all were equal in Sanya's country, one could determine the social status of the deceased very easily. From the quantity of wreaths, flowers, and musicians, the children learned to comment very accurately on the circumstances of the final march. "Look! Look!" excited shouts came from the students. "This must be a director of some sort. There's an empty bus riding in their wake to take everyone back to town." Or: "Look! Look, this must be an orphan, no music and only one wreath." And again: "Look! Look! This one's being carried by six men the whole way. He must have been a good man." And so on without end. The children knew more about funeral procedures than they did about geography or foreign history. As for Sanya, he did not wish to put up with this everyday occurrence, and, in his dreams, he frequently imagined his and Fedya's school in a city just like theirs, on a mountain just like theirs, on the shore of a river just like theirs, but without the fatal turn of the road leading to the city cemetery and the unpleasant presence on the other side of the fence.

He heard Fedya come back inside, moaning indignantly that it was all too cold.

"It has to be cold, my dear, it's winter," came Claudia's voice.

"Is it this cold all over Russia?" Fedya asked.

"Not everywhere, my friend, our nation is enormous, with different time zones and different climates. And what was that girl's name?" she wondered.

"Eh... Mashka," he drawled indifferently.

"Not Mashka but Masha," she corrected him tenderly. "And, better yet, in the French manner, Marie."

"Marie!" Fedya exclaimed. "Not bad at all. Do you still remember French?"

"I used to," she smiled meaningfully. "You see, my friend, a language is like an instrument: to play it well, one must practice."

Claudia was a very wise and discreet grandmother. With her few friends, she attended church, went into the woods to pick mushrooms and berries, and gathered in the evenings at her neighbor Lena's, sitting up late and playing a gambling game called "Russian Lotto," making token bets of twenty kopeks. Her grandsons loved her very much and, even though she was their actual grandmother, always addressed her in a polite and formal manner.

"Grandma," Fedya asked suddenly. "Why were you exiled to Siberia?"

"What are you talking about my dearest?" she said, growing worried. "No one has ever exiled anyone to Siberia. Everyone comes here happily of their own accord. You can see how pretty it is here, endless forests all around us. And winters? There is no winter like in Siberia. All the germs die in the frost. People come here to get healthy, like a resort."

"Then why do we have locals and exiles in our city?"

"The locals..." the woman explained as calmly as she could, "the locals are the ones who came here three hundred or more years ago. And the exiles are new residents, who came here a little later."

"So we are locals?" Fedya asked.

"See?" Claudia sighed in relief. "You understood everything correctly."

"Then why are they calling us exiled bourgeois?"

"Good Lord! Who's calling you that?" she asked, clasping her hands in confusion.

"The locals."

"No, my dear, they have it all mixed up, and don't you talk about this to them or anyone else. And what do they say at the school?"

"They say we are all equal, and that we would have had real communism long ago had the Germans not attacked. And they also say that we should be endlessly grateful to our state, which feeds us, clothes us, and takes care of us. In a place like England we would have long since died of hunger. Grandma Claudia, why did you leave Leningrad if it was so beautiful there? Mom played the violin; Grandpa lived in peace and happiness. You could have gone to church and prayed, since they have a lot of them there and they are probably all pretty, while there is only a single one here, and it's wooden."

"Fedya! Where did you get all that?" the woman said, all worked up.

"I've heard things," he said self-importantly.

Claudia hugged him by the shoulders and gave him a kiss. Smiling, she said firmly:

"We left, Fedenka, because we wanted to go to Siberia, my darling. To a resort in Siberia!"

Listening to the conversation, Sanya sensed the exaggerated optimism in Claudia's voice, concealing the truth.

After Fedya returned, he sat on Sanya's bed and said conclusively:

"See where we live? A resort. Everyone should live for a hundred years or more here." After a moment's silence, he added: "Mashka has a new name now, only she doesn't know about it yet. She's Marie now! Pretty, isn't it?" Sanya nodded along as he listened to him, leaning over his album and drawing something diligently.

That night, he dreamed of Alya. She was running down a long, sun-flooded corridor, while he was leaning against the wall and watching her. As she passed him, Alya grabbed his hand decisively and said: "Run!" He did not resist and ran next to her, feeling the warmth of her hand in his. Reaching the end of the corridor, they stopped in front of an enormous glass door. Placing her index finger to her lips, Alya whispered:

"Only be quiet," and with these words she leaned on the heavy door with her shoulder and pulled him inside. The room was completely empty, with a transparent domed ceiling, and in the middle of it was a small table with a book. Letting go of his hand, Alya dashed towards the book and opened it with a quick motion. He hurried after her and, glancing over her shoulder, saw two pages, shining with emptiness.

"Read," she asked him impatiently.

"Perhaps you can open another page? There's nothing written on this one."

"Read it," the girl repeated stubbornly.

"Maybe you can start reading?" he said suddenly. Closing the book, Alya turned to him and asked:

"You can't see anything can you?"

"I can't. And what can you see?" Sanya asked.

The girl placed the book on the table, retreated to the door, and ran out.

He opened the book once again in confusion and, to his surprise, discovered that the pages were crisscrossed with tiny letters. Shouting: "I see! I see!" he ran after her, but she was nowhere to be found...

Opening his eyes, he lay there, half asleep, trying to understand what was going on. He heard Grandma Claudia, who was beginning her day, as usual, with a morning prayer.

"God forgive us. In the name of the Father, the Son, and the Holy Ghost. Amen," came from her room. His grandmother never shared with anyone which god she worshipped. It was forbidden not only to talk but even to think about it. In Sanya's country, everyone had to be an atheist and believe in the party leaders, in the Communist Party, in the Young Pioneers and the Komsomol. The elderly were permitted to go to church, but only the elderly.

Sanya heard the anthem of the Soviet Union, which meant it was six in the morning. Now he could hear how grandma Claudia, having completed the prayer, began her morning exercises, performing them to the heart-piercing sounds of the anthem pouring from the small radio hanging on the wall at the head of her bed. Walking into the kitchen and opening the small iron door, his father began to toss pieces of coal into the furnace, which had cooled almost completely overnight. Sanya felt warmth flow from the furnace, crawling under his blanket, enveloping him and putting him to sleep. Yesterday, they had received a new telegram from his mother in Tofalaria; she wrote that the weather had improved slightly, and there was a chance to return to the city for two weeks by helicopter.

Sanya liked the early morning, when the adults, upon waking, would move noiselessly through the house on their business, giving the kids a chance to sleep in while on break.

He realized that he had probably fallen in love, and did not know what to do about it or how to live with it. The emotion he felt did not resemble any of the ones he had experienced to this day. He returned to their conversations again and again, reliving them several times and imagining what would have happened if he had said something else or responded differently. Again and again he would see her sweet face and the stubborn look of her green eyes. Sanya promised himself that he would at least not think about her during New Year's Eve, or else the vengeful Fedya would never forgive him.

At nine in the morning, just as it happened every year, the brothers and their father boarded the number five bus and headed out of town. There were many firs growing in the woods, and it was not forbidden to cut them down. They took the same route back. The spirits of the other bus passengers were lifted when they saw the tree, and smiles appeared on their faces. Forgetting tiredness and cold, the people began to talk amongst themselves and even crack jokes. Reaching their home street, the brothers pulled the tree along the ground, leaving the large tail track of an incredible beast behind them. Good news awaited them at home: their mother had finally come home after a three-month absence. She was already fussing around in the kitchen and helping Claudia with the holiday dinner, telling various stories about her life in the north. The house smelled of coziness and jam pies.

Commotion reigned around their green guest. Positioned and fixed in a special basin with water, the guest was being decorated. The tree was adorned with a small number of tree decorations, snowflakes made by the boys from shiny colored paper, and various sweets. A plastic Father Frost and Snow Maiden appeared under the fir, surrounded by pristine white cotton to mimic snow, sprinkled with sparkles. Fedya managed to count all the sweets on the branches, in case his brother was to start eating them first and without any warning.

Their mother, happy and carefree – which did not happen often – whirled around the house, appearing here and there, finding time to speak to everyone or simply to hug her sons and sit quietly with them for a moment. Everyone said that his mother was very beautiful, but Sanya, understanding nothing about women's beauty, simply took the statement at its word, admiring her as she whispered about something with Grandma Claudia, tilting her head. She never parted with her work pouch, which resembled a travel bag and was packed full of various medicines. Inside, one could find: vials of Brilliant Green and Iodine, bandages, tablets, syringes packed in glass cases, ready for sterilization at any minute, glass vials with penicillin, ampoules of Novocaine, and much, much more. When she was home, the neighbors knew that they could receive first aid here and would knock on her door demandingly and without hesitation. For Sanya and Fedya, their mother was the most important person in the world. Restrained in praise, she always managed to give that special, even if accidental, glance that would for many days remind the brothers of her deep love.

On New Year's Eve, the parents were hastening to a ball at the local recreation center. The mother stood before a small oval mirror in the front hall, wearing a long dress of soft green color and fitting a crown decorated with various shiny trinkets. The brothers lay on the floor beneath the tree, watching her every move through the open door.

"Guess what my costume is," she said, turning towards them with a gleaming smile.

"Que-en!" Fedya shouted out playfully.

"Not a queen at all. What do you think, Sanya?" she continued, smiling mysteriously.

He did not know what to say; he only saw the pretty dress that she had designed and made herself, and thought one could wear something like this to a real ball at a palace.

"All right, remember what my favorite fairy tale is, I've read it to you many times."

"Mistress of some kind of mountain!"

"Not 'some kind,' but Copper Mountain," the father corrected Fedya, watching with a smile. "So, are you ready?" he asked, handing her a coat and a down shawl. Their father did not like costumes and was wearing a suit and tie, as usual.

"Don't open the door for anyone, don't play with fire," came her final instructions, and then, happy, she disappeared behind the door with their father.

Behind the wall, on the neighbors' half of the house, an exciting game of "Russian Lotto" was in progress. They heard laughter and loud voices, and occasionally they could even discern the dominating voice of Grandma Claudia. This is how, lying under the tree and eating sweets till they were sick, to the sound of voices from behind the wall, the boys met the new year of 1977.

The Fire

After two weeks of break, the brothers returned to their state-provided stomping ground, trying to make it until spring with their last ounces of strength. Sanya could not even imagine the profound shock that awaited him. It was all the other kids talked about. Yes, everyone talked about her, Songbird, who would never sing for them again, having proudly departed to represent their school at an amateur art competition.

The news that Alya had left to the distant city of Khabarovsk shook him to the core. It turned out that the school had long been in negotiations with Alya's aunt, who lived there, but no one had told the girl anything until the last moment. On the one hand, Sanya was happy at this turn of events. On the other, how could she leave without saying goodbye? And as soon as he thought this, an excited Fedya ran into the room and showed him a piece of paper folded into a triangle.

"Sanya, I have a note for you, Songbird asked Marie to give it to you."

Taking the note with a heavy sigh, he began to read:

"Hello Sanya. When you read this letter, I will be walking in a new, faraway land called Khabarovsk. I will have a house, an aunt, and two cousins, and perhaps I will be able to love New Year's and the school breaks like you do. My parents were geologists; they died during one of their expeditions. For some reason, I can tell this to you now, but only to you. My aunt told me that Khabarovsk is far bigger than our city, but for now it doesn't mean much to me because you remain here, in City N. I always liked you very much, even when I was just a regular Songbird to you. I know that I will miss you, and I'll write to you. My address: First Soviet St., building #10. Alya."

Rereading the letter again and again, Sanya spilled tears, weeping for the love that had not managed to take root. He did not believe in writing letters. He believed that the most important events in life could only happen here in City N. Everything that happened outside its bounds had no meaning.

Unbearable days began to drag on, with a firm desire to be rid of any thought of her. Not to draw her, as he did daily, not to dream of her, not to talk to her in his thoughts.

After several days, another staggering piece of news flew round the school thanks to Marie's efforts. The news was that, after reading Songbird's note, Sanya had wept like a child. And now, all the girls, including ones from other classes, recognized him as a romantic hero and wanted to be friends with him, showering him with notes signed with different nicknames. "Let's meet under the staircase after lights-out. The Owl." "Let's go to the movies on Sunday, I'll buy you a ticket. The Tooth." "Sit next to me on the ride to the *banya*..."

Gathering the notes, Sanya gave them to Fedya without reading them, with the words:

"Be my secretary. Answer them if you want, throw them out if you don't."

But Fedya, who dreamed of adding even more variety to life, had other plans entirely. During recess, he slipped into the Goblin's office and left the love notes on his principal's desk. He did not have to wait long before three short rings of the bell deafened the school, announcing an urgent event. The classes lined up instantly in the hallway, and when silence fell, the Goblin suddenly approached Sanya's class and demanded:

"Owl, step out of the lineup!"

No one moved.

"What's your name?" asked the principal, jabbing his finger in the face of the girl standing in front of him.

"Marie," came the proud, ringing answer.

"What the hell is Marie? Nicknames are forbidden!"

"It's not a nickname, it's my new name."

"Silence!" the Goblin shouted, raising the pieces of paper over his head. "I order the authors of these notes to voluntarily step out of line and walk to my office."

"'Forget that fool, I can also sing. The Goat,'" the Goblin read loudly, stopping occasionally and looking over the assembled students with his different eyes. Some of the students, thinking this was some sort of surprise performance, began to laugh.

"What's so funny?" the principal turned red. "You think it's okay to write me notes of this sort?" he asked. "I saw your bare bottom, and I liked it. The Booger."

At that moment, Sanya glanced suddenly at Galina Petrovna, realizing that once she heard about the bare bottom, she would surely guess what this was all about, and he was not mistaken. Approaching the principal, the housemistress whispered something in his ear, and then they approached Sanya's class together without any further discussion.

"Vetkin!" a thunderous echo came suddenly. "To my office, march!"

Sanya stood in the middle of the principal's office, on an ornamental Eastern rug, with his head downcast.

"All right, Vetkin, tell me why you did this," the principal said, leaning back in his chair.

The boy lowered his head even further. What could he tell this heartless man? About his unfortunate love? About the silly girls? About Fedya, who had pulled such a dumb prank? What about? Sanya remained silent.

"Don't be silent, Vetkin. Tell me who wrote these notes, and why. Tell me their names, and I'll let you go."

"I don't know their names."

"What's the matter, did you lose your memory? Don't be shy now, my dear," the Goblin mocked.

Fedya and Marie spun around behind the door, peeking into the keyhole and wishing to help the unfortunate Sanya. Rumors circulated among the children that the principal occasionally punished the students using a soldier's belt with a large metal buckle, a gift of friendship to the school from the local military unit. The kids who had experienced this on their own skin had warned that, if the Goblin were to open the lower left drawer in his desk, it meant you had to run, save yourself as quickly as possible.

Sanya watched the Goblin's every move with incredible tension.

"I am asking you for the last time," the principal said with an unpleasant smile, opening the bottom left drawer.

"I am telling the truth, I don't know," the teenager lied as sincerely as he could, his voice breaking.

Someone knocked on the door, and, the next moment,

Sanya saw the concerned faces of Fedya and Marie on the doorstep.

"Comrade Principal, may we enter?" they said in unison.

"Come in," the principal replied with the same devilish smile, waving his hand in agreement.

"Comrade Principal," Fedya began, walking almost right up to his desk. "The city kids wrote these notes, you know, the ones who live in normal families. We know we aren't supposed to use bad nicknames. But they call each other whatever. And we... we'd never."

Sanya's eyes brightened and he kept marveling at his younger brother. Yes, if it weren't for all these extreme situations created by Fedya himself, Sanya would have never found out what his brother was really capable of.

"Even Mashka, I mean Marie," Fedya corrected himself glancing sidelong at her and continuing in an angelic voice, "even she can confirm this."

The Goblin motioned for the girl to come closer and, placing a pen and paper before her, commanded:

"Write it. Write everything you know about this. But if it turns out to be a lie, I'll have you sent to a labor camp."

Blushing, Marie picked up the pen with a trembling hand.

"Comrade Principal," Fedya asked suddenly. "Can I write it? I know for sure what happened."

"Who brought the notes into my office?" the principal shouted, banging his fist on the desk.

"The watchman!" Fedya blurted out, frightened by his shouting. "The watchman! He found them and... brought them here, thinking it was something important. He can't read, after all."

"What do you mean, he can't read?" the Goblin said in

indignation. "Everyone knows how to read in our country."

"Everyone but him," Fedya defended himself as best he could. "I personally heard him ask the first graders: 'Read this for me, I don't understand a thing.'"

"Get out!" the principal shouted, getting up from his chair and pointing at the door. Then, turning to Sanya, he added: "Remember. You're on the hook."

From that day, Sanya tried to avoid him, imagining a giant hook and himself dangling on it helplessly like a marionette.

After the incident with the notes, bleak days returned, interspersed with various small joys such as sledding down the steep bank of the Ut River or playing hockey. Due to the absence of a coach, the kids shared their experience, passing it on to the beginners. They skated on a temporary ice rink between the older kids' dormitory and the dining hall, slapping the puck like madmen. Fedya was the goalkeeper, wearing a plastic bucket on his head instead of a helmet and waving his stick like a sword. He twirled his head awkwardly, peering through the eyeholes that had been cut neatly in the bucket, looking like a funny sort of creature. Naturally, most of their days were taken up by classes and homework.

Returning to the cold classroom, Sanya looked with nostalgia at the empty spot where Alya had sat not long ago. And he would again be visited by thoughts and feelings that he could not suppress. Sharing his desk with the smallest boy in class, named Gosha, he would try to calm himself down by turning away and writing numerous letters to Alya. Writing them, and then tearing them to pieces and hiding them in his pocket.

"I won't copy, I already finished," Gosha would say,

peeking over Sanya's shoulder.

"Then do something else."

But Gosha did not have enough imagination, and he kept pestering Sanya with questions.

Gosha was the most harmless boy in the entire school, because even a first-grader could easily harm him. His nickname was Filipok, like the hero in the story of the same name, about a boy who was so small he could crawl into one ear of a cow and out the other.

"Sanya?" asked the boy. "You think I'll be taller some-day?"

"Of course you will," Sanya reassured him. "A man keeps growing until old age. You have plenty of years to go."

Funeral music came from beyond the bridge.

"Finally," Romka exclaimed. "I just got really bored for some reason. Was wondering what I could be missing today."

Giggling, the girls jumped from their seats and became glued to the windows, peering at the unfortunate soul who had left the earthly abode in such cold. Galina Petrovna was not angry, allowing the children to participate in the "lawful" parts of life. This time, the procession did not walk but practically ran at a speedy pace. It ran so as to somehow preserve some degree of warmth and survive the cold. Reaching the foot of the mountain, the musicians stopped playing and tossed their instruments on the truck. The procession turned left and stretched out beneath the school windows.

"Oy!" a girl named Tonya exclaimed suddenly and burst into tears. "That's our aunt Sonya being buried."

The students turned to the plump Tonya, who had now become not only an observer of the proceedings but also a participant. Like the Vetkin brothers, she was a visiting student who lived with her sick mother and the mother's sister aunt Sonya, moving to the orphanage during winter.

"Is she nuts, dying in such frost?" Romka commented with an expression of sympathy, interrupting the silence. Ordering the children back to their seats, Galina Petrovna turned to the weeping Tonya and summarized:

"See? You have no business looking out the windows. If you had been sitting in your spot like Vetkin, you wouldn't have known anything about your aunt Sonya."

In the evening, Sanya felt very tired and waited impatiently for lights-out. The dormitory gradually fell silent, and only occasionally would he hear the quiet shouts from the night attendant, hurrying along the dallying students.

At midnight, the bell rang suddenly.

"Hurry! Hurry!" the night attendant yelled in a hoarse voice, running up and down the hallway with a flashlight, bathed in a crimson glow. "Put on your warm things and get downstairs!"

Getting dressed, Sanya jumped out into the hallway in search of his brother, bumping into the other students as they ran around in a panic.

Reaching Fedya's room, he found him sitting alone on the bed in complete darkness.

"Get dressed, quickly! Why are you sitting around?"

"What's the matter, some kind of war again?" Fedya muttered, dressing himself unhurriedly.

"Doesn't look like war. Get dressed!" Sanya pleaded, trying to make out what was happening outside through the frosted-over window.

"Fedya! We're on fire!"

"What do you mean, on fire? Why isn't anyone saving us?" Fedya sniveled.

Grabbing his brother by the arm, Sanya pulled him along towards the staircase.

"Sanya, I... I'm scared," Fedya whispered.

"Stop whining already, I'm scared myself."

The sinister glow was pushing inside through the window, piercing the empty hallway and pouring into the empty rooms. The brothers descended the stone staircase in pitch darkness, joining the others who had gathered below. The night attendant tried to count her charges by the heads as they sat on the floor.

A bustling noise came from behind the door, and the attendant from the younger kids' dormitory appeared on the doorstep.

"I brought the little ones," she said. "It's safer here."

The castigated youngsters walked in, two by two, and stood in the darkness sniveling and crying.

When asked: "What's on fire?" the newly arrived attendant said that it was the clothing storehouse.

"Great, now we'll have to wear the same underwear for half a year," someone's voice commented.

"Is the school on fire, by any chance?" Romka wondered. "It's right nearby."

Realizing that only the storehouse was on fire, the students calmed down somewhat, scarcely believing what happened. After all, the fire station, with its two engines and a tall, promising-looking fire tower, was right next door across the road. The sheaf of fire dashed across the sky, and it seemed that, in a moment, the wooden schoolhouse would also catch fire, and then the younger kids' dormitory. Sparks twirled over the orphanage, winking out high in the air. Trucks rolled into the hospital courtyard one by one, ready to evacuate the seriously ill at any moment.

A girl of the first grade wept on the floor next to Fedya.

"What's the big deal, it's just the storehouse," Fedya tried to calm her down.

"My housemistress says I'm growing very quickly," the girl would not let up. "What am I going to wear? I don't have a mommy or daddy."

"Don't cry. We have all those patrons: Auto Depot, the military unit, the beer brewery. They'll help us again and buy new clothes."

"For real?" the girl quieted down.

"Ask the attendant if you don't believe me."

The next day, Marie flew around the rooms like a magpie, spreading the latest news, gushing about what happened. No one knew what started the fire, but when the fire engines arrived, the water did not flow because it had frozen solid in the barrels. Then they hooked up the hose to the fire tower across the street and started spraying, knocking over the flame from the direction of the school. They worked until morning, when everything had burned to the ground.

"They say that Goblin helped put it out," Marie chattered. "They say his boot caught fire. Maybe he's not so bad," she pondered, "or else why would he risk his boot?"

Classes were canceled for three days. A thick layer of ash lay on the snow. Many of the schoolhouse windows had cracked from the high temperature, and the schoolhouse itself was powdered with ash and looked like an ancient building.

The story of the fire circulated the city, from mouth to mouth, collecting new details along the way, and a month later it was impossible to find the smallest bit of truth in it. Here was that famous trait of Russian character – exaggerating the significance of events.

Fedya

The rage of winter subsided; the mad dance that had locked the residents of City N in their flimsy dwellings was over. Spring was gradually reconquering its lands, bringing back the birds from warmer countries, and scattering its first flowers – snowdrops – on the outskirts of the city. The Vetkin brothers livened up somewhat, for they had lived through another winter and would soon be able to go home.

At night, horrible crackling could be heard over the city, beginning somewhere upstream on the Ut River and hurtling down to places unknown. The ice was crackling, breaking up into giant pieces. Breaking away under the water pressure, the blocks of ice jumped out onto the surface of the river and glided along, crashing thunderously into one another. The old bridge, having survived numerous parades and funeral processions throughout its two hundred year lifespan, could not bear it and began to creak. The pyramid supporting it in the middle began to rotate, threatening to fall over, and a broad, ugly crack opened across the bridge.

The left side of the city became completely isolated from the right. The confused inhabitants ran helplessly up and down the two banks, waving at each other meaninglessly and shouting something. The students crowded around the windows of the school, observing with great interest. And if it weren't for the *banya*, which was located on the opposite bank, this would not concern them at all.

"Great," Marie sighed, "first the clothing storehouse burned down, so we have to wash all ourselves, and now don't even have a place to bathe. Trouble comes in threes, so now expect a third," she sniveled, being superstitious.

"Stop croaking, Marie," Fedya pleaded.

And of course all the students took an active part in discussing what would happen with the funerals. While they debated this, the military went into action, being fortuitously located on the right side of the river.

The soldiers were waiting impatiently to be allowed to do something. First, the engineering corps got to work, blowing up the ice and breaking it into small pieces. Then, the infantry took over, laying a pontoon bridge made up of square metal pieces filled with air. Three days later, when the work was over, a tank drove across the swaying bridge and back again with a fluttering flag of the Soviet Union on it, showing the citizens that there was nothing to fear.

Driving onto the temporary bridge, the buses crawled slowly to the opposite shore. Deathly afraid, even non-believing passengers openly called for help to God and various unknown saints. On *banya* days, Sanya would sit next to his brother, clutching his hand firmly and shutting his eyes just in case. This continued for almost two months, until the same soldiers from the engineering corps restored the central support pyramid that had been knocked out by the ice.

An apple orchard began to bloom in the orphanage named after Lenin, and swallows and swifts returned to their nests beneath the roofs of the dormitories. The heavy smell of hospital and chloroform appeared again in the air, mixed in with the scent of the first greening plants and the city dust. At the end of May, Sanya received an unexpected letter from Alya. Marie followed by a hopping Fedya, found Sanya sitting in the apple orchard, on a wooden bench that had been completely covered with writing.

Handing over the letter, Marie settled in next to him with a look of concentration.

"Read it," Fedya asked, hurrying his brother along.

"Right," Sanya said, glancing sidelong at Marie. "'Read it,' and tomorrow the whole school will be quoting it."

"Okay, we're leaving," Fedya said, offended, pulling the girl by the arm.

Breathless with excitement, Sanya opened the envelope:

"Hi Sanya, I wonder if you've lost my address, or perhaps you did not get my note. The city of Khabarovsk has humps like a camel; it's built on three hills. My aunt is very nice. She told me about my parents, because I don't remember them at all. My cousins are a little nasty, but then again they are cousins. Everything is different here: the climate, the people and my new school. Very often, I wake up, and I can't understand where I am. Is this a dream? Awaiting your response, Alya."

Placing the letter on his knees, he pondered this. Before, it had seemed to him that only City N existed, along with its small joys and numerous problems. And now, this Khabarovsk appeared, resembling a camel. Sanya turned the letter over and drew a three-humped camel on the back, with the caption: "Khabarovsk." He wanted to reply, but it did not happen. Everything in his life remained the same. He still lived in suffering from that incurable illness known as first love. And if someone had offered him a trip to the three-humped city, he would have accepted without hesitation.

The end of the school year drew near, and the students, class by class, marched over to the barbershop at the foot of the mountain, getting their last haircut before the summer break. The brothers were sitting on the porch, waiting, watching the barber Vitek through the enormous window. He cut hair quickly, lightly touching the kids' overgrown heads and occasionally trying to crack a joke in a language only he understood:

"Prosze Pana, co sie stalo ze Pan sie nie usmiecha?" * Vitek asked, smiling.

A deathly silence was his response. No one dared utter a word.

"Do you hear that traitor, *sprech*-ing in German?" Fedya whispered, jabbing his brother in the side.

"That's not German, it's Polish."

"Yeah right, of course it's German. I could tolerate Polish, but this makes my ears hurt. *'Prosze pana, prosze pana,'*" Fedya mocked him. "Do you know what that means in our language? It means: 'Sit still or I'll cut off your ear.'" Fedya got up and brought his face right up to the window glass, expressing contempt for the large man with his entire being.

Several days later, concluding with a triumphant lineup and parting words from Goblin, another school year came to an end. Fedya could not bear saying goodbye to Marie, who, along with other children, was departing for a Young

---

* Sir, what happened that you are so glum? (Polish)

Pioneer camp for the three months of break. With a quivering hug, Marie promised to remember him and write hi-m about everything she saw and heard.

The house on Third Proletarian Street greeted the boys warmly, with cabbage and apple jam pies made by Grandma Claudia's caring hand. Their mother came from Tofalaria for three weeks on vacation, not hiding her joy at seeing her sons again. Soon, an unexpected piece of news flew through the neighborhood: Grusha's husband, nick-named "the Con," had been released early under an amnesty. For several days, their house rang with glasses, bottles, and happy shouts. But soon, the laughter turned into fighting and breaking dishes.

"Damn speculator!" Grusha shouted. "You should have never come back! What's the point of having you around?"

Just go and try to understand the contradictory Russian soul: "Husband in prison – no good. He gets out – even worse." However, the suffering was short-lived. After drinking himself blind, the Con fell asleep and did not wake up.

Again a torrent of tears and wails came from Grusha about her loss. Due to Grusha's heart problems, the speedy funeral was set for the very next day. Unable to accompany her wayward husband on his final journey, Grusha stayed home, sighing and lamenting.

The procession took off, carrying the departed, who had not had time to enjoy his freedom, to his final destination. Passing the bridge, the truck started uphill, towards the well-known bend in the road leading to the cemetery. A horse appeared suddenly in front of the procession, hauling a barrel of water. The waterman, sitting on the driving box, pulled on the reins as hard as he could to try stopping the cart and direct it to the side of the road. The horse got spooked and darted towards the group of people carrying wreaths in front of the procession. They scattered, dropping the wreaths, while the truck driver drove off the road unexpectedly, causing the vehicle to lean and eject the coffin containing the deceased from the open truck bed.

The crowd began to wail upon seeing such an unusual situation. As for the deceased, he suddenly propped himself up with his elbow and began to shake his head, as if waking from a deep sleep. Then, sitting down next to the overturned coffin, he placed his head on his knees and began to come to his senses. The people, who had gathered a safe distance from the resurrected man just in case, stood paralyzed. The Con, seeing the coffin, the wreaths, and a tombstone with his picture on it, opened wide his eyes and looked around. He tried to get up, falling repeatedly and rising again, until he finally regained his footing. He walked around in a circle, swaying his arms still folded on his chest, frightening people with the pale, lifeless color of his face. Finally, finding strength in his legs, he dashed off suddenly towards the river. Snapping under the unbearable tension, the people shouted and gave chase. Seeing the crowd running after him, the Con, who had almost reached the middle of the bridge, tossed off his uncomfortable new shoes and took off even faster. No one and nothing could stop the deceased from escaping his own funeral.

Grusha, not suspecting a thing and having come to terms with her status as a widow, was fussing around the memorial dinner table when the gate flung open loudly, and she heard the heavy steps and the gasping shout of the dead man:

"Grusha save me! They want to send me to my grave!"

With these words, he appeared before his wife and sank to his knees. As for Grusha, she saw the dead man in front of her, froze in mid-motion, and fainted.

The neighbors arrived and tended to the poor woman for a long time, glancing cautiously at the resurrected man and reproaching him with carefully chosen words for not waiting and just showing up without warning.

Grusha came to, and the memorial dinner turned into a celebratory one. There were even those who believed it was a real resurrection, asking:

"Tell us, what's it like in the next world? Don't be shy, tell us."

"Citizen Comrades, I don't remember a thing. I fell asleep at home, woke up on the road, that's all there is to it," the Con replied, growing mellow after the latest in a series of shots.

The feast went on for a week, until everyday life set back in, and the early morning brought sounds of:

"Go work, you damn speculator! Can't you see the potatoes need weeding?"

Placing the hoe over his shoulder in a businesslike manner, the man marched to the far end of the garden, where about a hundred potato bushes were planted every year.

Settling in on the porch, the brothers watched their neighbor through a hole in the fence. The Con, who had already raised waves in the city with his resurrection, was in no big hurry to work. Taking out a tobacco pouch and rolling a cigarette, he squatted amid the potato plants, overgrown with weeds, and began to smoke.

"See, look at him," Fedya whispered in his brother's ear. "Neither prison nor death can get him, so why was Grandma Claudia so upset? Sanya, do you think he was really resurrected?"

"Of course not, you heard what mom said: he drank too

much and was in a lethargic state, so deep in sleep that he did not show any signs of life."

Hearing their whispers, the Con lay down on his stomach and crawled up to the fence. Fedya pushed his brother away with his shoulder, peeked into the hole, and yelped in surprise. The colorless, smiling eyes of the resurrected man were staring at him.

"Hey fellas," he said hoarsely. "Can you run and fetch some beer? I'll croak if I don't get some hair of the dog." With these words, a paper ruble note, rolled into a tube, dropped onto the porch through the hole.

"Buy a plastic bag," the man commanded, crawled back, and picking up the hoe, commenced work as if nothing had happened, whistling and glancing at the neighbors' fence.

"Sanya, let's go I guess, or else he'll really die."

Appearing in the open window like a cuckoo clock, Grusha said loudly:

"Why are you loafing around in one spot? Work, if you want to eat!"

From early spring and until late fall, a barrel of beer was set up at the corner of Proletarian Street. The saleswoman, wearing a white coat over her clothes and resembling a hospital worker, sold the warm, frothy beer. After running to the store for a plastic bag, the brothers sidled up to the other customers, and, when their turn came, the saleswoman glanced suspiciously at Fedya and asked:

"Who are you buying beer for?"

"For my father," he lied.

"So what, he sent you for beer and didn't give you glassware?" she kept pestering him, blowing into the plastic bag and testing its strength.

"He gave me a ruble but no glassware," came the heartfelt confession.

Filling the bag with the frothy golden liquid and tying it firmly with a knot, she handed it to Fedya and ordered:

"Carry it carefully, don't spill it. We don't accept complaints."

The waiting Con was already pacing near the fence, pretending to earth up potatoes. He grasped the bag with trembling hands and, trying to untie it, he almost lay down on the ground.

"I'll die, to hell with this," he cursed. "Honestly, I'll die, what sort of idiot tied it like this?"

"Soup's getting cold!" Grusha shouted, appearing in the window once again, and the Con tossed the precious bag among the mounds and trudged off towards the house, cursing. The bag of beer burst as it fell on the ground, and the golden liquid, streaming around the potato plants, was absorbed quickly into the dry earth. But the Con did not die, and the boys saw him alive and well the following day.

Several days later, Sanya came down with an unexpected case of the mumps and spent almost a week in bed. Fortunately, his mother was home at the time and saw to his treatment, isolating him in his room and forbidding him to go outside. Recovering somewhat but still suffering from headaches and fever, Sanya got up at last from his bed. He sat on the windowsill, watching his brother through the wide open window as the latter loafed around with a ball in his hands, mad at Sanya for getting sick. Overcome with boredom and the midday heat, Fedya did not know what to do with himself. Placing his hands in his pockets and whistling, he kicked the ball against the fence as hard as he could.

"Sanya, let's go to the park," he asked suddenly. "The gypsies are in town, they set up their tents there. Let's go take a look. No one will notice you're gone."

"No, I can't, I'm sick," Sanya replied, putting on a serious expression. "You can't go alone either."

"I'll just go have a look," Fedya shouted, tossing his ball into the bushes. "I'll be back soon," he said, already running off.

Time passed, but Fedya did not return, and every minute seemed an eternity to Sanya as he waited. Around three o'clock in the afternoon, he could not bear it and jumped out the window to go search for his brother. Gypsies were a commonplace occurrence. They would always appear suddenly for a few days in the beginning of summer, and then disappear just as suddenly for the rest of the year. Neither the police nor the city authorities harassed them, even making peace with the existence of such an entity. No one could imagine a gypsy operating a factory machine or working in the field. Moreover, the appearance of the camp brought some variety into the familiar rhythm of provincial city life.

Even from far away, Sanya noticed the tents among the trees and heard the heart-rending sounds of the guitar accompanying a hoarse woman's voice as she sang. People crowded around encouragingly, clapping to the beat of the songs and dances. Sanya whirled in the confusion, searching for his brother and imagining how Fedya would soon appear out of nowhere, saying: "Why did you drag yourself out here to infect decent people?" Only that didn't happen, and the physically ailing Sanya kept making his way through the crowd, senselessly repeating his brother's name.

Laughter surrounded him. The guitar clattered, and a racy gypsy woman, with her eyes half closed, was giving her all to the song in a fit of passion. The people swayed from side to side, echoing the song emotionally, singing along with the soloist. Almost all of her songs began slowly and worked up a devilish rhythm towards the end, bringing the audience to ecstasy.

Elbowing his way forward, Sanya found himself in the very center of the gypsy dance without noticing it. He wanted only to get back home as soon as possible and relay to Fedya all his pent-up complaints. But the inexplicable motion that reigned all around was sucking him in like a vortex. He no longer looked for Fedya or called to him. Turning, trying to change the direction of this motion, he tripped suddenly and fell.

Rising, Sanya saw two gypsy teenagers standing before him with insolent smiles and legs planted broadly apart, and realized that he fell because he had been tripped. The crowd pushed on him from behind, and in front were the guitars, the dancing, and these two, speaking an unknown gypsy tongue. For a moment, Sanya completely forgot why he was here. One of the boys grabbed his arm and began to twist it behind his back, while the other struck him suddenly under the knees, sending him falling back to the ground. Not paying attention to what was going on, the people no longer swayed but danced along with the gypsies among the colorful kerchiefs that flickered everywhere and created a festive mood. Yes, it was that moment when, at the end of the dance, coins and even rubles were to fly into the wide open, worn guitar case lying in the middle. Trying to rid himself of his assailants, Sanya shouted helplessly:

"I'm sick, I have the mumps! And I'll infect all of you, and you... you'll die like mangy cats!"

He barely finished his sentence when a deathly silence fell. The next moment, the racy soloist, covered in artificial bead necklaces, jumped up to him and snatched him by the collar, lifting him from the ground.

"Repeat what you just said!" she demanded.

The hooligan teenagers evaporated like smoke, while Sanya had a silly grin on, failing to understand how anyone could have heard him in this delirious madness.

"Say again, you damn scabies rat, what you have?" the gypsy would not relent.

"It's not scabies," he defended himself; "it's the mumps. Nothing scary, just five days of fever close to forty, and a ninety-five percent chance of survival."

"That's it! That's it, my good ladies and gentlemen, the show is over!" the soloist cried.

The people clamored in displeasure, while the gypsy grasped Sanya's collar even harder and began to drag him through the crowd.

"Step aside, now. Let this citizen go infect someone else and not us." She leaned closer to his ear and whispered venomously: "You ruined everything with your scabies, you damn filthy bastard."

Happy to regain his freedom, Sanya trudged back, confident that Fedya was probably back home already. He returned and climbed back quietly through the window, just as he had left. Feeling tired, he lay down. The clock showed five. Hearing a noise in the room, his parents appeared:

"Where did you two go?" his mother asked discontentedly. "And why did you leave without permission?"

"Tell Fedya to stop hiding in the bushes and come home," his father demanded on his way out of the room.

Sanya lay back down, thinking about what a horrible day it had been: the mumps, Fedya, almost beaten up by gypsies, and now his parents were bugging him.

Grandma Claudia walked quietly into the room, sat down on the side of his bed, and asked:

"Sanya, why did you have to go outside while sick? And where is Fedya?"

"How should I know where that dunce has vanished!" he shouted in a fit of impotent rage. He wanted his brother to return as soon as possible so that everyone would leave him alone. The mumps was a serious thing, after all!

"What do you mean you don't know?" Claudia began to worry. "And when did this happen?"

"At noon," he said, and became frightened himself at his own words. Indeed, it had happened at noon, and it was now almost evening.

"He'll come back shortly," he said, reassuring both Grandma Claudia and himself, then sank on his pillow in exhaustion and dozed off.

He dreamed that he was a tightrope walker, walking on a cable stretched high beneath the dome of a circus. He had almost reached the middle when the cable began to sway back and forth. He woke up, opened his eyes, and saw his father. Leaning over Sanya, he was shaking him as hard as he could, trying to wake him up.

Sitting up, he saw the entire family assembled around him, gazing at him with unbearable tension.

"Where is Fedya?" his father asked with concern in his voice.

"Papa, I honestly don't know. I told him not to go to the park, I told him… I went to look for him and could not find him. I thought he'd come back…" Sanya started crying, having realized suddenly that something strange and frightening was happening.

"Why did you take him with you?" his mother said with reproach, not understanding a thing, and when Sanya tried to explain, the adults left the room in a hurry, leaving him alone. Two minutes later, the front door slammed shut, plunging the house into a ringing silence. An icon lamp burned in Grandma Claudia's room, while she knelt with her head down low, praying. That evening, a tradition of many years was broken. For the first time, the window shutters were not closed for the night. Sanya had the chills, and he could not determine whether it was from his passing illness or from the fear, lodged somewhere deep in his stomach, that he felt for his brother.

Heading to the police station, the parents met with colossal disappointment. The young policeman on duty explained insistently that he could not accept their report of a missing teenager until at least twenty four hours had passed.

"If he's not back by then, we'll begin the search. Who knows, maybe he didn't like it at home and ran away, and tomorrow he'll be back. Happens all the time," he summed up firmly and indifferently.

"What are you talking about, young man?" the mother repeated worriedly. "I demand that the search begin to-day!"

"Don't make noise, citizen, or I'll have you kicked out," the response came.

An older man appeared from the neighboring room, his appearance and behavior suggesting a superior. Joining them at the table, he smoothed his disheveled hair and gave the on-duty policeman a stern look. The latter softened his voice and reported:

"This citizen wants us to look for her son."

"How old is the boy?" the supervisor wondered.

"Thirteen."

"Nikolai!" came a sudden command. "Nikolai, prepare the car!" Already in the doorway, he stopped, turned to the policeman, and said didactically:

"Remember, you don't need to do it by the book all the time, you have to look at the specific circumstances. Understood?"

Sitting in the car, the supervisor got steamed up, criticizing young staff that could not be trusted to make decisions independently. Then he moved on to the subject of children – it turned out he had five – and, finally, having had his fill of talking, he asked:

"So where do you think he might be?"

"Our older son said he ran to the park."

"Aha! That means to the gypsies. Nikolai, turn around, we're going to the park," he ordered the driver.

It did not matter to Nikolai, an older man who was used to taking orders, where they had to go. The car drove into the park and, turning on the high beams, pushed back the darkness around five gypsy tents. Hearing the noise, their inhabitants began to emerge. Children began to cry, and dogs started barking.

"Looking for someone?" someone's voice asked.

"We are!" the supervisor shouted confidently. "We are looking for a teenager, and he was last seen here," he said with overwhelming confidence.

Then, taking out a megaphone and raising it to his lips, he shouted loudly:

"Everyone outside, we are about to conduct a search! That's an order!"

Clustering into a group, the gypsies spoke amongst themselves. The daytime soloist appeared before them out of nowhere; walking up to the supervisor, she asked insolently:

"What's this, citizen? Why are you waking us honest people, scaring our children?"

Walking right up to him, she acted like a person with

nothing to lose. The supervisor snatched his gun out of the holster, its silhouette flashing menacingly in the air.

The woman burst out in laughter:

"The bullets you have in there are plastic!"

The supervisor tried to move forward, but she blocked his path. Men rushed out and tried to lead her away from trouble. Nikolai ran back to the car, grabbed the first metal object he could find, and stood next to the supervisor just in case, ready for battle. The parents quieted down and huddled together.

The gypsy woman broke free and ran up to the supervisor again, shouting:

"Plastic, your bullets are plastic! Who would give real bullets to an idiot like you?"

The next moment, a thunderous gunshot rang out deafening everyone, and then a deathly silence fell.

"We are searching for a teenager!" the supervisor's voice came again. "Anyone resisting will be placed under arrest!" With these words he turned on his flashlight and moved forward. Nikolai and the parents followed in his footsteps.

The first three tents turned out to be empty, and the flashlight's beam wandered in vain over piles of clothing, dishes, and various random items. An elderly woman was in the fourth. She was sitting in a corner on the ground, next to someone lying entirely covered on a mat. Turning her face, distorted with fear, to the visitors, the woman put her hands out warningly and whispered in broken Russian:

"Don't come, sick, sick..."

The supervisor stopped:

"If 'sick,' then you need to go to a hospital. Who do you have there?"

"Husband, sleep... Sick, sick..." the woman persisted,

blocking the way to the sick man with her body.

Not a single sign of life came from under the blanket.

"I'm a doctor, I can help," the mother said, quietly but insistently, and approached the head of the sick man's bed. She leaned down, pulled back the covering with a quick motion, and drew back. A pair of legs appeared where everyone had expected to see a head; they were dressed in torn, oversized socks with an unbearable smell of sweat and dirt. The old gypsy threw herself on the bed, covering with her whole body whatever lay beneath the piles of clothes and shouting what sounded like curses. The rest of the camp had gathered tensely by the entrance, portending very unpleasant things to the nighttime visitors at any moment.

"If you don't want help, so be it," the supervisor said indifferently, heading towards the exit. And if he had looked more carefully into the faces surrounding him at that moment, he would have noticed incredible relief and even joy.

On her way out, the mother stopped for a moment, wishing to return, but the gypsy noticed her intention and jabbed her in the back, whispering sternly: "Leaving, leaving."

The supervisor entered the fifth tent himself. After exiting it, he announced that the search would continue the next day.

Around midnight, when a police car drove up to the house, Sanya ran happily to the window, thinking that Fedya had at last returned home. But the happiness was short-lived. He shuddered upon hearing his parents' muffled voices and seeing their hunched-over silhouettes.

His mother cried incessantly, while his father tried to comfort her, saying:

"Please, calm down. He'll come back tomorrow, you'll see."

"Why didn't he come back today?" she sniveled hopelessly.

"Anna, what do you think you are doing?" Claudia raised her voice suddenly at her daughter. "Sitting here and wailing. Once, when you were little, you got lost during a parade."

"You never told me about this," the mother said, calming down somewhat.

"I didn't, and now I am."

Sitting in his room and listening to the conversation, Sanya felt gratitude towards Grandma Claudia at that moment for having stopped his mother's weeping, even if what she said wasn't true. No one remembered him or came to visit him. He could not sleep until dawn, and when dawn broke at last, he jumped out the window and ran to the park. Where gypsy tents had stood just yesterday, only emptiness remained. Only the trampled grass and rubbish lying everywhere, served as reminders of what had been here. Usually, the gypsies left the place clean, giving no cause for complaint. The picture before him spoke to the fact that the camp would never come here again.

They looked for Fedya everywhere. The group of ten police officers was joined by volunteers: neighbors, acquaintances, and strangers. They searched hospitals, railway stations, bus stops; they searched anywhere a man might set foot. The entire military unit was put on alert and combed through the woods around the city in columns. They searched for a day, two... three... They searched until the days began to run into one another, turning into one single anxious day.

Photographs were posted everywhere: on lampposts, at bus stops, in stores. And even on the large board near the train station, among flyers for missing animals, a large photograph of Fedya hung with the caption "Missing teenager." No one had seen him. No one had run into him. Even though, it seemed impossible to get lost in this small city. And few could know, during these warm summer days, when everything all around bloomed and exuded fragrance that hope was dying in house #17 on Third Proletarian Street.

Sanya, unable to explain the cause of what happened, tried to avoid his parents. And even such an important detail as his illness had been firmly forgotten that fateful day. Disappearing daily from the house, he would sit motionlessly by the river beneath the wooden bridge, tormenting himself with unending questions. Why did this happen to him? Why not someone else? Why not any of his school buddies? Why not the Goblin, in the end?

Grandma Claudia, torn between the icon lamp in the corner and her distraught daughter, felt powerless. His father, who had tried to maintain his composure during the first week, became more and more detached. The unbearable burden laid on his shoulders pushed him further and further down. He would lie for hours in Fedya's bed, his face to the wall.

Two weeks later, the search was called off, returning the people to their everyday lives. And a month later, everyone had forgotten what happened, and only the photographs on the lampposts, words washed completely away by the rain, reminded them of bygones.

A Friend

A year passed since the day that peace and happiness vanished from the Vetkin family forever. And the family itself, as a whole, was no more. Of the legal residents of house #17 on Third Proletarian Street, only grandma Claudia and Sanya remained. Soon after the incident with Fedya, his mother suffered an unbearable mental break-down. One day, after bringing someone else's child home and calling him by her missing son's name, she was hospi-talized. Grandma Claudia would not discuss where she was or how she was, leaving occasionally for several days to visit her daughter in the Big City.

The summer morning caressed Sanya tenderly with fresh scents of greenery and African flowers that decorated the city flowerbeds with their bright yellow heads. That morning – just like the previous one, in fact – Sanya was in no hurry to get anywhere, loafing around the nearby streets of the awakening city. Stopping by the wooden church with its open gates, he watched the Mother; for some reason, that's what everyone called the priest's wife. Moaning and groaning, she walked up and down the courtyard around a flowerbed, watering the flowers with a watering can. After standing there for a bit, he headed towards the bus stop. Hearing footsteps accompanied by the jingling of empty bottles, he turned around. A girl of about eleven years of age walked down the street, wearing sandals that were too large and clothing that she was meant to grow into. The girl was carrying precious cargo to the store: her left hand held a string bag with empty champagne bottles, while her right had a smaller bag with beer and vodka bottles. Passing by, she gave him a happy, mischievous glance. And this glance told him a lot: 20 kopeks for champagne bottles, 12 for the beer and vodka, today we're celebrating! "

Good for her!" he thought. "She knows how to live."

The girl walked on, and from far away she looked even more fragile, almost invisible between the misshapen string bags as they swayed from side to side.

The city streets were filling imperceptibly with sleepy citizens. Sanya sat aimlessly on the bus stop bench, trying to guess the number of the bus that would come next. When the approaching commotion flickered in his eyes, he jumped on the footboard, bought a ticket for five kopeks, twisting it out of a metal box bolted to the wall, and settled in by the window, watching the outside world.

The bus stopped at a crosswalk, and Sanya saw the girl he had met earlier. She walked across, seemingly unaware that she was on the road, hopping now on one leg, now on the other. Her hand was firmly clutching two paper bags full of sweets. He suddenly waved at her, even as he realized she would not be able to see him.

Approaching the next stop and seeing a lot of people waiting, Sanya tried to get off, but this proved impossible, and it became so crowded that he had to stand with his face plastered against the window and his arms raised. The bus crawled more slowly than ever, and it seemed like it would never reach the next stop. A strange commotion ensued behind his back, forcing him to turn his head with difficulty.

"Bastard! Thief!" he heard the exclamations of a young woman and then saw her trying to take her hand out of a pocket, which she finally managed to accomplish. A man standing next to her was grasping her by the wrist and trying silently to open the palm of her hand. The woman resisted, making a fist and cursing:

"You thug, and I thought you looked like a respectable citizen!"

Unable to use her hands, the woman tried to strike him with her head. Turning towards them with difficulty, Sanya was witnessing theft in broad daylight. First the man tried silently to open the woman's hand, and then suddenly he let go, flushed red, and turned away. When the bus reached its stop, the young woman raised her clenched fist high in the air and headed for the exit, and Sanya hurried after her.

"What a pest," the woman said indignantly. "Trying to steal ten rubles from my pocket, only it didn't work."

The passengers around were outraged as well, checking their pockets just in case and trying to understand who was trying steal what, and from whom. Sanya kept following the woman. Still reliving the events of the bus, she ended up on the bus stop surrounded by a crowd and was explaining herself with passion.

"See, see," she said, opening her palm at last and showing a crumpled ten rubles. "My money was here, in my right pocket. Well, I thought, I'd better take it out and hold it in my hand, or else someone will snag it. I put my hand in my pocket, and then this criminal element grabs me by the hand and won't let go." Sighing, the people expressed their indignation and contempt for someone who acted so villainously, as they listened rapturously to the young woman's tale. As for her, she tried to reenact what happened, placed her hand in her pocket, and suddenly another ten-ruble note appeared in her hand. Seeing this, the woman squatted down, clutched her head with her hands, and exclaimed:

"God! What's going on here?"

The people glanced at each other and shrugged their shoulders, failing to understand anything, while some thought this was some kind of strange trick. But Sanya understood very clearly that it was she, not the man, who put her hand in the wrong pocket, mistaking it for her own and taking what was, perhaps, the man's last money. "Imagine," he thought, recalling the man's face, "what a coincidence that he had the same ten-ruble note in his pocket." Sometime later, walking along the road leading to the bridge, Sanya saw the face of the predatory woman in the window of a passing bus; she was pensive and sad.

Crossing the bridge and stopping by the blue kiosk to buy two rice pies, wrapped in paper, he started walking wherever his feet would take him. And they took him to the porch of the barbershop, where, settling in comfortably and consuming the hot pies, Sanya watched Vitek through the large window. The barber was sitting in the empty barbershop room in a barber's chair, with an open "Ogoniok" magazine. All the lamps, but one, were turned off to save electricity. Sanya studied the large man with interest as he sat motionlessly with the magazine on his knees. Finishing the last pie, Sanya crumpled up the paper and tossed it on the ground, but then suddenly noticed the face of the saleswoman looking at him from the window of the blue kiosk. Her neck stretched out instantly, and she placed her hands on her rounded sides, assuming a battle stance. Jumping up and picking up the paper from the ground, the boy shoved it in his pocket and showed her his clean hands from afar, thus preempting the brewing conflict. Cleanliness! That's understandable, but what could he do if the nearest trash can was, for some strange reason, located on the other bank? The saleswoman returned to her seat, and Sanya thought he saw a smile dress up her face. "Of course, she didn't have to say a word and still everyone understood – that's how tough she is!"

Climbing up the steps, he stopped and peeked again through the window. Hearing steps, Vitek got up and stood in front of the mirror, smoothing his hair. The door to the shop remained open, and the only barrier to entry was a gauze drape that protected important clients from bothersome flies. Not sure why, Sanya stepped forward, greeted the barber, and stood in front of him.

"How would you like it, young man? With a trimmer or with scissors? With a hair wash, or without? With conversation, or silently?" Vitek said, not surprised at the young visitor.

Having no intention to get a haircut, since there was nothing to cut, Sanya said in embarrassment:

"Well, I... I only wanted to ask..."

"Of course, of course," the barber said, fussing, taking his visitor by the shoulders and sitting him down in the barber's chair. "It costs two fifty with cologne, a ruble cheaper without."

Draping the sheet over Sanya and picking up the scissors, he stood over the boy, ready to perform his work dutifully at any moment.

"I don't want a haircut!" Sanya exclaimed in a breaking voice.

"Well why didn't you say so right away, instead of messing around with me?" the barber said, removing the sheet and tossing it on the neighboring chair.

Taking advantage of the pause, Sanya wanted to dash to the open door, but his accursed legs seemed to fuse to the chair, so he remained sitting.

"Well, then," Vitek said pensively, turning off the lights except for one lamp, "I don't charge for sitting. If you'd like to sit here, go ahead."

Clutching his knees tensely, Sanya felt his palms grow sweaty. Caught off guard, his mind seemed to hasten every which way, not knowing how to continue the conversation. Then he thought of Fedya, about what his brother would do in this situation.

"Uncle Vitek, do you like beer?" he blurted out suddenly.

Hearing a question unrelated to his work, the barber pricked up his ears.

"And where are your parents?" he asked in a serious tone.

"I don't have any parents," Sanya lied without blinking an eye, thinking that he was going too far and that Fedya would not have said this; in fact, he wouldn't even have wandered in here.

"I don't have any parents on this side of the river..." he corrected himself, "they are... on the other side."

Sitting down on the faded sheet in the neighboring chair, the barber clasped his hands together and tried to understand what this meant.

Only now did Sanya notice that Vitek had a large face with red cheeks and blue eyes – all in all, a very kind face.

His age was difficult to determine, but the barber's occupation did not suit him at all. He should have been director of a confectionary factory or a beer brewery, for example. Anything, really – a born director.

For his part, Vitek was also studying the boy, contemplating that "another problem had come to him on two legs." In this heat, one should be sunbathing on the riverbank or playing with friends, not taking in the barbershop sights. He found Sanya likeable for some reason, perhaps due to the boy's unusual pensiveness, which distinguished him from other young people of the time.

"You know my name, but what is yours?" Vitek asked.

"Alexander Vetkin, or just Sanya," the boy introduced himself, and for some reason this made him happy. "Everyone knows you, Uncle Vitek, even on the other bank."

"Well then, Sanya," the barber drawled. "You seem like a stand-up lad, but why are you loafing around with nothing to do?"

"I'm not loafing, I'm searching."

"What are you searching for?" the barber inquired.

"I don't know myself," he lied.

"Well, that's just like the fairy tale: 'go I know not wither and bring me I know not what.'"

"Is it true what they say about you?" Sanya asked suddenly.

"And what is it they say about me?" Vitek asked in surprise.

"They say you fought for the Germans in the war."

Hearing this, Vitek leaned so far back on his chair that it creaked miserably. Raising his large hands in the air, he shook them and let them fall to his knees. Sanya regretted asking the question, but everything had happened all by itself somehow.

"You see, laddie," Vitek said finally, after a long and exhausting pause, "I was captured by the Germans." And to support his words, he raised his left pant leg above his knee, displaying an ugly scar.

"See?" he repeated. "They wounded me and then captured me."

Sanya sensed that the man was telling the truth, and now he wanted to know what happened next.

"My leg healed a little, and I escaped," Vitek continued cautiously. "I returned somehow to our side. Ah! How happy I was to hear Russian again. Only our side didn't take me back. They said 'Polacks can't be trusted' and branded me a 'traitor to the motherland.' I sat in an old stable all night under guard, and on the morning I faced a court martial and was sent to a penal battalion. A penal battalion, Sanya, is a group of people they use to break through enemy lines, they are sent to the very front. We had to run forward, and if any of us stopped, we would be shot in the back by our own."

Tense and motionless, Sanya listened to Vitek's every word, trying to imagine the full hopelessness of the situation.

"And so I ran, without a weapon, holding my hands out in front of me, trying to defend myself with them somehow. And, believe it or not, my final thought before I fell was the desire to turn invisible, to just disappear in that horrible moment. I woke up in the hospital, having washed off my earlier disgrace with blood and earned life once again. My wounds got better, I returned to the front, and, soon afterwards, the war ended. After the war, since I had been in a penal battalion and, by some suspicious miracle, survived, they decided I was a 'dangerous element to society,' and sent to live here, in Siberia."

Vitek fell silent and sat there, drained, unsure of what happened to make him tell everything to a random boy. He knew that many bad things were being said about him, and he wanted at least one person on earth, if even this teenager, to know the truth, so that he could be free of the daily torments that consumed him from within.

"Do you have a wife?" Sanya asked, shocked by the barber's vivid and truthful tale.

"I don't have a wife," the latter replied quietly. "Besides, what woman would marry a man with a past like mine? Now imagine I had a son, Sanya, someone like you. And everyone in school would tell him that his father fought for the Germans, and no one would want to be friends with him. What would you do?"

Unable to come up with an answer, Sanya remained silent.

"*Widzisz przyjacielu jakie to jest zycie?*" * the barber exhaled in Polish. "I have no family and no homeland. Yes," Vitek confirmed, "my homeland is where I was born; where my parents are buried, on the shores of the Vistula."

Listening to him, Sanya understood that the barber was very lonely and perhaps even suffering from the same ailment as himself. The ailment was called "eternal longing." Vitek longed for his lost homeland, just as he longed for Fedya. Except that, one day, Vitek could get on a train and go see his homeland, while he had no idea which train to take and where to go to find his brother. Realizing that he met a man who suffered as much as he did, Sanya got up, approached him, and hugged him firmly. The latter also placed his arms on the teenager's thin shoulders, and his

---

* You see, my friend, what sort of life this is? (Polish)

eyes began to glisten. For the first time in many years in a foreign land, Vitek felt compassion and was delighted to meet a friend; even if they would never see each other again.

Seeing him to the door, Vitek patted him on the shoulder, said goodbye, and returned to the barbershop.

"Hey, kid!" the shout of the saleswoman from the blue kiosk stopped Sanya in his tracks. "What's this?" she asked loudly. "Is that traitor your relative or something?"

Looking at the barbershop and seeing his friend sitting in the barber's chair, Sanya waved at him and replied in a ringing voice:

"Of course, he's my relative. Didn't you know?" Detecting overtones of Fedya in his voice and pleased with his reply, he resumed walking, heading towards the school.

The wooden door leading to the school grounds was unlocked. He pushed it with his foot and it swung open with a creak. He took a step forward, looking now at the road, now at the orphanage grounds. "Why are you standing there like a sheep?" Fedya would have said in this case, "Come in, now that you've trudged over here," Sanya thought, looking at many things through the prism of Fedya's thoughts.

A heavy smell of paint hit his face. The schoolhouse stood with all its windows and doors wide open, undergoing annual repairs during summer break. He walked a bit further and turned into the apple orchard, although that was really just a name. In actuality, it was filled with trees that were not particularly attractive. They were stubby, their branches sticking every which way. Small, wild rennet apples grew on them, ripening long into the fall and only becoming edible after the first frost. The rennet apples were soft and transparent, with a unique, particular taste.

They hung on the branches, enticing the students during recess, filling the orchard with noise and laughter.

Walking into the depths of the orchard, Sanya sat down on the wooden bench covered with writing. Everyone who sat there even once had left a name, or at least initials. There were no voices of workers or janitors coming from the school, a ringing silence hung in the air. He lay down on the bench and closed his eyes, trying not to think about anything, but uninvited thoughts kept intruding, one after another. He thought of Vitek, of how big and kind he was, and that he trusted him. Why was it so difficult for others to trust him? It was so simple; one just had to look a man in the eyes. And if that had happened, his life would have changed completely. He would have returned from the war a hero, married, and had many kids.

Turning onto his stomach, he examined the inscriptions scratched into the bench. Soon, he was no longer examining, but searching feverishly. Getting down on all fours, he crawled around. Finally, he stopped and sat down in front of an inscription, in red pen: "Fedya was here."

His fingers passed over the uneven letters again and again, until he stopped seeing them. His tears obscured everything – the letters, the garden, and the school in the distance. They obscured yesterday, and today, and, it seemed, his entire future. The tears gave way to impotent rage; jumping up, he began to kick the bench with all his might, screaming:

"Traitor! You're a traitor, Fedya!"

Tearing a clump of grass out of the ground, he rubbed the words Fedya had written, trying to erase them. Then, exhausted, he collapsed on the ground and fell silent.

He lay there, watching a grasshopper fussing nearby, peering at the life in the grass.

"Can such a grasshopper feel or experience anything?" Sanya wondered. "Does he know peace or fear? You can't tell by looking at him. He is his entire world. He's cleaning his wings cautiously with his rear legs, and then he'll hop onward and keep hopping until fall." So did he and Fedya once, hopping around, making carefree plans, dreaming, and accepting every new day as a gift.

Rising, Sanya limped towards the empty school and walked up the stone staircase to the second floor. He stood there for a while and walked downstairs, strolling through the broad hallway of the first floor. A portrait of Grandpa Lenin stood outside the principal's office, leaning against a wall. For some reason, Sanya did not like his face and his brown polka dot tie. He found a piece of chalk, walked up to the portrait, and drew some additional hair, making Lenin resemble a hedgehog. Then, long ears and a nose appeared, but even this seemed insufficient. Enthralled, he did not even hear footsteps behind his back.

"Oh... Uh..." he shouted, frightened, when someone's heavy hand was laid on his shoulder. The next moment, he received a hard push in the back. Unable to look behind him, he took off running. Heavy footsteps came from behind his back, chasing him. Sanya felt that, any moment now, he would run out of breath from fear and collapse. Reaching the end of the hallway, he ran up the staircase, trying very hard to look backwards. It would have been better not to look.

"The Goblin..." Sanya shouted in horror, tearing off even faster, and thinking only of how he could cross the second floor and get downstairs. He had never wanted so much to be outside the door. Jumping over the final three steps, he dashed towards the door, but it was locked. Panicking, Sanya did not realize that the principal had not chased him upstairs but merely returned to his earlier position, waiting by the entrance. Staggering backwards, he felt the same tenacious hand grasp him by the shoulder.

"I've got you now, my dear," the principal whispered conspiratorially, stating the obvious, and dragged him off to the office.

Sanya followed him, balking and not even trying to imagine what Fedya would have done.

The office was half dark. Pushing him into the middle of the room, the principal turned on the light, locked the door, and hid the key in his pocket.

"That's so you don't run off," he said snidely. "You know what I'm going to do with you? I'm going to lock you in here for the whole night, and tomorrow we'll talk."

"You can't do that!" Sanya said fearfully.

"I can do anything!" came the response, and the Goblin walked out, locking the door from the other side.

"Let me out!" Sanya shouted, banging his fists on the door. "Please!" he added quietly, hearing the principal's receding footsteps. The schoolhouse door slammed shut, and a deathly silence ensued.

He walked up to the window, which was covered with a finely spaced metal grate, climbed up on the windowsill, and, standing on tiptoes, tried to peek over the nearby fence onto the sidewalk and the road. Stretching his neck, he leaned close to the open vent pane, gulping the fresh air from the outside like a fish, because everything reeked of paint. Evening was approaching, and occasional passers-by were hurrying home. Seeing the face of an elderly woman walking by, he gathered as much air into his lungs as he could.

"Help!" he shouted, and his voice rang out piercingly in the quietness of the city as it prepared for sleep.

"Help yourself. Slacker," came the response.

Sitting down on the windowsill, Sanya asked for help each time he saw the rare passerby, but no one paid any attention, and his voice became quieter and more hopeless every time. Only once, a young man stuck his head over the fence and asked:

"And how can I help you?"

"The principal locked me in here and I... I want to go home."

"You think I'm an idiot?" the man replied. "You probably snuck into his office to steal something, and the door closed on you. Only the police can help you now." And his face disappeared just as suddenly as it appeared.

At that moment, with the last glimmer of hope, Sanya thought of his new friend.

After another boring day at work, as he locked up the barbershop, Vitek suddenly heard a distant, piercing cry. The old soldier thought he heard someone call his name. He moved towards the riverbank, thinking the noise was coming from there. The cry quieted down but then came again, and Vitek, thinking of Sanya for some reason, changed his direction and headed up the mountain. Out of breath, he crossed the road, stepped onto the sidewalk, and continued to walk along the fence in the dark, not hearing anything else.

Having had his fill of shouting, Sanya grew afraid of the dark and turned on the light. Climbing onto the windowsill, feet and all, he tucked his face into his knees and accepted his circumstances. As for Vitek, he paced by the schoolhouse fence, convincing himself that he had imagined it all, until he saw the light in the first floor window.

"Sanya?" he asked, just in case, coming closer and peeking over the fence.

"Uncle Vitek!" Sanya replied rapturously, not believing his eyes.

"Help me get out of here!" he shouted, jumping up to the vent pane.

"But who locked you in there, laddie?" the barber said in surprise.

"The Goblin!"

"A goblin?" Vitek asked distrustfully.

"The principal, that's what we call the principal," Sanya explained, collecting himself. "I'll tell you everything after; just help me get out of here. Maybe there's a watchman nearby."

"There's no watchman," Vitek declared.

"How do you know? He's always here."

"He would have come here long ago upon hearing you yell. Even I heard you at the foot of the mountain."

The barber disappeared briefly and, after reappearing, announced that the gates were locked. Realizing the full difficulty of the upcoming rescue mission, he tried to climb over the fence with incredible effort.

"Don't even try, Uncle Vitek," Sanya begged him warningly. "Go to the very end of the fence, there are two detached boards that are just leaning on the fence. Perhaps you'll be able to climb through."

Wasting no time and testing every board just in case Vitek walked a short distance and found the secret passage. He wanted to climb through, but the hole was too small. The barber's hands, thinking faster than his head, were already testing the nearby boards for strength.

"To think what I've lived to see," Vitek grumbled. "By God, they'll throw me in jail for breaking government property in the middle of the night."

The boards creaked and fell away under the powerful

thrust of his hands. Finding himself on the other side, the barber rushed to the ill-fated window and asked Sanya to turn off the light so as not to attract attention.

"What are we going to do?" Sanya asked cautiously.

"Break it!" Vitek said decisively, testing the grate and realizing that it was far stronger than he anticipated. Sanya opened the window, pushing the metal object from the inside with all his might, helping his friend, but in vain.

After several attempts, Vitek admitted that he would not manage this without his tools.

"Look," he said, "you wait here, and I'll run home quickly, get what I need, and come back."

"And where is your house?"

"An hour's walk, there and back."

"No!" Sanya implored. "Don't leave me here alone, I really am scared."

Vitek believed him, not knowing what else to do and involuntarily recalling his military past, after his return from captivity. Back then, he, too, was sitting locked up in an old stable house and weeping like a child because they would not believe him. It was dark and damp in there, and the only light reaching him was starlight coming in through the roof, destroyed by a shell. Clouds floating over would sometimes obscure this distant flickering, and then it became even more unbearable. He could have found a way to escape that night, of course, but he had nowhere to run.

Vitek sat down on the grass under the window and stretched out his tired legs.

"So what are you in for?" he asked.

"For nothing, really. I did a number on Lenin's portrait."

"Cut it up? Tore it or what?" the barber kept prying.

"No, I drew on it with chalk, it's behind that door," Sanya waved to support his words.

"And what did you not like about our leader's portrait?"

"I don't even know. I didn't like his tie."

Vitek thought about this, while Sanya wanted to keep him nearby by any means necessary, feeling different somehow in his presence, perhaps calmer.

The moon rose in the clear sky, and all the scents became fresher and sharper. Through the smell of paint and of medicine from the infectious disease ward, he detected the aroma of his favorite yellow flowers. Acacias and poplars were flowering by the road, and the situation would have felt a lot more romantic were it not for the metal grate.

"Uncle Vitek," Sanya inquired, sitting down more comfortably. "Back in the war, when they locked you in the stable, were you also afraid?"

"Of course, laddie, of course..." Vitek replied, laying down on the grass and crossing his hands under his head. "How could one not be afraid? You only live once, and no one knows what happens afterwards."

"But my grandma said that this God would take everyone in after they died. You don't think it's true?"

"I don't know, I've never been there," the barber replied, trying to make out his companion's face. Although the moonlight was spilling copiously on the earth, illuminating everything around, Sanya's face remained in the shadows. He sat, clutching his knees with his hands, his chin stuck in his knees. Vitek sat up, and his shoes, polished daily to brilliance, glittered silver in the moonlight. He did not even want to look at his watch. He felt that something very important was happening in his life, filling his heart with warmth at the thought that someone needed him. Moreover, Sanya seemed special to him, unlike all the others.

"Why are you so quiet?" Vitek called out. "Have you fallen asleep?"

"No, I've been thinking."

"About what, might I ask?"

"About your shoes," Sanya laughed.

"Better this than talking about death," Vitek thought.

"My father used to polish his shoes every day, but they never shone like this."

"Perhaps he uses a different polish?"

"It comes in a little round tin, it's called 'Red Dawn.'"

Cicadas and grasshoppers put up an incredible racket under the intoxicating influence of nightly warmth, forcing the companions to raise their voices. Stretching out his tired legs, Vitek lay down once again. Thinking about the principal's behavior in indignation, he said suddenly:

"Oh, I'd give him a good cut, I would..."

"What? Whose hair do you want to cut?"

"Uh, this one neighbor of mine, only he can never make it over..."

The sound of an ambulance came from across the river, disturbing the night. Driving onto the bridge, the car sped towards the hospital.

"Why scare the people, turning on the siren on an empty road?" Vitek was exasperated.

Indeed, the city appeared dead after nine o'clock. Only a stray cat or dog could ever cross the road. The ambulance wailed even louder as it drove into the hospital gates.

"They drive it every day," Sanya commented, "either an emergency or a funeral."

"Do you like school?" Vitek asked.

Sanya thought about it. When Fedya was around, it was tolerable, but now he didn't know.

"You keep calling me laddie, but no one says that around here."

"That's what they say in my homeland."

"Where is it, your homeland?" Sanya inquired, pressing against the grate.

"Far away, laddie. Oh, how far away. Poland... can you hear how beautifully it sounds? I can't even imagine how it looks now. There's one city there on the river, and it's full of *kosciols*."

"*Kosciol*, is that like a hostel or something?"

"No, Sanya, it's a kind of church where people go to pray."

"Did you go there as well?"

"I did when I was a boy your age, every Sunday for confession."

"But it's forbidden! My grandma wouldn't even pick us up because of this."

"No, back then it was allowed. Us? Who's us?" Vitek inquired.

"Us... means me and... me again..." Sanya lied, angry at himself for not even being able to share. Even though, he would have told Vitek the whole truth, unlike any other man. Suffering all alone recently, he could not just imagine that he could talk about it with somebody.

Seeing that something was eating at the boy, the barber did not pry and changed the topic.

"I was a history teacher before the war, Sanya."

Pressing first one ear against the grate, then the other, so loud were the grasshoppers, Sanya listened, trying not to miss a word.

Vitek spoke unhurriedly. He had sat up again, resembling a large, clumsy bear in the moonlight. He opened his leather bag, extracted a small bottle, took a gulp, and put it back.

"Is that vodka or something?"

"No. A medicine called Valerian. Have you heard of it?"

"I haven't, my grandma takes Corvalol."

Vitek sighed. All he knew about his young friend was that he lived on the opposite bank of the river, possibly with his grandmother who took Corvalol, and also that his father polished his shoes every day but they didn't shine. "Not much," thought the former soldier. As for Sanya, he was tired from the day's events and lay down on the windowsill, tucking in his legs.

"Don't leave, Uncle Vitek, okay?" he asked.

The latter got up, approached the window, and said quietly:

"Sleep, li'l one, sleep!"

"Li'l one, li'l one," Sanya repeated, falling asleep. "They don't say that around here either."

Falling into the abyss of dreams and not even trying to arrest his fall, it seemed he could fly like this forever, until he saw Fedya. His brother was sitting on the very edge of the abyss with an open book on his knees, he was waving and smiling. Finding strength out of nowhere, Sanya dashed back up, drew near, and sat next to Fedya. His heart felt light and peaceful all of a sudden, and the book turned out to be one they had read together once, about forest dwarves. The brothers gazed at each other in silence, smiling. Words could be seen on the open page next to a picture of a small dwarf:

"Kindly dwarf in woods of pine, hiding treasure 'neath the trees. Show me but a single sign. Speak a word to me, o please!" The little dwarf was sitting cross-legged beneath a tree and smiling as well. Through his dream, Sanya recalled that, after reading the book, Fedya really started to believe that treasure was hidden beneath pines, checking every single one, and was even ready to dig at one point. Unfortunately, that pine was located in the park, next to the Eternal Flame in memory of those who perished during the establishment of the Soviet government. Then Sanya tried to explain to his brother that it was fiction, make-believe.

"You don't understand anything," Fedya insisted. "It's magic."

Unsure what his brother meant by that, Sanya kept checking pine trees along with him, just in case, until Fedya finally became disillusioned. The book about the silly dwarves guarding treasure under pine trees was the first and last book they read together.

"Why waste time on stupid books," Fedya said in outrage, "when everything in them is a lie?"

A wind blew out of nowhere, sending flocks of multi-colored autumn leaves spinning around the boys. Fedya got up and slammed the book shut. He let it go, and it tumbled into the abyss, turning and opening its pages in different places. He laughed, and his laughter echoed somewhere far, far away. The leaves merged into a single fabric and kept spinning, pushing the brothers apart.

"Fedya," Sanya shouted. "Fedya! Don't go!"

But his brother, wrapped in the leaves like in a speckled shawl, was already flying over the earth, rising higher and higher. From far away, it resembled a gypsy camp flying through the sky. Suffocating and trying as hard as he could to get a breath of air, Sanya woke up.

Every day as he went to sleep, Sanya begged his brother to visit him in his dreams, but it never happened, and today, unexpectedly, it did. The dream was so strange, so troubling and mysterious. Sanya lay with his eyes open for a long time, not knowing where he was and what was happening to him, until he saw Vitek sleeping on the ground in the rising dawn. But even this seemed like a continuation of the dream. The barber was laying on the ground in a very uncomfortable pose: one arm under his head, the other over his neck, his body on its side, and his legs scattered, as if he simply fell down and went to sleep. His shoes were standing nearby, waiting for their master to awaken. Sanya got the desire to draw his friend, and, finding a pencil and paper on the principal's table, he began to work. It was so easy: first a sketch, then the lines get clearer and clearer. "Hmm, it's turning out well!" the youthful artist thought in surprise, seeing a lot of resemblance. The barber began to toss and turn.

"Don't move! Freeze!" Sanya shouted to him. "I'm drawing you."

He barely managed to finish his drawing when the watchman appeared.

"Hey! Who are you and what are you doing here?" he shouted, seeing a man lying on the ground.

Raising his head, Vitek said happily:

"Where have you been all night, my friend? What's the state paying you for?"

The watchman slowed down and stopped in his tracks. At five in the morning, in the schoolyard, the barber was surely laying around drunk.

"Where I've been, I'm long gone," the watchman said. "I'm no fool to breathe this filth all night and guard an empty school. And you, why are you cooling off in here?"

Coming closer and noticing Sanya in the principal's office, the watchman gasped:

"And what are you doing in there, you brat?" he exclaimed. "Well then, it seems we won't be able to avoid calling the police."

Glancing at his friend, who was calmly putting on his shoes, Sanya remained silent. He folded his drawing neatly and placed it in his shirt pocket.

"And would the gentleman happen to have his keys?" Vitek asked.

"What sort of watchman would I be without keys?" the watchman replied proudly.

"Then open the door and let the boy out."

The watchman looked at him in confusion. Many things had happened over the years of his faithful tenure at the school – fires, burglaries, and fights – but this he was seeing for the first time.

"How did he get in there?" the watchman asked, testing the grate for weakness. Recognizing the teen, he added:

"Vetkin, what are you doing in the principal's office?"

"Sitting," the boy replied calmly.

"Listen, my friend, so the boy was a bit naughty, drew on Lenin's portrait. But why lock him overnight in an empty school?" Vitek said in an explanatory tone.

"Aha, I'll let him go and then they'll fire me. The principal locked him in there himself. And what's your relation to him?"

The barber glanced at Sanya and, intercepting the boy's testing look, said firmly:

"I'm his uncle, his real uncle. Now don't stand there idly, and go open the door. And if you don't open it, they'll surely fire you for spending your work hours by your wife's side."

Sanya could already hear the uneven steps behind the door. A moment later, a key picked out hastily by the watchman's hand turned in the lock, restoring his freedom. Vitek paced under the windows of the schoolhouse waiting for him with his bag slung over his shoulder. When Sanya appeared, he hugged his shoulder amiably, and they marched off together towards the hole in the fence.

"Hey!" the watchman shouted after them in displeasure. "Exit's the other way."

They heard a heart-rending anthem of the Soviet Union from a car driving past. Trying to wake himself up, the driver shouted the universally known words: "Unbreakable union of free republics, great Rus has welded together to stand..."

"No, he's not crazy," Sanya said suddenly. "My grandma does her exercises to the anthem every morning."

"Your grandma's a champ," Vitek smiled.

The man in the car disappeared behind a turn, while the two friends kept standing in the same spot.

"I have to go home and change," Vitek said. "I have to be at work in two hours."

"I have to go too," Sanya lied, putting on a serious look and realizing that he didn't want to go anywhere. He wanted to see where his friend lived, to spend even a little more time with him. But the night had passed, and new day was beginning, intruding on and destroying the valuable things that happened at night.

"So why are we standing around, wasting time? Come along, I guess," Vitek said suddenly, noticing his young friend's apprehension. Sanya's heart lightened and the most important thing was that he didn't have to invite himself over.

They walked briskly, finding their way along the riverbank through the morning fog, listening to the water splashing on the stones. The city was waking up from its nightmares. A horn sounded from the confectionary factory "Dawn" on the opposite bank, making a very serious announcement to all: the night shift was being replaced by the day shift, allowing the factory to work unceasingly.

Threads of streets with leaning wooden houses were spreading from all directions from the military base. Vitek lived in one of these houses, right on the riverbank.

"Come in, door's open," he invited, letting Sanya walk ahead over the sidewalk, made of three wooden boards. Sanya smelled shoe polish, a scent familiar to him since childhood, and he found himself in a tiny foyer with a door leading to the bedroom, next to a living room that transitioned into a kitchen. There was a coat hanger with three hooks next to the door, and two windows covered by drapes with small flowers. For some reason, that was precisely how Sanya had imagined the dwelling of his best friend on earth.

"Do you have any bread?" he asked, feeling unbelievably hungry.

"Of course, have a seat," the master of the house invited him with a gesture, and then bread, cheese, cookies, and apple juice appeared on the table.

Saying that he needed to change, Vitek disappeared in the bedroom, while Sanya, in good spirits, set upon the food.

"Can you interpret dreams?" Sanya asked suddenly, recalling his nighttime dream.

"Dreams?" Vitek asked, appearing in a clean shirt, exactly the same as the old one, and joining him at the table. "Why interpret them? Dreams are just foolishness."

"No, this was definitely not foolishness."

"What did you dream about?" the barber inquired.

"Foolishness, just like you said," Sanya replied, and his face contorted with dismay. "Gypsies, gypsies," he whispered. "Why gypsies, there weren't any... but... it was them... it was them."

Sanya sat there with his mouth full of food, and tears

were pouring down his cheeks. Of course, Fedya had been trying to tell him something, and those leaves, resembled gypsy skirts.

"Sanya, my dear laddie, don't you frighten an old man, tell me why you are crying," Vitek said worriedly, moving closer.

"You'll be late for work," Sanya muttered, running out the door and leaving his friend in confusion.

At noon, he returned home and was met with Grandma Claudia's question:

"Where have you been disappearing?"

"I... was at the school," he replied, slinking into his room, tossing off his sandals, and laying down facing the wall. Claudia followed him and sat down on a chair next to the bed, but Sanya pretended he was asleep. Sitting there for a while, she returned to her room, stopping by the icon, as usual. Sanya suddenly wanted to yell right in her face that she was a foolish, backward old woman, and that she shouldn't be praying to some guy on a cross, much less calling him "God." If Grandfather had been alive, he would quickly set things straight around here. Sanya could not live like this anymore, knowing that things would never get better. Powerless before the flood of thoughts and feelings, he wanted to run away, dissolve and disappear forever. Then, fumbling for the drawing of his friend Vitek in his pocket, he took it out and looked at it carefully. In the drawing, the barber looked large and poignant as he slept on the grass in a strange pose. Once again, he suddenly got an unbearable urge to draw something, anything at all.

"Grandma, let me draw you," he asked quietly, appearing before her.

"Sashenka, why would you want to draw me?" she smiled at such an unexpected suggestion. Sanya had avoided interaction with her practically all year, and this was the first sign of attention from him, which made her immensely happy.

"Sit here and don't move," he said, sitting her down in the living room.

And once again, he felt something incredible. He felt like a weightless feather, flying over his own hand as it created, and he found it insanely pleasing. He peered carefully into the blue-gray eyes of Grandma Claudia, trying to pick up on her mood and her kind, mysterious smile. It was this that he wished to immortalize. Someone knocked on the door, and their neighbor Lena appeared on the doorstep without waiting for a response.

"I baked a bunch of pies, brought you some to try," she said, placing a plate on the table. "But what are you doing here? Oy!" the woman exclaimed, drawing nearer to the artist. "Claudia, it looks just like you."

The neighbor hurried home, worrying that her remaining pies would burn, while Claudia took the drawing from her grandson's hands and studied it in silence.

"You don't like it?"

"You're talented, very talented," she replied. "Only your talent frightens me." Realizing what she meant, Sanya tried to calm her down.

"Don't worry, if I go somewhere to study, it won't be far, or for long," he said, thinking that his grandma was the wisest person in the world, and that perhaps her God was not so bad.

Returning to his room, he lay down on the bed, looking at the photographs on the wall and whirling away into memories of Fedya. Of how good and happy it had been. Fedya jingled like a bell from morning till night, now here, now there. And now everything was different, everything seemed useless and unnecessary. Sticking his head into the pillow, Sanya tried to hold his breath until he felt his head spinning. He finally fell asleep, and when he woke up, the house was dark. Feeling his way along the wall, he fumbled for the switch and turned on the light. Getting up and closing the door to the neighboring room, trying not to wake up Grandma Claudia, he lay down again, folding his arms under his head. His gaze paused on a photograph of his father, smiling, in the company of two unknown men dressed in military uniform, perhaps his brothers or his friends. His father had lived with his large family before the war, but he was the only one to survive, returning severely disabled, carrying the nightmares of war in his head like shrapnel and never speaking of it.

"Every situation has a way out," his father would say often, slapping his sons on the shoulder, but it turned out that not every situation did. After Fedya's disappearance, his father would lie on Fedya's bed, repeating: "Please leave me alone, let me die in peace."

In his memories, Sanya saw his father sitting on a small bench in the kitchen, clutching his knees with his arms. It happened several days before New Year's. Grandma was trying to lighten the mood, brought a small tree and placed it on the table, decorating it with snowflakes and silver glitter. Seeing his father sitting helplessly without changing his pose, Sanya experienced unbearable pity and sat down next to him, hugging him awkwardly by the neck.

"Papa, Fedya will come back and... Everything will be good again."

Grabbing his son's arms and throwing them off, his father got up suddenly and shouted:

"You fool! This is the end! Things will never be good again!"

He had thrown in his son's face, mercilessly, something the latter was afraid to even think about. Dumbfounded, Grandma Claudia looked on, frozen in place with a tree decoration in her hands. Jumping up to her, his father snatched the silver glitter from her in rage and tossed it on the floor.

"All this! Who is this for? Who?"

With these words, not bothering to put on a hat and throwing on his coat along the way, he ran out the door. Several days later, a postman brought a card with a brief note: "I'll be back when I can." Days passed, but he never returned.

Now, half a year after his departure, Sanya was not angry at his father. He preferred not to know where his father was or what happened to him, so long as he did not have to see him nearby, dying daily of despair.

Departure

Barely managing to make it to the end of the school year and receiving a certificate for completing school, Sanya began to think of leaving. He could not even imagine that he would be able to find his missing brother if he stayed here, in City N. He shared his thoughts with Grandma Claudia and was surprised at what he heard:

"Going to search for Fedya is not a good goal. When the time comes, he will return. Go study, my friend, you have a talent for drawing," she said and then added, smiling: "Go to Leningrad, there is a good art school there."

"Leningrad?" Sanya even grew frightened. "It's on the other side of the earth, it's so far."

"Far?" Claudia repeated. After a brief silence, she continued: "There is no such thing as 'far' on this earth my dear. It's time to go home..."

Claudia was trying to restrain herself from crying, and Sanya could not understand at that moment that it was she who really wanted to go out on the railway platform, get on a passing train, and return to a place without pain and loss. Where life was just rising like a rosy haze over the water well shaped rooftops of a distant, mysterious city. Where the sea air, mixed with dust, penetrated far into the lungs and left a taste of wind and silt on the lips.

"I won't go so far without you," Sanya said. "I was planning to go to the Big City. It's nearby, practically next door."

"No, my friend, I'm going to stay here and wait for you. Perhaps someone will remember our old address and come back home."

After the conversation, life was reinvigorated somewhat at the house on Proletarian Street: Sanya was preparing for departure.

No, he could never come to terms with the idea of going to the other end of the earth, not even in his mind; he would only go to the Big City to see his mother and try to get admitted to study.

Gathering all of Alya's letters, of which he had collected about fifteen, Sanya tied them with a ribbon and put them in his backpack, along with his carefully rolled up drawings. He had managed to reply to four of the letters, so their correspondence continued. In her most recent letter, Alya wrote that she wanted to study geology in memory of her deceased parents.

Two days before departure, Sanya visited his friend Vitek. It was around six o'clock in the evening, and Vitek was locking the door of his barbershop. Seeing Sanya and not concealing his joy, he joked:

"Do you need a haircut, young man?"

"Uncle Vitek. I... I... came to say goodbye."

Placing his hand on his young friend's shoulder, Vitek said:

"Let's have some tea, shall we?"

And once again, as before, they started off down the

riverbank, drowning in the descending nighttime fog. All that Vitek had in the house appeared on the table in the small kitchen. And only when they sat down and wisps of steam appeared above the hot tea did Vitek ask cautiously:

"Going far, Sanya?"

"I'm going to study, Uncle Vitek. Maybe to the Big City, and maybe even to Leningrad," he said, surprising even himself.

"Ai-ai-ai..." Vitek laughed. "You're leaving already, and you haven't even decided where?"

"I haven't," he said and then asked: "Uncle Vitek, you should visit our Proletarian Street sometime to check on Grandma Claudia. She's going to be left all alone; maybe you can cheer her up a bit."

"I'll stop by, even though we haven't been introduced," Vitek promised, realizing the seriousness of the conversation.

Rising, he got up and walked into the neighboring room. Sanya heard him opening and closing drawers in his dresser. After returning, he sat back down, caught his breath, and extended his hands in front of him, his fists closed. Smiling slyly, he asked:

"Guess which hand."

"The right," Sanya blurted out without thinking.

"Wrong," the barber smiled.

"The left."

"Also no." He reached into the pocket of his blouse and took out a round, seemingly gold watch on a long chain. He placed it on the table before the boy, and said:

"How are you going to live without knowing the time, laddie? You'll be late for all your trains." Sanya sat there in surprise, alternating between looking at Vitek and at the shiny object on the table.

"Take it," the barber said. "This watch is yours now."

Pulling the watch carefully by the chain, the boy lifted it over the table, examining it from all sides, and then placed it on his palm and read the pretty engraved inscription: "To Alexander, in eternal memory."

"Uncle Vitek!" he exclaimed. "Did you scratch this on here just for me?"

"No, Sanya," Vitek replied sorrowfully, looking somewhere, into the distance over the boy's head. "It's a coincidence. See the year on the side?"

"I see it. 'Leningrad, 1936,'" read Sanya, glancing at Vitek questioningly.

"This watch was not meant for me, but I have it," the barber continued, as if in confession, placing his palms on the table.

"At the beginning of the war, in 1942, I was transferred to an artillery division. It was full of young and inexperienced soldiers: Ukrainians, Russians, Czechs, Poles, all sent to the front after two weeks of training. We kept retreating and retreating, losing our positions and our men until we were encircled. We tried to break through, now crawling along, now charging, until we finally managed it, on the outskirts of a birch forest. Everyone started running, while next to me was a young soldier that I had walked with for several days, shoulder to shoulder. At one point I looked, and he was gone. I turned and saw him curled up on the ground, waving to me with his hand, telling me not to go back for him."

Vitek fell silent, while Sanya froze with the watch in his hands and asked impatiently:

"But you came back for him, right?"

"I did," the barber continued. "That's when these hands of mine came in handy." He raised them in the air and shook them proudly. "I picked him up with these paws, Sanya, loaded him on my back, and crawled onward until my head started spinning from the silence, which happens so rarely at the front. The young man moaned, wounded somewhere near the hip. I gave him a drink from my flask, told him: 'hang on,' put him back on my back, and this time walked instead of crawling. He kept repeating, like a wound-up toy: 'leave me here, leave me here, I have no one to live for.'"

Vitek fell silent again, while Sanya was clinging on to his every word and implored:

"What happened next, Uncle Vitek? What happened next?"

"Then... I said to him: 'You're talking nonsense, fellow, everyone has someone to live for, if only himself.'

"Then, a true miracle happened. When I had no more strength, we came across an ambulance truck with a group of survivors, heading rearward. My wounded companion quieted down on his stretcher in the truck, or maybe he passed out. I don't know how long we traveled before we found a field hospital. I warmed myself by the fire, drank a glass of hot water, and collapsed right where I sat and fell asleep. I woke up, recovered, and went off to search for my new friend, knowing neither his first nor last name. At war, Sanya, you barely make friends, and then you look and see someone else walking next to you.

"I found him nonetheless. He lay on his stretcher in one of the tents, all quiet-like, and looked at the sky through the torn fabric of the tent. I sat down next to him, and only then did I get a good look at his young face, contorted with pain. He recognized me and smiled, but when I asked him his name, he would not reply; he only took out this watch, pressed it into my hand, and begged me to accept it. He said that he would not survive anyway, and that I was the closest man he had on earth because I had tried to save him. At that moment, a commotion ensued. The Germans were approaching, and a speedy evacuation of the hospital began. There was not enough room, and the wounded were being tossed onto the flatbeds, each one practically on top of the other. I helped arrange my friend's stretcher on the side, so no one would disturb him, and the truck started. I never saw him again."

Vitek drank several gulps of cold tea.

"Now, Sanya, you know all about this watch. You see, he had the same name as you, Alexander. Take it and keep it safe, don't show it to anyone."

Around ten o'clock in the evening, Vitek saw Sanya to the gate.

"Write me every once in a while, my address is simple enough. My house is on the riverbank, so the street is called 'Riverside,' and my house number is 100. See how easy?"

"I'll write, Uncle Vitek, I'll definitely write," he kept repeating, wiping tears with his sleeve and clutching Vitek's gift firmly in his hand.

Sanya tried to not think about what the day of the departure would be like, until that day arrived. In the morning, he ran to the store to buy bread, milk, and cottage cheese for Grandma Claudia. On his way home, he bumped into the Con, who was running to get some beer.

"Hello!" Sanya greeted him unexpectedly. "I'm leaving to study in the Big City."

"When are you leaving, then?" the Con asked in surprise, peering into his neighbor's face and trying to figure out if the boy was lying. It sounded so strange. Who would ever want to leave this wonderful place?

"I'm leaving today, at seven o'clock in the evening, on

the passing 'Moscow – Vladivostok' train."

The Con drew nearer, looked in all directions, and whispered conspiratorially:

"Don't trust anyone, Fedya, they will all cheat and betray you."

"I'm not Fedya, I'm Sanya. Fedya's my brother."

Taking a step back, the Con furrowed his brow, clearly trying to remember that summer day when he had also joined the search for the missing Fedya.

"Of course, Sanya," he corrected himself. "Listen, don't hand out money for trifles and buy yourself some bread instead." He burst out laughing and, with the words: "All right, then, I'm off, or else I'll be the last one in line again," he ran to the store, slapping Sanya on the back as he ran.

Long before her grandson's departure, Grandma Claudia had gone to the nearest collective farm and bought two buckets of sunflower seeds. After toasting them on a cast iron pan until they were golden in color, she would sit at the train station from morning till night. Trains would stop, and passengers would jump out of the cars to buy the seeds. What could be better on a long journey, when you'd rather not even see the face of your compartment-mate, much less speaking to him? You chew on some seeds, saying with your entire being: "Leave me alone, I'm very busy." Ten kopeks for a small cup, twenty for a large one; in this manner, she earned a little money for the departure, adding them to whatever she had saved. Altogether it came out to 35 rubles. Sanya had never held so much money in his life, and he was filled with gratitude.

"Have a seat," Claudia said, "your train is in two hours, check your ticket, hide the money somewhere safe, and your papers. Don't forget to write."

She got up suddenly and took out a small pink piece of

paper from behind a picture frame hanging on the wall. Placing it before him, she said:

"Here's the address of the hospital, you can visit your mother."

Soon, they were walking together to the train station, located fifteen minutes away from the house. It felt like they had said a lot, but so much more was left unsaid.

The train arrived on schedule, and when the doors opened and the footboards were lowered, he suddenly felt scared, more scared than ever before. He turned and looked at Grandma Claudia, who was smiling a little. She pressed him to her and whispered:

"Everything will be well, Sanya, everything will be well. Don't be afraid of the future."

"I... I don't want to leave you," his voice trembled.

"Then stay, don't go," she replied unexpectedly.

The boy lifted his head in surprise.

"No, I can't. I have to go," he said apologetically.

"Then go," she smiled, pushing him towards the train doors.

A whistle came from far away, and the conductors began to close the doors one after the other. Dallying a little, Sanya jumped up briskly on the footboard.

"I'll write straight away," he had time to shout.

The door slammed shut, and Claudia, raising her right hand and paying no attention to the passersby, openly made the sign of the cross over the departing train until it vanished from view. Tossing her shawl over her head and covering almost half her face, she returned to an empty house for the first time in many years. She went into the bedroom and lay down without undressing.

Settling in on the top bunk, Sanya looked through the top part of the window at the lights flickering past. Fear and worry for Grandma Claudia receded, and he thought how he could always go back home, although the thought of returning did not fill his soul with happiness.

"I was born there, and Fedya's footprints and mine are on almost every pavestone and every sidewalk," he thought, "so let it stay in my memories. Goodbye, Claudia, goodbye Vitek..." With these thoughts, hugging his backpack with one hand and clutching his watch in his pocket, which had been sewn shut, with the other, Sanya fell asleep.

He woke up from a commotion and from the shouts of a conductress who was standing next to him and pulling off his blanket:

"How many times do I have to say it? Get up! Turn in your bedding! We've arrived already!"

The clock on the platform in the Big City showed seven o'clock in the morning at the moment that Sanya stepped into the unknown, joining the crowd streaming towards the exit. He noticed that he was not experiencing any particular euphoria from his first train journey. Looking around and remembering Claudia's instruction that all important places were located in the city center, he saw a streetcar with the sign "Central Market." Without thinking, he jumped up on the footboard, bought a ticket, and sat by the window. The half-empty streetcar crawled slowly through the city, and Sanya kept spinning his head around, looking at the streets and houses. The female driver, watching him in the mirror, asked:

"What's your stop?"

"I don't know."

"I can see that you don't know. Where are you headed?" she persisted.

"To the center."

"That's the next stop. City Center!" she announced into the microphone.

Saying goodbye and jumping off the footboard, he crossed the streetcar tracks and stopped in an enormous square. Yes, it was unmistakable. "Central Market" shouted the letters on a two-story brick building. Next to the building was the "Central Department Store," on the opposite side of the street "Central Bank," then "Center Street." Putting on his backpack, Sanya headed towards the fairly spacious market. Walking from counter to counter, he acted like an interested customer and tasted everything that could be tasted – berries, cottage cheese, pieces of fruit, nuts – until he was full. Then he walked through the streets and alleyways of the unfamiliar city until noon, languishing from heat and dust. Finally, stopping a passerby, Sanya inquired about the location of the art school and was surprised at the answer:

"But it's right here, you are standing in front of it."

Indeed, a sign hung by the front door, speaking for itself.

Walking along the broad hallway of the first floor, he stopped in front of a door with the sign "Admissions Committee," and knocked.

"Come in!" he heard the response, along with a ringing slap.

A young blonde secretary was standing in the office, holding a rolled-up newspaper.

"Finally killed him," the girl exhaled happily, tossing the newspaper in the trash. "Killed the fly," she laughed and continued inquisitively, "Who did you think I killed?"

Then, sitting down at her desk and assuming a business-like look, she asked:

"Why are you here?"

"I came to apply."

"Very timely, there is a colloquium tomorrow," the girl announced proudly.

"Colloquium, what's that?"

"It's a type of meeting. The applicants meet with an instructor who is admitting the new class and present their work. That's how they make the first round of selections."

"The first?" Sanya exclaimed. "How many are there?"

"There are three. Did you fall from the sky or something?" the girl said in surprise. "There are only twenty-five spots and hundreds upon hundreds of applicants, that's how much talent we've bred in this country. Then comes the second round, where you do a drawing on some assigned topic. And the third round is for those who passed the competition and are practically admitted. They just have to pass exams in language, literature, and history."

Suffering from a lack of attention, the secretary launched into quite a conversation: about books, about movies, about neighbors... at that moment she could have bored anyone but him. Feeling a brief respite after his long walk, he sat on the chair nodding obediently, not listening to the young chatterbox at all. Having had her fill of talking, she introduced herself solemnly as Alla Borisovna. Then, taking a pen and opening a notebook, she asked in an official tone:

"Surname, first name, middle name, address?"

"I have a name and surname, but I don't have an address."

The secretary raised her eyebrows.

"So where do you live?"

"I am from out of town, I just arrived today."

"Aha!" the young chatterbox understood. "You need a spot in the dormitory?"

"I do, actually, do you have any?"

"No, all the spots are taken," she said, tapping her long fingers on the table. After a brief delay, she started writing.

"Here," she announced after finishing. "This is the address of the dormitory and the room number. The graduating class has one spare room. Tell them I authorized you to take it."

Thanking Alla Borisovna as he left, Sanya suggested a better way to hunt flies.

"Some advisor you are..." he heard in response. The door closed behind him, and he did not hear the end of the secretary's farewell phrase.

Identifying the requisite bus stop and bus number, Sanya continued his journey into the unknown without fear or regret. "After all, Fedya is somewhere out there right now, also alone," he thought, not yet missing his home City N. And the feeling that Grandma Claudia and Vitek were somewhere here, right nearby, did not leave him.

"Lisikha!" the driver announced, and the boy stepped out of the bus and looked around. Twilight was approaching, and he barely made out a small, two-story milk store with a restaurant on the first floor.

Hurrying to the dormitory along the broad sidewalk, leading uphill, he walked about fifty steps and then stopped, not believing his eyes. On the other side of the road, bordered by a light-colored fence, was a real cemetery. Yes, this had once been the outskirts of the city, and the city grew, engulfed the holy spot, and moved onwards, placing the boxes of its houses all around.

The dormitory, which was located right there, next to the cemetery, did not have a single unlit window. It was occupied by students of theater, dance, art, and music, and it looked like a real wasp nest in the darkness.

After a brief conversation with the attendant lady, Sanya found the assigned room on the third floor, knocked, and entered timidly without waiting for a response. Everything here spoke for itself: canvas stretchers hanging on the walls next to paintings in progress, brushes and paints scattered everywhere, even in a plate with unfinished fried potatoes. There were four beds in the room, one of which did not have a mattress, blanket, or pillows. Looking round, he sat down on the empty wire mesh bed and waited, but no one showed up. Taking off his backpack, Sanya lay down without taking off his shoes, and, feeling tired, closed his eyes. Noise came from everywhere. Someone was playing the saxophone, someone was laughing, someone was shouting at someone else in the hallway. Used to life in the orphanage, none of this bothered him, and one could even say he liked it. Life boiled all around, and he could become a part of this life without much participation. It was a free and independent life, like he and Fedya had once dreamed – do as you will.

The occupants of the room returned at last. Seeing the greenhorn and reading Alla Borisovna's passionate request, they set him up with something to sleep on and something to cover himself.

"What's your name?" asked a red-haired graduate.

"Sanya."

"Wow! It means we're namesakes, my name is also Alexander. Well, Sanya, hold on! You have a big day tomorrow."

But right now, Sanya was thinking about something else entirely. He took the small pink piece of paper out of his backpack, and, handing it to his redheaded namesake, he asked:

"Is Sogra far away from here?"

The artists exchanged glances and burst out laughing:

"You haven't even been admitted yet, and you're already hurrying to Sogra," one of the students shouted, choking with laughter. "Wait till you spend some time with our professor, then they'll take you in with full state support."

The redheaded namesake returned the piece of paper to Sanya and yelled:

"Hey, no laughing, it really says Sogra." Sitting down next to Sanya, he continued cautiously: "It's actually not too far from here, on the other side of the river, an hour and a half by bus with two transfers. Who do you have in there?"

"My mother," the boy smiled awkwardly. He knew that his mother was suffering from depression, but he had no idea what exactly was wrong, or where she was.

Exchanging glances, the artists changed the topic.

"What's your medium, oil, tempera, or watercolor?" asked the redhead.

"Pencil," Sanya replied, still deep in thought.

"Good on you!" said the redhead, failing to think of a response, then shrugged his shoulders and suggested that Sanya go to sleep.

In the morning, it rained for a long time. Wearing a clean shirt and tossing on his father's rain jacket, Sanya hurried to the so-called – by an incomprehensible, foreign word – "colloquium." Young people were crowding in the foyer of the art school. Despite the open windows on every floor and staircase, the building was very stuffy. Finally, a door opened into the large hall, and the applicants, trying to mind their manners, walked inside without pushing each other and took their places on wooden benches and chairs placed in the middle of the hall and along the walls.

When everyone was seated, the admitting instructor appeared in the hall, surrounded by the graduates. Among them, Sanya recognized his redheaded namesake and his other two roommates. The instructor, a short man in a light jacket thrown casually over his back, sat down, leaned back, and said in a hoarse voice:

"Answer the questions quickly and intelligibly, leave the envelope with your signed work on the table."

He waved to the side, where Sanya saw the already familiar fly huntress sitting at a desk with her head raised proudly. Settling on a bench by the window, Sanya sat clutching the roll of drawings in his hands. The applicants walked out to the middle of the hall, trying to respond to the questions in loud voices. Sanya wanted to be last, and, seeing that the instructor had begun the questioning from the window side, he got up and slicked towards the door, where he sat on the floor.

"Young man! You... you," came the instructor's insistent voice.

Sanya raised his head to see whom the instructor was addressing and saw that it was him, and that the instructor's index finger was hovering in the air in anticipation. Looking behind him just in case, Sanya got up and walked into the middle, grasping his backpack in one hand and his drawings in the other.

"Why are you hiding, young man? Please introduce yourself."

"Sanya, Alexander Vetkin," he said, quietly but distinctly.

"Well, now, Alexander, answer me this. What's the most important thing for an artist?"

Straining, Sanya went through all the possible options in

his head: "money, brushes, paint…" The redheaded name-sake, sitting behind the instructor, tried to help him by pretending to draw with a brush.

"To draw!" Sanya replied.

"Correct," the man rasped. "The process! That's the most important thing for an artist. And what must an artist feel when the work is completed?"

Oh, these silly questions. Sanya looked to the redhead again for help, and the gent made a sad face, almost crying.

"Sadness," said the teenager.

"Correct!" the instructor shouted, pronouncing in syllables: "Dis-sat-is-fact-ion! A true artist must always be searching, always dissatisfied, even when the work he creates becomes a masterpiece. What's in your backpack?" he asked suddenly.

"Nothing, just some trifles." The applicants laughed.

"You are free to go, Alexander, leave your work here."

Returning to the dormitory in the evening, he heard hints of approval from his roommates. In the morning, he went again to the art school. By the bulletin board, no longer minding any sort of manners, the applicants were clambering forward, shoving each other away, to see the posted list of those who had made it to the second exam. He heard tears and tantrums from those who had not passed the first test, and joy from those who did. Leaning against a wall, Sanya stood waiting until everyone left. He passed his finger down the list and stopped on his name. He felt his heartbeat in his temples from unexpected happiness. "I passed, I passed!" he kept repeating, and even though two more rounds and the exams lay ahead, he was happy. It suddenly became important to him that someone had noticed him among this vast crowd, that someone had paid attention to his drawings.

A week remained before the second exam, and Sanya decided that he would go to the hospital to see his mother every day. He bought a small watermelon in advance, remembering that she liked them, and the next day he went to visit.

He feared this meeting; the last time they saw each other was a year and a half ago, back when he felt reproach directed at him over every little detail. June marked two years since Fedya's mysterious disappearance.

Reaching the Middle stop and switching buses, he passed over the broad river. Turning and dodging left and right, the bus reached, at last, the final stop. Sanya walked, carrying the watermelon carefully, and struggling with the emotions engulfing him. "What to say? How will she meet me? What to talk about?"

At the end of the alley, overgrown with cottonwood trees, he saw a rather huge three-story building of red brick and hurried to the front door. It was locked. Looking round, Sanya saw a doorbell on the right side of the door. Pressing it, he jumped aside, so startling, sharp, and loud was the ringing behind the door, resembling a scream. A short while later, he heard approaching footsteps. A small window in the door opened and the face of an elderly woman appeared in it.

"Why are you bothering me for nothing?" she asked, looking down at him.

"I came to see my mother, here..." Sanya muttered, showing her his watermelon as confirmation.

"Can't you read? This is a closed facility; visits are by preliminary registration only."

"My grandmother didn't tell me about any preliminary registration; please let me in for a short while, just for five minutes."

"Don't you understand that it's not possible?" grumbled the old woman.

"So register me for today," Sanya pleaded.

"Registration occurs once a week, on Tuesdays between seven and eight. Today is Wednesday, so come next week," the old woman replied dryly, shutting the window. Approaching the plaque hanging on the wall, he read: "Restricted Access Regional Psychiatric Hospital." Only now did he begin to realize that his mother had something far worse than depression, that this was a genuine prison.

Returning to the dormitory with nothing, he decided to wait till Tuesday. The desire to see his mother was becoming unbearable. Recently, Fedya had been displacing all thought of her, but now, knowing that she was here, nearby, he could not get a minute's rest from thinking about her. Sanya's roommates ate his watermelon, praising its sweetness.

With difficulty, he made it until Tuesday. At six in the morning, he was the first to arrive on the hospital porch, awaiting registration. By seven, a long line had formed behind him. Finally, the window opened, and a man's unshaven face appeared. Placing a thick notebook on a stand in the window, the man said:

"Who's first, come up. Name, identification..."

Sanya handed him his passport. The man opened the document, closed it just as quickly, and returned it to the owner with the words:

"Visits are permitted from age of eighteen; come in two years. Next," he said imperviously.

"What do you mean, from eighteen? Register me!" the boy demanded. The crowd standing behind him murmured, pressing on him and pushing him aside.

"Don't be yelling here, got it? Or else we won't let you

in at eighteen either," the registrar shouted, sticking his head through the small square of the window. All the people fell silent, as if on cue, waiting for their turn, lowering their heads obediently like children.

Sanya wanted to disappear from that horrible place as soon as possible. He walked through the bushes and shrubs indifferently until he found himself in a birch grove. The tops of the trees were covered in thick foliage, sifting the sunlight through like a sieve and allowing a paltry amount to fall to the ground. Coolness and quiet reigned here, and only the birds in the round trash bins next to a broken bench violated this peace. Sitting down and bowing his head to his knees, he began to cry. Something shifted under the bench, under a piece of tarpaulin, and hissed:

"Get the hell off my ter-r-r-ritory."

Jumping to the side, Sanya observed with interest as a man emerged from under the tarpaulin. It was difficult to estimate the age of the man who had appeared before him – it could have been fifty years, or it could have been a hundred. Despite the summer day, he was wearing a sheepskin winter coat, torn in many places. The top part of the man, generally termed the head, resembled a bush. He had short rubber galoshes on his bare feet; more of a hobgoblin than a man, really. Emerging from under the bench, he sat down on it, sprawling to occupy as much space as possible.

Finally, he regained his sight, and, seeing that in front of him was no intruder but merely a lad, no big deal, he said indignantly:

"What are you looking at? Get out of here. I don't come into your house without permission."

"Are you homeless?" asked Sanya.

"Sh... sh... sh..." the man hissed, pressing his fist to his lips and glancing round.

"We don't have homeless people in our country, I just lay down for a rest, got it? And you, why are you hanging around here?"

"I also sat down for a rest. Forgive me!"

"Well, all right, don't apologize. No one comes here but the police, only they can't catch me, I've got this..." – placing two fingers in his mouth, he whistled, and a reddish dog resembling a fox came running – "See this animal? She can smell them a kilometer away and starts to whine, never wrong. What's your name, then?" asked the man.

"Sanya."

"Mine's Nalim*," the interlocutor smiled.

"Why Nalim? That's a nickname, not a name!"

"Because I keep swimming here and there, spinning around like a fish in an ice hole. And I used to be one of the best employees at a meat factory. On the honor roll. Have a seat, then, why are you standing there?" Nalim suggested and moved aside, crossing his legs and flashing his bare ankles from his galoshes.

Sitting on the edge of the bench, Sanya eyed the man with interest. He had not yet met anyone who had sunk to this level of freedom.

"So what happened?"

"To whom?" Nalim asked, glancing round.

"To the honor roll," the boy reminded him.

"Oh, things happened, things happened." The man scratched his head and picked up a tiny twig, scraping out the dirt from under his fingernails.

"I worked like all honest men, two and three shifts, and like all the others I smuggled in my pockets and under my

---

* Nalim (Russian): Burbot, a slippery, cod-like freshwater fish

coat all I could: sausages, wieners... The wife kept telling me: bring them, plenty of customers. She sold them to neighbors and acquaintances for half price or traded them for other merchandise. So I kept bringing them, until they got me.

"I am walking through the checkpoint one day, and I see that the director has come to check on the doorman. I'm walking along, pretending to be honest, and holding a two-foot 'Moscow' kielbasa through a hole in my pocket that I made there just for that purpose. Would have looked suspicious to turn around, and the director sees me and shouts: 'Let me say hello to our top employee.' So he walks up to me, extending his hand, and I do the same – it's the director, after all – with my right hand, which I was using to hold the 'Moscow,' and it falls right on the floor, sticks out of my pants. That's how my triumph turned to tragedy.

"First they moved my photograph from the honor roll to the shame roll, and then they fired me entirely, said: get out of here, or you go to prison. Soon, my wife didn't need me anymore either, sausages and wieners weren't enough for the damned wretch, she wanted the 'Moscow.'"

Delving further into his memories, Nalim worked himself up, swaying his foot in the air and kicking it forward abruptly. Then he calmed down a little and asked:

"Everything is clear with me, but how did you get here?"

Seeing this fallen citizen before him and not wishing to conceal the truth, Sanya told him what happened by the hospital door.

"Your mother must be very sick," Nalim said, inhaling.

"Must be," Sanya assented and continued: "My brother disappeared, and she became ill after that."

"What do you mean: disappeared?" Nalim said in

surprise. "I wish I could disappear so no one could find me or bother me, but I just can't seem to be able to do it."

"He left and never came back," Sanya said quietly, surprised that he was so calm, speaking about it for the first time. Afraid of his own emotions, he continued: "I'll find him, just wait and see. I'll definitely find him."

Narrowing his eyes and watching the teenager, Nalim asked:

"You want to see your mother?"

"Very much."

"You're in good hands!" Nalim exclaimed optimistically. "Having an 'in,' my friend, that's a great thing. You can't go anywhere without an 'in,'" he said, underscoring the significance of the word. The boy listened carefully, trying to understand his interlocutor.

"Now, Sanya," the man continued, smiling with his toothless mouth, "I have a big 'in' with the cook at this nuthouse... that is to say, the hospital. When her assistant is away on Saturdays and Sundays, she calls me, she yells: 'Come! Come here, Nalim, take out the trash bins!' So, tell you what, just wait until Saturday and I'll talk to her."

They arranged to meet on Saturday. Sanya headed to the dormitory, trying along the whole way to understand this great power of an "in" that Nalim had talked about. He built an entire pyramid in his head: Nalim knows the cook, the cook knows the chef, the chef knows the guard, the guard knows the nurse, the nurse knows the doctor, the doctor knows the lawyer, the lawyer knows the assistant secretary of the Regional Committee, who knows the secretary, who knows someone else. And thus, it's a stone's throw from the homeless Nalim to the leadership of the Central Committee of the Party.

The most important thing in our country is to be in good

hands, Nalim had said, and then you'll be fine. And even though it is not written in any books and not taught in any schools, everyone knows how to make out in this life. "Long live the 'in!'" Sanya exclaimed. "Long live the 'in,' if only it helps me see my mother."

He lived without paying any attention to his surroundings, lived in anticipation of Saturday, making trips between the dormitory and the art school, stopping every now and again in front of the wooden mailbox with small alphabetized slots, attached to the wall with large nails. The second round occurred on Wednesday, and he passed once again. The next exam was scheduled for next Thursday at eleven o'clock in the morning.

Sanya sent two brief letters, one to Claudia, which read: "Dear Grandma Claudia, I am doing well and have almost made it into the school. I cannot visit mother due to the fact that I don't have an 'in,' which is necessary for visits if you're under eighteen. Yours, Sanya." The second letter was for Vitek: "Uncle Vitek, please do not forget about Claudia. Your friend, Sanya."

In the dormitory, the young people would, quite frankly, go nuts in the evenings. Those who had graduated walked around like kings. The newly minted actors, dancers, artists, and musicians sat up late in the communal kitchen with wine and guitars, singing until they lost their voices. The disco on the first floor stayed open until three, the records were worn to the point of the sound disappearing entirely, and then the dancers would sing in different voices, trying to recreate the lost melody. The new applicants were assembling in groups, trying to figure out what was going on and which group it was better to join. Not joining anyone, Sanya took his own path, leaving the dormitory in the morning and wandering the city till evening, making drawings and sketches, returning late, and thinking only about Saturday until it finally arrived.

He took the familiar route to Sogra early in the morning. Nalim was nowhere in sight, and Sanya began to wonder whether the man had deceived him. He could do nothing but wait, and as he sat there waiting, he lost track of time. Now he definitely had nowhere to hurry. Taking his remaining money out of his pocket, he began to count it, smoothing it out neatly. He had ten rubles and two more in small change; no matter how thrifty he tried to be, the money vanished quickly.

Nalim's dog appeared, running up and wagging its tail, letting him know the master was nearby.

"Ah…" he heard. "You're here already? Why so early?"

"Better early than late," Sanya said in confusion. "We agreed, no?" he glanced inquisitively at Nalim.

But Nalim was fussing around and acting as if he had forgotten everything. Sitting next to Sanya on the bench, he jabbed him in the shoulder and, not bothering to hide his good mood, said:

"Why are you sitting there like a mummy? Smile or something."

Sanya did not know how to address the man. Saying "Nalim" would be like calling names. Uncle Nalim? Also not quite right, and yet he did not know his real name.

"Mister," he said finally, "how about that 'in?' Did it not work, or what?"

"Ha… ha… ha…" came the response. "As if things don't work with me. That doesn't happen… well, maybe sometimes…" Nalim sighed and fell silent.

"Sometimes means right now, doesn't it?"

"No, it doesn't," Nalim said, clowning, and then, moving closer to Sanya, he announced triumphantly:

"This time, I managed without a big 'in.' There is an old lady registering next Tuesday; it turns out she's the cook's sister. She'll register you."

Not hiding his joy, Sanya grabbed Nalim's hand and began to shake it, repeating:

"Thank you, mister. Thank you so much. But how will this old lady recognize me?"

"You're the only dunce to loaf around places like that. Trust me, she'll recognize you," he assured Sanya before getting up from the bench and extending an invitation: "Shall we go visit my home, then?"

"Home?"

"What, did you think I lived under this bench?"

They walked near the tall hospital wall and, on the back side Sanya saw an entrance leading to a fairly spacious inner courtyard. He saw flowerbeds dotted with the same yellow flowers that grew everywhere in his hometown, City N. Seeing his new friend dallying, Nalim pulled him into the bushes by the sleeve.

"Keep walking and don't draw any attention to yourself," the old man grumbled in displeasure.

"But there's no one here," Sanya said, turning his head in all directions and not seeing any signs of life.

"You'd think there isn't, and then these strongmen come out, grab you by the arms, and lead you off."

Sanya was having trouble understanding what he was saying. Seeing this, Nalim paused, put his index finger to Sanya's head, and instructed:

"Don't ever approach the grate or look through it unless you are called. I kept looking one day, until these two muscle-heads grabbed me, no idea where they came from. They took me for one of theirs, you know? For two hours I had to sit in a small empty room with a square window on the door, and it's completely impossible to tell what idiot is watching you. Well, of course I pretended as hard as I could that I was sane. Good thing the cook helped, she recognized me. God grant her good health!"

After this revelation, he turned and continued walking on the narrow path, which led them to a collapsed barn.

"This is my house," he said, waving his hand.

Not surprised, Sanya walked in; seeing holes in the ceiling and the floor, he inquired if it was cold here in the winter.

"Winter?" Nalim burst out laughing and then exclaimed: "Are you taking me for a fool? This is my summer residence. In the winter, I wander through the railway stations, pretending to be a solitary gypsy."

The barn's only window was nailed shut with plywood. In the corner, where the roof looked more or less solid, there was a pile of rags lying on top of a straw mat on the floor, serving as a bed. The door was missing. Next to the entrance, on a coat hanger hanging on a large nail in the wall, resembling a visitor from an alternate reality, hung a dress suit: white shirt, tie, pants, and a jacket with three pairs of glasses sticking out of the pocket. Catching his guest's glance, Nalim smiled and commented:

"I wear that when I go to work, only I've been lazy of late, don't feel like working."

Sanya had difficulty imagining work of any sort for the fallen Nalim, who looked like a character from a movie that had just finished filming; only the actor had grown so attached to the part that he could not stop playing it.

"Mister," he said. "Can I draw your portrait?"

"What's that?" Nalim said indignantly. "What for?"

"I'm an artist. Well, not yet, but I can draw," Sanya insisted.

"All right then. Bring all those brushes and easels of yours next time…"

"Pencils, I draw with pencils."

Nalim asked his guest if he was hungry and then, not waiting for a reply, went to the corner across from the bed, lifted a board on the floor, moved it aside, and exclaimed happily:

"I have everything in my fridge."

Glancing into the shallow pit beneath the board, Sanya saw many cellophane bags with food, tied with knots. Leaning down, Nalim pulled out one bag after another, saying:

"Here's a piece of kielbasa, here's bread, and this one has cheese, sweets, and cookies. I have everything, pick what you like."

"Where did you get all this food?" the guest asked in surprise.

"Where, where," the master imitated him. "Maybe I just like to eat."

Taking the bags, they walked out of the barn and, sitting down on a fallen tree, began to eat. They heard an ambulance drive up to the hospital gates; the gates opened with a creak and a short while later closed with the same pitiful sound. The dog spun around Nalim in anticipation of its share. He fed it kielbasa and anything else he came across from his palm without reservation, saying: "Eat, my friend, eat, you've earned it."

After eating their fill, they lay down. Closing his eyes, Nalim was humming something under his breath. Placing his hands under his head, Sanya lay on his back and looked at the sky, thinking about Fedya and about the fact that, perhaps, his brother was also staring at the sky right now and seeing the same clouds, resembling different giant animals, and that the sky was their only point of contact. He also thought about how everything that had taken years to build fell apart in a second. He had a family, his mother, his father, Claudia. "See, Fedya?" he muttered. "It turns out that everything revolved around you; you were the axis that held us all together. And now Claudia is alone, mama is in that horrible place, father has run away from everything, or perhaps he is already dead." And as for him, Sanya, he had not been his own master for a long time now, chased to places unknown by an unknown force. The only hope was to find Fedya, and then everything could be as before. Nalim pushed Sanya in the shoulder and asked:

"Hey, are you crying or something?"

"No, I'm not crying," he replied. "I've been staring at the sun too long."

"Then don't stare at it, or you'll go blind. I never look at it; let it warm me, and that's good enough. When is your next exam, then?" Nalim inquired.

"On Thursday. If I pass it, I will only have literature, Russian, and history left," Sanya replied dejectedly.

"See? I can tell you are a real artist. You'll make it in, receive a stipend, so why are you sad?"

Not answering the question and thanking Nalim for his hospitality, he said goodbye and went to the dormitory. Waiting for Tuesday, Sanya killed time by wandering the city aimlessly and washing his socks and his only backup shirt several times. Rising at dawn on Tuesday, he left the dormitory and, after walking past several stops on foot, got on a bus.

This time, there were a lot more people crowding by the hospital door. Those awaiting registration had formed a long line that ended somewhere far away in the poplar alley. Standing first in this line, Sanya picked at his passport nervously, and when the window opened finally, he extended the document silently to the old woman who appeared. She stared right at him, marked something in her notebook, and returned the document without opening it along with a small, stamped piece of paper, which had the time and date of the visit.

"Show this at the door, don't be late," she said and then shouted loudly: "Next!"

The happy Sanya rushed to Nalim, clutching the piece of paper in his hand, scarcely believing that everything had worked out. Finding Nalim asleep in the barn, he began to chatter.

"Mister, get up! They registered me, imagine, they registered me!"

Without concealing his smile, the sleepy Nalim repeated:

"See the great power of the 'in?' For what time did they register you?" he asked.

"It says Thursday, Thursday at eleven. Oh no! That can't be! That's awful! I have my exam at that time," Sanya exclaimed.

"I did my job," Nalim said, rubbing his hands. "I won't ask a second time for you. It's up to you to decide. An 'in' is like a firebird, brother: you have to grab it by the tail or it'll fly away."

In low spirits, Sanya returned to the dormitory. It had been over a month since he arrived in the Big City. He had barely any money left, and he did not buy anything anymore, only visiting the market occasionally to sample fruits and nuts. The graduates passed their last exams, received their diplomas, and each went his own way, leaving Sanya the master of his room. In the evenings, he went to the communal kitchen, gathering everything that had been forgotten or left unfinished. After the insane parties of the graduates, the new applicants relished the quiet as they prepared for their next exams.

Sanya found it difficult to choose where to go on Thursday: to the next exam, or to visit his mother? How was it even possible that two events of such importance could coincide?

On Wednesday, Sanya visited Nalim once more, cajoling him to sit on a bench and pose. The latter resisted, saying that he was feeling down and had a lot to drink. Sanya stubbornly forced him to sit in the same pose and not move. Finally, Nalim fell asleep, allowing the young artist to make several more sketches and drawings. That same day, he made numerous drawings of the city, taking pleasure in transferring to paper the charm of the streets overgrown with large poplars trees and the houses with carved shutters, reminding him of his past. It seemed to him that Thursday would never come. But when it did come, Sanya woke up in the morning without a trace of doubt. The desire to see his mother outweighed everything else. Putting on a clean shirt, wiping his shoes, and buying a quarter of a watermelon with the last of his change, he appeared at exactly eleven o'clock before the hospital door and pressed the doorbell. When the window opened, the teenager silently passed the precious pass-sheet into the black square. The door opened, and a young nurse, dressed in a clean white robe, whispered:

"Follow me and don't stop anywhere."

Petrified with fear and expectation, Sanya glided noiselessly on the plastic squares, seeing only the white cloud of the robe flying in front of him. Passing through a narrow corridor, they turned to the right and walked up to the second floor by means of a broad staircase decorated with a carpet. Not noticing anything around him, Sanya followed his guide obediently until she stopped before the right door. Picking out the key to the lock, the nurse said that he had only fifteen minutes and let him in, locking the door behind him. The walls, painted a heavy green color, gave the small room a dismal look. There was a small grated window high above near the ceiling, a metal bed in the corner...

"Mama," Sanya called out, clutching the quarter of the watermelon so hard his fingers hurt. "Mama, it's me," he said, without coming closer.

The woman lying with her face to the wall got up quickly and sat on the edge of the bed, placing her bare feet on the floor.

Seeing her dear face, which had changed so much, Sanya could barely contain the emotions choking him. Smiling, he stepped towards his mother, holding out the watermelon:

"Here, this is for you, it's the sweetest one."

"Fedya," she whispered. "My son's come back."

Approaching and placing the watermelon on her bedside table; Sanya sat by her feet.

He did not care that his mother had not recognized him. "Perhaps I really do resemble Fedya, he's my brother after all," he thought.

The mother held his face tenderly in her hands, not taking her eyes off him, and shook her head:

"Fedenka, how you've grown."

Placing his head on her knees, he grew quiet, holding back his tears with the last of his strength. The mother's hands stroked his shoulders and back, trying to take him all in, to hold him and not let go, gliding along his hair and his face.

"Fedya," she asked pleadingly all of a sudden. "Now take me home."

Not knowing what to say, he took his mother's hand, squeezing it in his palms, muttering incoherently:

"Mommy, I... just you wait, I will definitely take you home. I... I will come back, I..."

The key turned in the lock and the nurse walked in, announcing the end of the visit, and how timely this was. Sanya rushed to embrace his mother, pressing firmly against her cheek. He could not remember how he ended up in Nalim's barn. Falling upon the pile of rags in the corner, he began to howl, and he howled as only parents do when they bury their children. Seeing this, Nalim was taken aback, not knowing what to do. He went outside and, placing his hands in the pockets of his torn sheepskin coat, paced back and forth for a long time, listening to the wailing of his young friend until the latter quieted down at last.

Returning to the barn, Nalim found him lying on his back in detached silence, staring into the ceiling. A poor psychologist, Nalim did not say anything either. Sanya lay motionless until evening, then sat up and said decisively:

"I'm leaving, mister."

"Of course, of course," Nalim agreed.

"I am going to Leningrad," he said firmly.

"Oh, how far. Have you got enough money for the road?" Nalim asked.

"Not yet, but I'll find some."

"Where are you going to find it? Money doesn't grow on trees," Nalim smiled slyly.

"All right, I'll help you," he said. "Ah, I promised myself I'd get out of this business, but it seems my fate decided otherwise, it won't let me."

"Help me how, mister? And what's your real name, anyway?"

"I'm Nalim, understand? I don't have a name, just a nickname, for secrecy. Maybe I don't want to remember my name," he added, grimacing.

That evening, Sanya did not return to the dormitory and stayed the night with his friend. They lit a fire and toasted bread on it, sticking it on twigs. The warm, starry night reminded him of the night he spent locked in the school. The grasshoppers shouted just like they did back then, and even the sound of the ambulance and the creaking of the opening hospital gates were familiar. Only the air smelled different. Then there was Nalim, his new friend, sitting across from him with the reddish dog lying at his feet in anticipation of affection and food, reminding Sanya of the new setting. Without fully realizing the consequences of his decision, Sanya contemplated the fact that he would not be able to live near his suffering mother without being able to help her. It would be better to run as far away as possible, and perhaps the distance would erase the pain and the frailness he had encountered that day. Interrupting the silence, Nalim asked:

"When do you want to leave?"

"I would leave tomorrow if I could. I did not make it into the school, so I'll try in Leningrad, but first I will go work as a loader at a railway station for two weeks. I'll earn some money and go."

He recalled that many of the men in his home city earned extra money as loaders. As for Nalim, he burst into laughter upon hearing this:

"A loader? Who'll take you? They lift loads weighing ten times as much as you over there. I said I'll help you, so I will," he summarized, scratching the back of his head.

"How can you help me, you are homeless."

"Homeless but not brainless," Nalim said proudly.

He got up and headed for the barn. He came back with a plastic bag and poured out its contents on the ground in front of Sanya.

"That's your passport!" Sanya exclaimed and read loudly: "Zaytsev, Pavel Petrovich. Aha! Your name is Pavel Petrovich!"

Nalim turned away. Then Sanya picked up a different document, for there were about ten lying in front of him, each with the photograph of their owner, Nalim, but with different names. One had Nalim with a moustache, another with a short haircut and wearing eyeglasses, Nalim with a beard, everywhere Nalim, Nalim, Nalim...

"I don't understand a thing. Are these yours or what?" Sanya asked.

"They used to be theirs, and now they are ours. That's the nature of my business," Nalim replied. "Have you read 'Dead Souls' by Gogol?" He was lying down, having settled in comfortably by the fire next to the dog, and waving his bottle in the air.

"I did, in eighth grade."

"Well, that book is my inspiration, my friend! Praise Gogol! This great writer gave me a brilliant idea."

He put his mouth to the bottle and took a drink.

"Nikolai Vasilievich Gogol wrote about this no-nonsense merchant lady who got all the dead people in her village listed as living and then sold them to another merchant and businessman. So the merchant comes to the village he bought, and there is not a single person alive there. So he bought dead souls. What a fool!" the narrator laughed.

"That's not right, she was not a merchant but a landlady,

and it's a made-up story. And the plot is a little different, anyway."

"You see?" the drunken Nalim laughed. "A made-up story, and yet it drove an honest man like me to crime. If rich people can do it, we definitely can."

Seeing Nalim finish one bottle and pick up another, Sanya begged him:

"Mister, don't drink that filth, you're drunk already." Squatting, Nalim replied jauntily:

"Don't you teach me about life. I need five like this one to get drunk."

Suddenly, Sanya extended his hand sharply and demanded:

"Let me try, I guess."

"No, I won't..." Nalim said in surprise. "Look at me, at your comrade. What do you see?"

"Nothing," Sanya grumbled in response.

"Exactly. Nothing!" Nalim exclaimed, throwing the bottle into the bushes so hard that it broke on a tree.

"You got it right. Want to be another Nalim? Drink up and there'll be nothing..."

Getting drunk even more and emitting completely incomprehensible muttering, he fell over on his side and began to snore. Tossing dry branches and twigs into the flames, Sanya sat by the fire until dawn and then lay down on the ground and fell into a deep sleep. Waking up at noon, he did not see Nalim. The work clothes of the latter had disappeared from the nail, and only the old sheepskin coat lay on the ground, resembling the discarded skin of the frog prince.

On his way to the art school to pick up his drawings and passing by the hospital courtyard, Sanya stopped for a moment, peered into the emptiness of the yard, and then ran for the bus stop without looking back and got on an empty bus.

Turning away, he looked through the window, seeing nothing, immersed in his thoughts about what he had experienced the day before. He tried to imagine his mother's face after his departure, and then... then he couldn't think about it anymore, fighting the grief and the tears that were stuck somewhere deep inside. A group of teenagers was crowding the bus stop. The kids were talking and laughing, perhaps reenacting a scene from a film to each other, or mocking someone. Looking at them, his peers, Sanya thought of how he would probably never again laugh as they did, never clap his hands in a carefree manner and jump for joy. All of this was and remained in the wooden house on Third Proletarian Street, in a small room with creaky floorboards. It remained in that summer day when Fedya, kicking the ball nonchalantly, was begging him to go to the park. It remained in their empty room, on the lonely bed standing in the corner where he wept at night, begging his brother to return. He knew that he would search for him everywhere: railway stations, bus stops, streets, everywhere and always, until he found him.

Exiting the bus, he thought he saw Nalim's face flash in the crowd but then, deciding it was just his imagination, he walked quickly onward.

Not even bothering to look for his name on the list of admitted students, Sanya asked the attendant where he could pick up his drawings. When she walked up to a cardboard box on the windowsill and handed him a yellow envelope where someone's caring hand had neatly placed his work, he smiled, thinking of the blonde secretary. Stopping by the post office, he sent Claudia a brief letter:

"Dear Grandma Claudia, I'm going to Leningrad, will

send you my address once I arrive. Do not worry; everything is going to be okay. If you see Vitek – you have probably met already – give him my warmest greetings. Your Sanya."

A pleasant surprise awaited him at the dormitory: a letter from Grandma Claudia in a surprisingly thick envelope. He did not even remember how he ran up to the third floor, shut the door behind him, and hastily tore open the envelope. Inside, he found a letter from Alya. First, he read the long-awaited note from Claudia. She wrote that she had met Vitek and that he was an incredibly kind man. They were meeting every Friday to play lotto. "My darling," she wrote, "your letters are so short, and I would like to hear more details. Don't be lazy now, and write." She wrote that she missed him greatly. Pressing the sheet of paper to his face, Sanya breathed in deeply, trying to sense the scent of his home.

In no hurry to open Alya's letter, he stood leaning on the windowsill with his elbows, watching boys playing soccer outside through the open window. Pretty printed letters on the envelope read: "Careful: photograph inside!" and that was precisely what was stopping him. After leaving for Khabarovsk, she never sent him her photograph, and Sanya still imagined her as a little, fragile girl with large, green, laughing eyes and a serious face. For some reason, everyone thought she'd become a singer, but no, Alya decided to become a geologist.

Finally, making up his mind, he opened the envelope in a single motion and froze upon seeing Alya's photograph. She had changed a lot in three years. She still had the same laughing eyes, hair to her shoulders, and one could say it was impossible to even wish to be more beautiful than she was. He studied her photograph, not believing that it was really his Alya, the girl sitting in the hallway by the radiator, trying to keep warm.

He tried to answer the question: "Why was she writing to him? When she could have anyone she wanted at her feet?"

"Sanya, my dear friend. Hello!" No, she had never written to him like that before.

"I'm so happy I was admitted to study geology! And you? Were you admitted to study art?

"Your letters are so brief, and I want to know everything that's happening to you. Perhaps you can come to Khabarovsk? It's very nice here, we even have grapes growing. I frequently go to the local theaters and see plays, familiarizing myself with culture. Please send me your photograph, because I can't even imagine how you look now. Kisses, Alya."

"Kisses!" Sanya repeated rapturously. "Does she really love me, even a little? This is the first time she wrote 'kisses.'"

He decided to write her a reply after his situation cleared up and he had a permanent address.

Walking up to the mirror glued to the wall, in a luxurious baroque-style frame painted around it by skillful artists, Sanya stood right next to it and tried to get a good look at himself. Of course, he had probably changed as well without noticing it. Would Alya like him now? At one point, the girls in the dormitory stopped him, asking if he was applying to the theater school, and were very surprised to hear he wasn't. "Go into theater," they suggested, laughing; "you'll make it in without an exam and play heroes, lovers all your life." "Do I really look like some sort of hero, much less a lover?" he thought in surprise. Over the last year, Sanya had grown a lot and had a fairly well-defined, sportsmanlike figure, causing him to look older than his years. Only the face, were one to look closely, betrayed his real age. His large, dark, attentive eyes and his long black hair stood in surprising contrast to his bright face. Straight features and a dimple on his chin softened the contrast, giving him a particular charm.

"I wonder how Fedya looks now. He must have changed as well, after all. How will I recognize him?" Asking himself this question, he immediately refuted it. "How foolish," he whispered, "how could I not recognize him? Of course I'll recognize him right away, he's my brother: his voice, his laugh, his gait, his habit of tossing back his head, as if trying to get a better look at something, and then again, the scar on his left index finger."

Sanya plunged into memories of how once, during summer break, Fedya cut his finger with an axe. That summer, their mother was sent to a distant Buryat settlement for two months, and she decided to take them with her. For the first time, they flew on a real helicopter, and the delight on Fedya's face was clear to see. Referring to the experience that evening, he commented: "Now, you are going to become an artist. And as for me," Fedya made a weighty pause and then continued, "I'd never want to be some sort of director, but only a fireman, pilot, or a military man. I really like uniforms. You feel so important right away. Remember the math teacher's husband? When he came to our school without his general's uniform, he looked so little, and no one would notice, but when he came in the uniform, even trees would salute him. I want to be important in this life, get it?"

"I get it," Sanya said out loud as he recalled the conversation, which once again felt near and dear to him. He no longer resisted the flood of memories as it whirled around him, picking him up and carrying him to the desolate Buryat village, to a wooden house called "Medical Post," where they lived with their mother in a small room allotted to the doctor. The door of the hospital stayed open even at night. She inoculated children, treated the sick, taught the villagers about diseases and hygiene. It was so fascinating, a completely unreal way of life, as if taken from some wondrous book. He and Fedya ran around the village for days on end, playing with kids who spoke Buryat better than Russian. And it was hard to believe that these people lived in the same country as they did. It was a true Siberian village, surrounded by taiga and mountains – mountains all the way to the horizon. The people brought them food, firewood, and warm clothes when the weather turned cold and rainy. Everyone wished to invite them to his house and treat them to something. The inhabitants liked their mother, calling her *"Sagaan Shubuun,"* which, in Buryat, meant: "White Bird."

An old, branchy tree covered with colorful ribbons grew outside the village, and the children explained that this tree belonged to a spirit they worshipped. The spirit was very happy to see people come to him with requests and tie a ribbon to the tree in gratitude.

Their mother worked with no regard for herself, occasionally falling asleep for half an hour as she sat on a chair, her head resting on the table. It was back then that he and Fedya first witnessed the birth of a child. Their mother did not leave the woman in labor for even a minute, until the latter gave birth to a tiny girl at last. The brothers peeked into the woman's room through a crack in the door, and when the child came into the world and began to cry, they could not believe their eyes. A day later, after recovering somewhat, Fedya said that he would never again believe that children are found in cabbage or brought by a stork. As for Sanya, the incident remained to this day one of the greatest shocks of his life, even though he had never discussed it with anyone. The newborn girl was named Anna, in honor of his mother, and it was the first Russian name given to a child in that village.

When they ran out of patients in the area, they started asking her to treat sick animals. Their mother resisted, saying she was not a veterinarian, but then went and helped anyway. One night, a man ran into the hospital, begging her to come with him and help his cow give birth. The man cried and lamented: "If the cow croaks, then I won't have any way to feed my kids, and I have five. Does it really matter if it's a cow or a woman? The principle's the same."

Yes, it was an unforgettable summer break, and when it came time for them to return to the city, the villagers lit an enormous bonfire outside the village. The children baked potatoes in the ash, the men chopped up branches in the area and tossed them into the fire, and the women, dressed in traditional Buryat garb, sang songs in their native tongue and danced.

Fedya, wishing to feel like an adult, sneaked up to the block where the men were chopping firewood, lifted a heavy axe, and, unable to hold it, misplaced his blow. The axe fell onto his left index finger, nearly chopping it in half. He screamed without respite, because it hurt, while their mother fussed around with his finger, giving him a Novocain injection. Boiling metal brackets to sterilize them, she attached them around the wound, closing it and sprinkling it with some strange white powder called penicillin.

"It'll heal in time for your wedding day, don't you worry," she whispered, kissing Fedya's hair. She said it very confidently, and indeed, the finger healed very quickly, leaving an uneven scar.

On the day of their departure, the entire village saw them off as if they were relatives, and their mother took off her light blue kerchief, walked outside the village fence towards the spirit's tree, and tied it to a branch. Soon, a helicopter came to take them back to the city. Their mother never returned to this village again, she was being sent north to the Chukchi and Evenki people. This happened three years before Fedya's disappearance.

Sanya was still deep in thought when the door into the room swung open abruptly, and the superintendent of the dormitory appeared on the doorstep, expressing her surprise that he was still here. Sanya promised her he would leave tomorrow, and the superintendent shut the door just as noisily as she had opened it. He could not fall asleep all night, fighting his memories, and in the morning, after packing his few possessions into his backpack, he headed to Nalim.

"I'm moving in. May I?" he said, appearing in the barn.

Nalim did not show any surprise, gesturing hospitably with his hand to invite him in. Stepping inside and sitting down on old piece of wood in the middle of the dwelling, which served as a chair, Sanya peeked at Nalim's work clothes and asked:

"You didn't work today?"

Cleanly shaven and with a short haircut, Nalim was sitting on a mat in the corner. He smirked at the question and replied:

"I don't have any days off, Sanya. My work is the intellectual sort. Tomorrow I'll give you money for a train ticket... and..." not finishing his sentence, he threw up his hand and waved it lazily.

Sanya shrugged his shoulders, feeling very uneasy because this man was trying to help him despite being in need of help himself.

"You don't believe me?" Nalim asked, staring directly at him.

Getting up, he extracted a passport and four photographs of himself from his inside jacket pocket and handed them to Sanya.

"Sidorov, Stepan Ivanovich! What's his relationship to you?"

"A direct relationship!" Nalim exclaimed with optimism and, taking back the document, continued: "It used to be him. And now it will be me. I just have to skillfully glue in my photograph, which I am very good at, and on we go! Tomorrow, I'll pawn comrade Sidorov like a watch, and this time I won't even regret it because this comrade fired me."

"Aha, so it's revenge?" Sanya shouted, "And what of the other comrades?"

"The others are just a random paycheck. I've lived for over three years like this, I've pawned a good dozen such comrades."

In the evening, they sat once again on opposite sides of the fire in complete silence. Wagging its tail, the dog paced between the two of them for a while and settled down off to the side. In the morning, Nalim disappeared along with his work clothes. He appeared in the evening in elevated spirits. Entering the barn and picking up a bottle of wine, he said:

"Shall we drink to your departure, then?"

Sanya looked at him without any particular emotion. Then Nalim took money out of his pocket and, counting off ten-ruble notes, handed them to Sanya with the words:

"Take it, there's a hundred rubles here. This will be enough for you to go there and also back, in case you don't like it."

Walking up to the boy, Nalim placed the money in the palm of his hand and closed it into a fist, then said in a demanding tone:

"Take it, I said! You're not going to live the way I do. Go! You're only getting in my way here. Why are you staring at me?" Nalim squinted. "I didn't steal them, and I didn't kill anyone. Oh, look at him torture an honest man. Here!"

He handed him comrade Sidorov's passport by way of explanation. Opening the document, Sanya saw Nalim's expertly attached photo. Leafing to the last page, he found an enormous square stamp with the words: "The body of the bearer of this document after his death, regardless of his place of residence, is the property of..." and then came the address of a medical establishment. There was also a small insert acknowledging the payment of two hundred rubles for the sale of the body.

"How horrible!" Sanya exclaimed. "You sold him, and he doesn't suspect a thing!"

"That's right, I sold him. I sold myself as well. Thank God we have plenty of medical establishments, and they all want cadavers. Who cares what happens to us after death?" Nalim said philosophically, opening the bottle and taking a drink.

Sitting by the fire in his good suit, Nalim took a piece of old wood from the pile the boy had gathered over the course of the day, and placed it on top of the burning fire. Sanya could not even imagine that this was his friend's line of business, or, for that matter, that such a line of business existed at all.

"Mister, I will definitely pay you back, you'll see."

"I'll pay you back, I'll pay you back," Nalim guffawed. "You won't pay me back a thing, and if you do, you should pay back comrade Sidorov instead of me. The product is his, only the idea belongs to me. Tomorrow you'll go to your Leningrad. I looked up the schedule for the passing Khabarovsk-Moscow train, it leaves at nine o'clock in the evening..."

Finishing the bottle, Nalim tumbled on the ground and fell asleep. Fall was approaching, a nighttime coldness emanated from the ground, while the air, not warmed sufficiently over the course of the day, carried a penetrating dampness. The leaves on the trees had also changed color considerably, reminiscent of the slow fade. Sanya had the idea to destroy all evidence that could implicate Nalim, and, finding the plastic bag with other people's papers in the barn, he tossed them all into the fire. Then, leaning over the sleeping Nalim, he pulled out comrade Sidorov's document and burned it as well, saying:

"This will be better for everyone, this will be better for him."

Sitting next to his friend, he looked at this face. After a haircut and a shave, Nalim no longer resembled the homeless, insane old man that had first appeared before him, climbing out from under a bench. Now, in the soft glow of the fire, Nalim's face looked humble and kind. Feeling in his pocket for the watch, Vitek's gift, Sanya mused that he managed not to be late anywhere even without it. A strange, new feeling crept into his heart. He wanted to share his most precious possessions with Nalim, and the only precious possessions he had turned out to be his memories of times past and the watch. Tearing open the sewn-up pocket and taking out the watch, he looked at it for a long time, just like the first time, and then, quietly, so as not to wake him, Sanya placed the watch in the sleeping man's pocket.

The next day, at eight in the evening, having bought a ticket, they sat on a bench in the waiting hall.

"I'd like to write to you," Sanya said, "but you don't have an address."

"I'd like to write you back," Nalim replied, "but you don't have an address either."

Nalim looked sad; it seemed he had really taken a shine to Sanya.

"Perhaps you'll try to find a job again?" Sanya whispered anxiously.

"Who would hire me with a conviction in my work record?"

"Maybe you'll go back to your wife? You're her husband, after all," he pleaded.

"She divorced me long ago, what good am I to her like this?"

With no further arguments, Sanya fell silent.

"Like an old friend once told me," Nalim said in a detached voice, "my life, Sanya, is like a suitcase without a handle – tough to carry, a pity to throw away. Don't worry about me; I still have some cards up my sleeve."

They heard the boarding announcement. As he said goodbye by the train doors, Sanya, without thinking about it, threw himself at Nalim and gave him a firm hug. Not expecting such a goodbye, Nalim pushed the boy away with difficulty and said:

"Farewell, Sanya." He turned around and walked quickly away, his bare ankles flashing from his rubber galoshes in the light of the streetlamps.

Leningrad

The wheels knocked faster and faster, piercing the twilight as the train picked up speed. Sanya stood in the passageway of the train car with an air of detachment, staring into the darkness. A passing conductress asked him what his seat was, then pointed out the appropriate compartment and promised to come back in a few minutes with bedding. The train was passing through, and only two passengers had boarded at this stop. The conductress returned with the bedding, and meanwhile he was still standing by the window.

"How many days till Moscow?" he asked indifferently.

"Five days," she said, pointing at the schedule posted on the wall. "Here are all the stops and cities we'll be passing."

Walking up to the schedule, Sanya perked up suddenly, seeing his home City N.

"We're passing through that city?"

"Yes," the woman replied. "At six in the morning, and we'll only be stopping for a few minutes." Setting up his bed and climbing quietly onto the top bunk, trying not to wake the three already sleeping passengers, Sanya stared at the ceiling and thought suddenly that perhaps he should get out in City N. Grandma Claudia and Vitek would be so happy.

When, at six in the morning, the train pulled into the station in his home city, he slung his backpack over his shoulder, just in case, and jumped off the footboard. He looked around, as if waiting for the people close to him to show up, realizing that they could not be here at this time, and yet standing and looking.

The whistle sounded, and the doors began to shut one after the other.

"Hurry!" the conductress shouted. "Hurry! We're leaving."

She was about to close the door when Sanya jumped into the already moving car at the last moment.

"If you're so absentminded, then don't go outside at all," the conductress scolded.

Now, he had nothing else to wait for, and, climbing onto his bunk, he fell into a long sleep. He woke up and saw an elderly woman sitting below. Sanya asked her what the next stop was.

"I thought you'd sleep the whole way. Novosibirsk is next," the woman said with a good-natured smile. Then, spreading butter on a piece of rye bread and placing two slices of fresh cucumber on top, she handed it to Sanya.

"Eat," his fellow traveler said. "You must be hungry. I see you barely have any things. Going far?" she inquired, and hearing Leningrad, shook her head and said that it was awfully far.

Not wishing to continue the conversation, Sanya looked outside through the top part of the window. And he kept traveling, day and night, day and night, and the further he traveled, the more anxious he felt. "Try and find a missing person in such a large country, this is not even a needle in a haystack or a drop of water in the ocean, this is something else... And Mama, Grandma Claudia, Vitek, Nalim... they have stayed behind, in the past." No, he never wanted to consign them to the past. Calming himself down, he imagined that they were here, nearby, on the same earth at the very least.

Fields and forests flickered outside the window, boundless, stretching into the horizon. Small villages, settlements, and towns flashed past. Rivers, lakes, mountains, and heaths flew by, and all of it had neither beginning nor end. Exhausted by everything that had happened, trying to regain his strength, Sanya did not leave his bunk without need, either looking through the window or laying in a slumber. His fellow passengers switched out almost every day, leaving him food and water, and it would have been difficult to find on earth a lonelier person than he. Again and again he revisited the unforgettable meeting with his mother, reconstructing and replaying everything to the smallest detail. Everything that had been noticed elusively during his visit now resurfaced unexpectedly: a scratch on her left hand, blue circles under her eyes, her nightshirt, stained by Brilliant Green, a metal bowl with a spoon attached to it by a long chain, a plastic basin in the corner, people behind the grated doors, waiting quietly. And this mental agony could not be stopped. His face grew lean, while the pants and shirt that he had worn the entire trip were wrinkled and devoid of any form.

On the fifth day, when the train finally pulled into the train station at the capital, the cars emptied quickly. Sanya slipped off the top bunk, stepped into the passageway, and walked, swaying, towards the exit.

"You're still here?" the conductress exclaimed in surprise upon seeing him. "I thought you had long since fallen behind somewhere."

He exited the train. "The capital!" he said indifferently. "If Fedya were here, then it would have been some great joy, perhaps, but now, who cares – the capital," he repeated.

Seeing a crowd flowing like a river down into an underground crossing and joining this flow, he was swept by its power to the other side of the square. An hour later, Sanya was already sitting in the express train that was supposed to deliver him to the mysterious city on the Neva River in seven hours. The train was called "Arrow," and, indeed, it flew like an arrow, piercing the cold, rainy fall day. He felt unwell, and, thinking that the change in climate was to blame, he did not even consider that he might be ill. The passengers, sitting in threes opposite one another, were preoccupied with their own business; someone was reading a book, someone a newspaper and many were simply staring into the space in front of them. The young girl sitting next to Sanya moved away from him, just in case, casting the occasional sidelong glance at his clothing, dusty and wrinkled almost to the point of indecency, and his bare feet clad in sandals. Pretending that he did not notice this, he sat with his head downcast, practically burying his face in the backpack lying on his knees, fighting nausea.

Sanya did not remember that final minute when, leaving the train after such a long journey, he ended up on Nevsky Prospect. Rain drizzled here, like in Moscow. Taking his father's old windbreaker out of the side pocket of his backpack and putting it on, he stood, thinking, not knowing which way to go. The gloomy weather made it seem as if it was nine o'clock in the evening rather than four in the afternoon, plunging the city into mysterious shadows.

Entering a drug store, glowing with neon lights, Sanya inquired as to where he might find the Academy of Arts.

"I don't know, kid, ask in the grocery," came the reply.

In the grocery, the saleswoman excused herself by saying that she had only been living here a month and suggested he ask at the candy store next door. At the candy store, it began to seem like a conspiracy.

"Sorry," the elderly saleswoman apologized. "All the time I've lived here, I've never even wondered where that might be. You should ask at the drug store, they probably know."

He had the chills; walking in an indeterminate direction, he tried once again to make inquiries and was finally given a detailed explanation. He walked on, realizing that no one might be there, and even if someone was, no one might want to speak with him. Perhaps had he felt better, he would have analyzed his circumstances, lost confidence, and grown embarrassed. But now, walking past the tall buildings of a kind that he had never seen before in his life, staggering from exhaustion and malaise, he did not care in the least about what waited for him behind the enormous front door of the Academy, which revealed carpeted marble steps leading to a second door, just as pretty as the first.

He opened the door and walked up the steps, his head hanging low. A man was descending the staircase, and they had almost passed each other when this man stopped and asked:

"So, young man, has no one taught you to say hello?"

"Hello!" Sanya said quietly, unbuttoning his windbreaker. The man, elegantly dressed, holding a briefcase in his hand, stood there examining the strange visitor closely.

"And who has allowed you to enter this sacred institution in such dirty clothing?" he said indignantly all of a sudden.

Lowering his head even more and thinking all was lost; Sanya gathered his last strength to reply and muttered:

"I… I came to study. Forgive me."

"To study!" the stranger exclaimed, grasping him by the arm and pulling him towards the door. "Where did you come from then, the other side of the city?"

"From Siberia! I traveled for five days!" Sanya tried to explain himself powerlessly, trying to stop the mad stranger.

"Lies," the man said sharply, but then stopped suddenly and ordered him to produce proof.

Taking the train ticket out of his pocket, Sanya handed it to the distrustful stranger and, unable to stand, sat down. The latter looked at the ticket and returned it to Sanya, seeing that the boy was unwell.

"You don't have anyone here, of course?" the stranger said in a puzzled voice, softening his tone and leaning over Sanya, who was sitting in the same position with an air of detachment.

"Why, you're sick!" the man said, touching his forehead lightly.

The man stood in pensiveness for a while and then made a sudden decision, ordering Sanya to follow him.

They returned to Nevsky, where they waited for the right bus for a long time and then, it seemed to Sanya, rode it somewhere for a long, long time. Seeing nothing around him, he dreamed only of laying his head down in some quiet spot. They exited the bus, walked silently down a broad street at first, and then turned into an archway. The man took him up a narrow stone staircase to the third floor, stopping in front of a strange door with four doorbell buttons and a different name next to each one.

The man took a long key out of his pocket, opened the door, and, after asking Sanya to follow him quietly, led the way inside. He lit a dim lamp high under the ceiling, illuminating a large foyer that, it seemed to Sanya, had numerous doors all leading in different directions. Crossing the foyer and entering a long hallway, they stopped at the end, in front of yet another closed door, which the man opened with a second key.

"Come quickly," the man invited, letting Sanya go first.

He closed the door firmly behind him and introduced himself as Grigoriy Petrovich. Sanya introduced himself as well, took off his sandals, placed his backpack on the floor, and, without undressing, lay down on a couch indicated by his caring host. The host poured some water from a decanter standing on the table, then poured some pills into his hand and gave them to Sanya, demanding he take them.

"Lay here while I go to the kitchen and make some hot tea," he said, walking out.

Sanya kept spinning his head, trying to get a good look at his new residence, which looked most unusual. It seemed like an entire apartment had been squeezed into one room. A massive wardrobe stood to the left side of the door, and next to it was his host's large, wooden, carefully made bed. To the right side of the door was a tall old sideboard full of various dishes. Next to the sideboard was a round table serving as both a desk and a kitchen table, with stacks of notebooks and books interspersed with plates left over from a hasty breakfast. Leaning against a wall was the single wooden chair in the room. In the corner, a television with a bulbous screen rested on a large stand, then came a bookcase full of books from floor to ceiling, and a truly enormous window covered with long, light brown drapes. In front of the window was the couch on which Sanya was lying, and between the couch and the bed was a large mirror on a stand shaped like lion's feet. The window and the tall molded ceiling created a sense of spaciousness. There was not a single photograph, or even a calendar, or any sort of picture on the walls, which were covered in gray wallpaper with tiny flower prints, peeling away in a few places near the ceiling. The parquet floor, worn and creaky, threatening to crack like ice, made the room even drearier. The host did not return for a long time, and Sanya closed his eyes and fell into a deep sleep.

Returning and finding his guest asleep, Grigoriy Petrovich placed a painted metal tray with two cups of hot tea on the table. Dallying a while, he took a warm blanket from the television stand and covered the sleeping boy. Quietly moving the chair, he sat down for his evening meal, eating both his and Sanya's sandwich and doing the same thing with the tea, drinking one glass after the other. Then, rising and turning off the light, he approached his bed and stood there motionlessly for a long time, thinking of something known to him alone.

Waking up the next day, Sanya felt much better. Stretching and opening his eyes, he saw his rescuer from yesterday eating breakfast. A smell, new to Sanya, was flowing through the room, the smell of coffee. Not a trace remained of his former indifference, and he suddenly felt very awkward in these indeterminate circumstances. Grigoriy Petrovich invited him to sit, extracting a small metal chair from under the table.

"Where is the bathroom?" Sanya asked.

"Down the hallway on the left. If you meet anyone in

the hallway, don't engage them in conversation. And if they ask who you are, tell them you are my relative," his host explained in a cautionary manner.

Sanya did not meet anyone but was even more surprised when he glanced into the small kitchen next to the bathroom and saw something he could not explain. Like obedient soldiers, lined up against the wall were four identical refrigerators, four identical wall cabinets, and four small tables covered with pots and pans. A cleaning schedule and a usage schedule hung on the bathroom door.

Returning to the room, Sanya asked the question Grigoriy Petrovich was already expecting:

"Is this a dormitory or something?"

"No," the host said calmly, "this is a real communal apartment. Do you understand what 'commune' means?"

"I do. It's when everything is shared, like in an orphanage."

"There was a time when this apartment belonged to one family," Grigoriy Petrovich continued. "And now, can you see the progress? Four families have found shelter here. What are you going to do next?" he inquired, changing the topic.

"Study."

"All the classes have long been filled," Grigoriy Petrovich said dryly. "Show me your work," he asked.

Extracting the yellow envelope with drawings from his backpack, Sanya handed it to the host, saying this was all he had. Laying out the drawings on his carefully made bed, Grigoriy Petrovich leaned over them and studied them carefully for a long time, not concealing his surprise. He did not expect to see such troubling, mature, and emotional pieces from a teenager who had not yet experienced anything in life.

"How old are you?" he asked, staring Sanya intently in the eyes.

"Sixteen."

"Who are these people?"

"No one in particular, just people," he dodged the question.

"How long it would take to tell him about everyone," Sanya thought. He felt that he had just laid out his entire life, all his precious memories about those he left behind, in front of this little-known man, on his unfamiliar bed. Here was Vitek sleeping on the grass, and Grandma Claudia, and Fedya with the ball in his hands, like he remembered him. The girls with their silly faces in the *banya*, covering their bare stomachs with metal basins. His mother dressed in the costume of the Mistress of Copper Mountain and his father, sitting on a low bench by the furnace. Here was Third Proletarian Street, powdered with snow. And the man of despair, Nalim. And much, much more...

Gathering up the pieces with a quick motion and putting them back in the envelope, Grigoriy Petrovich quickly prepared to leave. Walking up to the wardrobe and taking out athletic pants and a shirt, he tossed them to Sanya so the boy could change.

"You can wash your clothes in the bathroom," he said. Adding: "I'll be back soon," he left hastily.

Sanya heard the goodbye creak of the parquet floor in the hallway, and the front door banged shut behind his host. Approaching the window, which faced the round courtyard, shaped like a water well, Sanya saw his host walk quickly outside and disappear through the semicircular arch. Grandma Claudia sometimes spoke of these well-like courtyards, of drawbridges and canals. Even now, he could scarcely believe that he had reached this city; before, it seemed to him that it only existed in his grandma's fantasies. Now he had not only reached it but also met such a charming man, although Sanya still did not understand the sudden change that occurred after he mentioned the word "Siberia."

"Perhaps it's a magic word," Sanya pondered, "one that I must use more often." One way or another, something stopped Grigoriy Petrovich's firm, justice-seeking hand yesterday, turning Sanya from a vagabond into a resident of his modest abode.

Changing into Grigoriy Petrovich's clothes, he pulled what little clothing he had out of the backpack, preparing to wash it, and, to his immense surprise, discovered the watch that he had given Nalim on the bottom.

"Oh, Nalim! Oh, Nalim!" he repeated meaninglessly, opening and closing the shiny object, trying to remember when Nalim could have done this. The day of his departure, they had been together the whole time. Nalim got a worn chessboard from somewhere along with similarly worn, dog-nibbled chess pieces, and suggested Sanya play to unwind. They sat by the fire in silence, playing chess almost the entire day. Nalim was not only an excellent businessman, but also a grand strategist, winning one game after another, and saying:

"I can go easy on you, of course, but then you won't learn anything." Nalim was master of all trades, and it was impossible to figure out when he had put the watch in the backpack. Deciding not to use the watch and hiding it again, he tied the backpack firmly and tossed it on the very top of the wardrobe so no one could see it.

Gathering up his dirty laundry in a pile, Sanya headed to the bathroom and found several aluminum basins hanging on the wall there. Without thinking, he took the first one that came to hand and began to wash his clothes. He did not hear the bathroom door open softly, and then a child's voice asked loudly:

"Who are you?"

Turning around, Sanya saw a large-eyed girl of about five standing in the doorway. She stood there in a business-like pose, arms akimbo.

"I... I..." he stammered, trying to find the right words.

"Are you a thief or something?" the girl continued. "I've never seen you here before."

"Where have you seen a thief who comes into the bathroom to wash his clothes?" Sanya replied, squatting down in front of her.

"There are exceptions," the girl said and pointed to the basin: "This is our basin, and you stole it."

"Okay," Sanya asked, not seeing the difference as he pointed to the basins hung on the wall: "And whose is this one?"

"That one belongs to those actors, more like sideshows. The one on the end is the alcoholic's. And the one in the middle is the Professor's."

"Professor, that means Grigoriy Petrovich. And why do you call him that; is he really a professor?"

"Of course, he's a professor. Everyone calls him that because he works at the academy. And who are you, anyway?" the girl demanded once again, throwing her chin up like an adult.

Recalling Grigoriy Petrovich's request not to talk to anyone, he wanted to remain silent, but he had to somehow get rid of this little detective asking head-on questions.

"Yes, I'm a thief," he said unexpectedly. "Can't you see I stole your basin?"

Astounded, the girl opened her eyes even wider, took a step back, turned around, and ran off down the hallway. The next moment, he heard the door to one of the rooms slam shut and the key turn in the lock.

The Professor did not return for a long time, and when he did, he made a joyous announcement:

"Well, Sanya, you sure are a lucky fellow. You don't have enough material, of course, but I asked the painting instructor, and he agreed to give you a trial period. If you pass the first session successfully, you'll be admitted as a student and receive a spot in the dormitory, and for now you can live with me."

Even before he fully understood what the Professor had said, Sanya began to smile, and his eyes sparkled with joy like a mouse that had made it alive through the winter. Having no idea of what he would have to do, he was ready for anything. After everything that had happened over the last several years, he felt the hope for change for the first time and promised that he would try very hard.

Enlivened by these events, the Professor graciously helped the newly minted student with the purchase of books and supplies. He even took the desperate step of registering the boy as a permanent resident in his forty square meters of space, which, in Piter, as the locals called the city, was next to impossible. Placing a certain sum of money in an envelope, the Professor went to the passport bureau where these formalities had to take place, and handed it along with a filled-in form to a servant of the law, assuring him that Sanya was his very real relative. The servant of the law, finding the contents of the envelope un-impeachable, granted the Professor's complicated request without delay. Sanya, having already encountered the great power of the "in," bore witness to a new type of business relationship called a "bribe."

Two days before the start of the school year, the Professor invited Sanya on an evening walk through Leningrad. The evening was quiet and unusually windless. The sun, setting slowly somewhere on the other side of Nevsky Prospect, cast a farewell shine on the golden domes towering here and there over the mighty and stately city. Stopping on the bend of the Moyka River, they bought ice cream in waffle cups. Walking next to the short-spoken Professor, Sanya thought about how life here was completely different, full of such scope and space: not like his home City N. There were no streets with wooden houses here, no mournful music, no funeral processions. Perhaps life was so good here that no one died?

At night, he dreamed of the sculptures in the Summer Garden, of bridges, palaces, and canals, and marveled at how all these new things seemed familiar and natural to him, as if he had been born here and had lived here always. In his dream, he saw Grandma Claudia standing on the doorstep of the beautiful cathedral, grieving and calling to him:

"Look! Look who's come to us!"

Walking up the steps cautiously, he stretched out his neck, trying to peek through the wide open door of the cathedral to see whom she was talking about. Grandma Claudia was gesturing at him to hurry, and as Sanya walked up the final step, he saw a man sitting on a wooden bench with his back to the door. He was dressed in a dark green suit and large shoes of the same color. The man got up suddenly and walked briskly to the altar. Sanya hurried after him, merging with his shadow on the floor, trying to overtake him and get a look at his face.

By his firm gait, his straight back, and his proudly raised

head, Sanya could surmise that it was a young man. As he drew closer to the altar, the man disappeared suddenly, and then Grandma Claudia and the cathedral disappeared also.

Waking up, he stared into the darkness, listening to the Professor's heavy breathing and the various nighttime rustles, thinking about his new place of residence. Rain drizzled outside the window, and the wind carried the last leaves of fall from somewhere, flinging them at the windowpane. Sanya, one could say, had already adapted somewhat and begun to understand the internal laws of life in the communal apartment where four families lived together, and he was now an attentive observer and participant.

Two actors, Dasha and Alexei, lived in one of the rooms. They left for work around noon, returning usually in the evening and squabbling until late at night. The charming, always smiling Alexei spoke in a trained, confident stage voice. He would binge drink occasionally, vanishing from the house without a trace for several days. And then they could hear Dasha sighing and sobbing as she paced up and down the room and waited for his return or a telephone call. When the sharp ringing of the long-awaited call resonated through the apartment, Dasha would dash to the phone first, scaring the resting residents and shouting: "It's for me, it's for me!" to reach it ahead of everyone else. She looked very young, thin, and pensive; not an open book like her husband.

The next room was occupied by a single mother, a young Jewish woman named Simona, along with her five-year old daughter Katya, a curious little detective. No one knew where they got the means to live. Simona never worked anywhere and rarely parted with her daughter, afraid even to send her to kindergarten for a few hours. She regularly cooked breakfasts, dinners, and suppers for Katya, and took her for long walks through the city and on museum tours. Every now and again, they would receive letters and packages from their close relatives in Israel. Katya rolled through the long hallway of the communal apartment on her little bicycle, singing loud songs and inserting words that no one could understand. Simona, who spoke very little to her neighbors, met Sanya for the first time in the communal kitchen; with her eyes squinted playfully and said:

"Just don't tell me you're the Professor's relative."

"And why not?" he replied just as playfully.

"Because I can see right through you, got that? Do you know how hard it is to register someone as a tenant? And when you aren't registered, you can't study and you can't work. You have to get a 'temporary residency' and wait three years for a permanent one, and he went and registered you right away."

"How do you know?" Sanya said in surprise.

"How, how!" Simona mocked him, smiling. "We got a letter from the tenant association about a new resident. You are an out-of-towner, and all out-of-towners are 'temps,'" she declared proudly.

"Are you an out-of-towner?" Sanya asked.

"I..." she said indignantly, "I am not," and, turning sharply, she left the room.

Yes, here in Leningrad, Sanya first encountered a new terminology of existence that he had previously known nothing about. For example, 'temp' – a man with restricted rights of residence, 'the fringe' – a man not distinguished by a sharp mind, and 'backwater' – someone even more hopeless than the fringe.

The third room in the communal apartment was occupied by a single man, like the professor, an engineer about fifty years of age, named Victor. He was sent frequently on work trips, and there was not a place in Russia that he had not visited. But Victor's most favorite activities were books and alcohol. On weekends and large holidays, he drank himself into oblivion, crawling out into the hallway devoid of any human aspect. Usually, after a typical episode of relaxation, the neighbors would openly show him contempt and ignore him, and then Victor would quit for a short while and sit quiet as a mouse. He would appear in the kitchen to cook something to eat with a book in his hand and be so polite and intelligent that everyone would forgive him once again and not report him to the housing authorities. And if it weren't for the fact that he frequently left on work trips, giving his neighbors a break for a while, they would have long since turned him in to the police.

The chimes in Simona's clock rang three o'clock at night. Sanya lay in bed, recalling the neighbors' conversation with the stubborn Simona. They had begged her to turn off the chimes at least for the night, but she refused to do this, saying that the clock was her only memory of childhood, when she lived in a true family and not among a gang of idiots.

The front door banged and Alexei stomped heavily towards his room. Immediately, Dasha's whisper came:

"Where were you so late?"

"Re-he-ar-sing," he drawled out in syllables.

"Why are you lying, you're drunk again," Dasha sobbed.

The neighbors began to toss and turn as they woke up and listened to the nighttime quarrel. The voices of the actors could be heard clearly in the silence of the night, even though they tried to speak quietly.

"Come on, now, Dashka, forgive me. So I had a bit to drink, sat in the kitchen with some friends, we sang a little, that's all," Alexei tried to explain.

"You've been sitting there and singing for two days now, you could have at least called, you parasite!" Dasha's voice said hurtfully, but this time, to everyone's surprise and disappointment, everything resolved itself quickly and the old couch began to creak triumphantly, announcing a new peace, until the creaking was crowned with Alexei's final gasp, resembling an athlete reaching the finish line. And the silence resumed. Listening to this night life, Sanya thought of how simple it was to have intimate relations practically in public, without concealing them at all.

In the morning, seeing Dasha in the line to use the bathroom, Sanya stood behind her and stared at her pretty, athletic legs. Without embarrassment, she had walked out into the hallway in a short nightshirt and stood there, leaning on the wall with one hand, drumming on it impatiently with her long fingers. She sensed his gaze and turned around.

"Are you an artist or something?" she asked.

"An artist," he said, shrugging his shoulders.

"How old are you?"

"Eighteen," he lied for some reason.

"Would you like to draw me?" the girl said coquettishly.

"I would," he said without hesitation.

"Well then, come Friday evening, when I'm not working."

Her turn arrived, and she disappeared behind the door, while he returned to his room and announced to the Professor that he would be practicing with his first live model. The latter, hearing Sanya's delighted voice, replied that practice was a very important thing in his profession.

"Practice makes a talentless artist passable, a talented one a genius, and, conversely, without practice even a genius can become nothing."

Sanya had many things to do before Friday, and he barely thought about Dasha. He wrote and sent letters to Claudia and Alya, describing his initial impressions of Leningrad in detail, and asking them to send him letters to the address of the academy. He wrote about the Professor and about living in a communal apartment, explaining that it was a dormitory but for adults. He begged them to reply as quickly as possible and gave them his telephone number just in case.

Naturally, the most important priority in his new life was study. The academic year had just begun, and Sanya understood his shaky situation, trying to live up to the Professor's hopes and prove that he would be able to continue his studies. The truth was that he really took his chosen profession to heart, and everything they touched on during class left tiny seeds in his soul, sprouting quickly and producing visible results. The greatest reward for him was hearing praise from the Professor, who watched his every step. Meeting almost every day in the academy's broad hallways, they nodded at each other discreetly, not giving anyone cause to suspect that they knew each other very well as roommates, or that Sanya was there thanks to a huge "in." It was enough that other students wondered how he had found his way into the class list, given that no one could remember him during the entrance exams. And the Professor, a delicate and sensitive man, could see Sanya's embarrassment and did not admit how closely they were acquainted.

Yes! He was a real Professor who taught "The History of Russian Art" and considered it the most important subject at the academy. Pacing slowly through the auditorium, he explained the significance of concepts through comparison, making them more understandable and approachable: "Just as tomorrow has its beginning in the present day, so did our classical masters lay the foundation so that today we do not have to grope around in the dark, trying to feel out the canons of true art." Listening to him rapturously, Sanya would sometimes feel surprise that this charming, talkative man with a brilliant mind was the same person as the taciturn resident of the communal apartment.

The week passed unnoticeably, and on Friday evening, with notepad and pencil in hand, Sanya knocked quietly on Dasha's door. Hearing her voice, he came in and looked around, trying to appraise his surroundings. In the corner of the room stood an old couch, known to all by its creaking. Across from the couch was a wardrobe with its doors missing, full of clothing. A lamp covered with a tablecloth stood by the window, while the wall shelves were full of books, dishware, and other items. All the walls in the room were covered with theater posters from plays where the actors had performed. Dasha had positioned herself almost in the middle of the room in a rocking chair, one leg over the other, glancing haughtily at the expected guest.

"It's very dark in here," Sanya said. "I need more light."

Rising easily, Dasha pulled the tablecloth off the lamp with a single motion.

"Where should I sit?" she asked.

The room did not present much of a choice, and Sanya invited her to return to the chair.

"I would like to be drawn without clothes," Dasha said, tossing off her robe and revealing her thin, athletic body. Then, removing her hair clip and scattering her hair over her shoulders, she returned once more to the chair.

He sat down on the floor across from her, stunned by what was happening. Seeing his embarrassment, Dasha smiled and said:

"Get used to it, if you're an artist. Treat me like a client. Let's get started, please!" she commanded, placing one leg over the other, leaning back, and freezing in place.

And he began, putting to paper the graceful lines of the first life drawing in his life, trying to look at her as little as possible and drawing mostly from memory. They were silent, and he did not remember the moment when he finished the drawing, got up, and handed it to Dasha, trying not to look at her. She looked at it carefully and finally exhaled:

"I'll take it." She got up without embarrassment, walked up to the wardrobe, obtained twenty rubles from somewhere, and handed them to Sanya.

Seeing the nude model with a twenty in her hand, Sanya grew even more embarrassed and stepped towards the door.

Grasping his hand, Dasha said firmly:

"Take it, silly boy, you've earned it. This is how you'll make your living the rest of your life. Do you really think you'll be able to create art just for yourself?" She forced the money into his hand, and he walked out.

Revisiting what Dasha had said, he realized that she was right. Indeed, after the final brush stroke that completed the work, his art would no longer belong to him. It would become a means of survival and be transferred from the hands of the artist to the hands of the collector. He also realized that there was nothing more beautiful than the nude female body.

He felt delighted when, just before the winter exams, it was announced that the students would be trying life drawing. Sanya sat frozen with anticipation, imagining how someone resembling Dasha would walk into the room and sprawl freely in front of them. How deeply he was disappointed when, following the instructor and covered with a white sheet, a bearded man walked into the auditorium and took the assigned spot, throwing off his covering and revealing all his endowment. The girls frowned and turned red, glancing at each other and not daring to begin. As for the model, he sat there looking very content with himself and glancing at the students with a crafty smile: "See, here you are suffering through my unusual body parts, and meanwhile I'm getting paid for this."

Returning home late in the evening, Sanya ran into Simona.

"Perhaps you'd like to draw me as well," she asked, smirking.

He looked at her, biting his lip and trying to figure out if she was joking.

"I'll pay you fifteen rubles, how about it?" Simona burst out laughing.

"I'll... think about it," he said on his way out, not wishing to continue the silly conversation and thinking of how these walls truly had ears.

Living under the Professor's wing, Sanya read many books suggested by his mentor, and now he could finally determine his favorite artists, poets, and writers, and would not shy away from discussing history, art, music, or architecture. He saw a ballet – "The Nutcracker" – for the first time, reveling in the perfection and the capabilities of the human body. He compared the ballet to painting and found similar foundations. In painting, the artist was the driving force, while in ballet it was the performer. Precise composition and form could be found in both the former and the latter. The stage could be called the ballet's palette, while the music was the color gamut. He could find similar connections for the various significant and less significant parts that complemented one another and created an impression of wholeness. The Professor was teaching him how to express his thoughts in a vivid fashion, and Sanya was immensely grateful for the Professor's quiet assistance at every step. As for the Professor, he watched his charge and was sincerely happy that he had not been wrong about him.

When the winter exams came, Sanya passed them with flying colors and was officially accepted as a student. Now he could expect a stipend and have at least some money to support himself. When the question of dormitory space arose, it turned out that there was no room, and Sanya would remain with the Professor until summer, something neither of them regretted. Throughout this time, he had received several letters from Alya and from Grandma Claudia. Alya was happy at his success and reproached him for not yet sending her his photograph. She wrote of her plans for the summer, a trip to Altai with a large group of students. Her letters were amicable and tender, and she would always beg him to write about himself in more detail, promising to call someday.

Grandma Claudia's letters always sounded very optimistic and full of boundless joy for her grandson. She wrote of winter and cold, forty degrees below, of how she took in a dog with an injured leg and of her incredibly kind friendship with Vitek.

Russia was on the threshold of New Year's, 1981, one of the most significant holidays for its citizens. Running through stores and standing in lines to buy delicacies, the inhabitants of Leningrad prepared for the holiday, setting up and decorating trees and wrapping presents for the children. During that time of year, the city air became permeated with the scent of a foreign fruit – mandarin oranges – a requisite part of a New Year's gift.

Finally, the long-awaited day arrived. The residents of the communal apartment were lining up all the tables in the small kitchen, and covering them with a snow-white tablecloth. Everyone participated without exception, preparing their favorite dishes and adding them to the already full table. Sanya and the Professor bought a large cake called "Flight." Victor, the alcohol specialist, obtained a bottle of good wine and some real champagne.

At twelve o'clock, when the Kremlin chimes were echoing the clock in Simona's room, announcing the start of the New Year, the neighbors dashed to congratulate one another, hugging and promising that, if they had somehow wronged one another in the previous year, they would surely set things right in the new one. And, of course, everyone realized that these were only promises, but they were still nice to hear. After drinking some champagne and giving everyone a kiss, Dasha started a song, and Simona joined in, rocking an absurdly happy little Katya on her knees. Victor tried to control himself enough to be able to make it back to his room, discussing Greek mythology and the meaning of life with the Professor. Playing loudly on the guitar, Alexei sang in a low voice, accompanying the girls. At one o'clock at night, the phone rang, and the Professor, who was sitting by the door, went into the hallway and picked up the receiver. They heard him giving someone warm New Year's wishes, asking about the weather, and exclaiming: "That's cold! How cold!" Then he said goodbye, returned to the kitchen, and called out:

"Sanya, it's for you."

It was Grandma Claudia, and, upon hearing her dear voice, Sanya lost all control and began to pepper her with questions, pressing the receiver to his ear as hard as he could, trying not to miss anything she said.

"Have you seen mama at the hospital? How is she feeling?" Sanya asked with a breaking voice. "How is uncle Vitek? Has there been any news of Fedya? Has there been word from my father?"

The scheduled time slot of the phone call ended quickly, and, as he said goodbye, he told her would definitely come visit in the summer. He hung up and stood there, leaning against a stack of old boxes from German artillery shells, covered with oilcloth and serving as a stand for the telephone.

The phone call was a true New Year's present for him; Grandma Claudia's painfully near and dear voice, breaking and reappearing again, had flown here across six thousand kilometers to the city on the Neva River. Tears appeared, choking him, and Sanya went into his room and lay down on the couch, covering his face. He remembered the New Year's tree in his home, as well as Fedya, his mother preparing for the ball, and his father, waiting for her patiently in the foyer. He could have painted pictures from the past forever in his imagination had the Professor not walked into the room. Having eavesdropped on the conversation, he learned much more about his protégé than he had during almost six months living together, so private was Sanya.

"Your grandma called?" he asked tenderly. "Such a pleasant voice, very pleasant..."

"Everyone has drama in his life, Sanya," he continued quietly. "And no one but you can live through it, not even if you pay someone a lot of money. No one," he repeated clearly and walked out, leaving Sanya completely immersed in thoughts. Trying to grasp the Professor's words, Sanya realized that they did not pertain only to him, and he thought about it for the first time. Who was this man, who had shared all he had with Sanya? And what was his life drama?

He returned to the kitchen and found the neighbors sitting together as one big family, happy and considerate towards one another. Even the Professor had joined the group, eating and drinking. On that New Year's night, Sanya agreed with the carefree and coquettish Simona that he would draw her hands.

"If it's just my hands," she laughed, "then, so be it, I will pay you three rubles."

And the next day, as the inhabitants of the city slept until dinnertime, snow was sweeping over Leningrad. It swept over all the unfulfilled hopes and expectations, giving birth to new dreams, underscoring all this with the pure whiteness that covered the earth.

Sanya liked everything here, even the weather that would frequently displease the locals. There were not a lot of sunny days, so few that every other child, according to Simona, was born with rickets. Constant wind and endless drizzling rain creating depression even among the mentally healthy, have been becoming an inseparable part of life. But when the White Nights began, a single month was enough to forgive the city for an entire year of suffering and fighting the weather's nasty moods, and to live on, waiting for these nights to return.

In the second semester, Sanya enrolled in new classes and devoted all his days to his art, barely leaving the academy. The stipend helped a lot in terms of finances, but almost all his money went towards the purchase of canvas, pencils, paint, and everything else he needed to study. Everyone looked enviously at the fourth year students, who had it a bit easier. Familiar with the basic technique, they could make some money on the side by selling their art or doing simple commissions.

When he finally reached the long-awaited fourth year, standing out through his talent, his interesting ideas about art, and the execution of said ideas, Sanya felt an enormous sense of relief.

Dasha

Four years flew by quietly and routinely, but a lot happened in the course of this routine. Sanya turned twenty, becoming a young man with a good figure, a mysterious expression on his face, and a dimple on his chin that created a masculine yet tender effect liked by many of his female classmates. However, he did not dare to start a serious relationship.

Throughout these years, he wrote and received multiple letters from Grandma Claudia and Alya. They continued to remain his spiritual companions. He shared his impressions of Leningrad's life with them. He missed Grandma Claudia endlessly, not giving his emotions free reign and funneling them instead into his art, promising her every time that he would come as soon as an opportunity presented itself. But the opportunity did not arise, and life sucked him deeper and deeper into its vortex.

Sanya continued to live with the Professor, and they seemed to become like two trees grown together despite knowing very little about each other.

"Once you become famous," the Professor joked one

day, "you'll forget all about me."

"I absolutely have to become famous," Sanya replied unexpectedly.

The Professor took off his glasses and stared at his protégé.

"It's a joke, a joke," Sanya said quite seriously. "And don't you worry; I won't forget about you even if I do become famous someday."

"How could I forget about him?" he thought indignantly. "Or how could one forget Nalim, or Vitek?" If it weren't for them, the course of his life would have taken a completely unknown direction. And, moreover, during the last few years, his life had been consumed by a mad idea that would not leave him alone. The idea that, if he were to become famous all of a sudden, there perhaps would come a day, during one of his exhibits, when the door would open, just as it happens in the movies, and *he* would walk in. The one for whom Sanya had dedicated himself to art. Sanya believed steadfastly that only art could lead him to his brother. He did not lose the desire to find him, but he changed his tactics, realizing that searching for him would be fruitless. He wanted to give Fedya the opportunity to recognize him and remember him through the forms inhabiting Sanya's canvases.

The life in the communal apartment remained the same. The chimes in Simona's clock annoyed the neighbors day and night, bringing them to the verge of a nervous breakdown. Katya had grown up and was already in third grade. She loved to chat; when Sanya bumped into her one day as she made tea for her mom in the kitchen, she said with an air of detachment:

"My mommy keeps crying, and I feel really sorry for her."

"Why does she cry?" Sanya asked, afraid to scare her off.

"My mommy wants to move to Israel to live with her family. But they won't let her go, they say she has to live here and suffer," the girl sighed in a very grown-up manner.

Victor kept flying away on work trips and "relaxing" moderately after returning.

Enormous changes took place in the lives of the two actors. After four years of tolerating Alexei's escapades, Dasha's patience snapped one day, and she kicked him out, filing for divorce.

Not hiding the fact that she was not indifferent towards Sanya, the girl tried to provoke him at every opportunity. She would press firmly against his shoulder after hugging him to say hello, or stroke his hand, or kiss him playfully on the cheek. A new show was opening soon in her theater, and she proudly announced this to him and the Professor, giving them two complimentary tickets.

On the day of the premiere, they bought a bouquet of tulips and headed for the first time to Dasha's theater, located on the grounds of one of the oldest parks.

The captivating show incorporated the songs and dances of the past century, reminiscent of the times when the tsar himself, Nicholas II, would come to this theater with his retinue and watch its best music shows. Today, they sang romances, performed tricks, and enacted silent scenes in the style of Charlie Chaplin, bringing exuberant laughter to the audience. On a second level, above the stage, tables and mirrors were positioned on a small platform resembling a makeup room. After finishing their parts, the actors would climb up the steps to the platform to sit down in the dim light of the lamps, adjust their makeup, and try on costumes right in front of the audience before returning to the stage. Also on the second level was a quartet comprised of actors playing different instruments and accompanying one another masterfully.

Dasha, irreplaceable in many scenes, made an enormous impression on Sanya during an unrivaled dance called: "The Lady Vampire." She performed it with a partner who played a hooligan that tried to mug her and received a deadly kiss at the end. Strolling slowly, Dasha appeared in the spotlight that snatched her out of the darkness. She was wearing a transparent dress with slits on both sides, wrapped with a broad belt around her waist. After appearing on the stage, she walked haughtily right at the audience with a long cigarette holder in her right hand. Pretending to smoke, she tapped off the ash in rhythm with the music, flicking her hand to the side with a light motion and showing off her amazing ballet skills. Her face – cold, youthful, and unapproachable – made Sanya shudder and wonder at the transformation. "What's she really like? The way she is now? Or the way she is in the hallway of the apartment, with her charming, childlike casualness?" Alexei, also performing in the show, would occasionally cast long, meaningful glances at Dasha. As he performed the song of a solitary gypsy, he turned to her as she sat right there on the stage and sang: "Goodbye, my friend, goodbye! 'Tis so hard for me to leave at dawn..."

Then, everything began to spin and twirl like in an old, forgotten dream. A tall, blonde actress playing a gypsy walked up to the microphone. With a low voice, picking up the tempo, she began to sing a song that Sanya had heard before.

He sat and gazed with detachment upon the stage, where the actors were twirling and singing with all their strength, mimicking the gypsy temperament, creating an atmosphere of complete freedom. Meanwhile he, closing his eyes a little, could see the real faces from the gypsy camp in the summer flickering in front of him. He could see the face of the racy gypsy performing the same song.

Gasping and clutching the bouquet of tulips prepared for Dasha, he squeezed his way towards the exit and hastened to the hallway, leaving the Professor in utter confusion.

Lengthy ovations came from the theater after the performance, and members of the audience walked up on the stage to give the actors flowers. Coming to his senses somewhat and leaving the Professor in the foyer of the theater, Sanya hurried backstage with the bouquet. Walking through the long side corridor and climbing some steps, he saw the overjoyed actors anticipating a banquet and congratulating each other noisily on the successful premiere. Dasha's face flashed in the crowd. Raising his tulips high in the air, Sanya headed towards her and saw that she was also pushing his way towards him. Approaching, she silently hugged him, gave him a kiss on the cheek with her moist, hot lips, and then said demandingly:

"We have a banquet today, and I want you to stay."

"No, I can't..."

"I want you to stay," she repeated capriciously.

"No, I can't, the Professor is waiting for me," he said, handing her the modest bouquet, and turned to leave. Dasha followed him.

"Did you like the show?"

"Very much, especially your dance."

After walking him to the foyer and seeing the Professor, Dasha waved at him, said: "See you tomorrow," and disappeared in the hallway.

"Tomorrow!" Sanya commented. "That means they'll be partying all night."

"So it does. They've done well, they've earned it," the Professor said as they left the theater.

They walked slowly through the park, savoring the warm May evening in anticipation of the White Nights.

"Do you like Dasha?" the Professor asked suddenly, breaking the silence.

Sanya recalled how, many years ago, after a New Year's party, Fedya had asked him the same question. "Do you like Snowflake?" he said back then, and now Sanya heard the question for the second time in his life.

"I don't know," he said quietly.

He truly did not know. Whenever he thought of Dasha, Alya's image appeared, begetting feelings of guilt and stopping all his desires in their tracks. Perhaps that first love for Alya yet glimmered inside him, unextinguished, even though he understood the futility of these feelings.

Dasha attracted him through a completely different desire, a strong physical drive to possess her. She had come from Volgograd and, after finishing theater school, stayed to work in Leningrad at the request of the theater. Alexei, born in Kazan, would frequently joke that, "were it not for the boondocks, the great art of Russian theater would have declined. We, from the provinces, are its renaissance, because the capitals are all out of talent." And, indeed, most of the acting company consisted of actors from different parts of the country.

Around ten o'clock in the evening, the two friends walked out on Nevsky Prospect. Empty and glowing with neon signs, it met the late strollers in an unfriendly fashion.

"Let's go to a cafe," the Professor suggested, and, after finding the only establishment open at such a late hour, they entered the semi-basement where it was located. The Professor sat down and ordered a bottle of wine, surprising Sanya, who kept looking round in case someone from the academy saw them.

"You are grown up already," the Professor said, seeing his anxiety. "You can try it."

Indeed, all the processes in Sanya's physiological development seemed to flow more slowly than normal. While his classmates had seemingly tried every possible method of expressing their emotions, he kept away from the herd mentality, and there were many things that he had encountered only in his imagination. To the Professor, he remained the greatest riddle.

"Why did you come into my life?" the Professor said suddenly.

"Blown in by chance," Sanya smiled, unable to find a better answer.

"No, my friend, nothing in our lives happens by chance. Even a tree does not grow accidentally. There is hidden meaning in everything. You can have a thought right here, and someone on the other end of the earth will sense your thought." He had a sip of wine and fell silent.

"And do you really believe this?"

"Sometimes, there's nothing else left..." the Professor trailed off, picking up his glass again.

Sanya repeated the Professor's motion with the glass like a monkey, raising his own and taking a sip. And what if this was true? What if thoughts could be transmitted and sensed over a distance? Meanwhile, he had not devoted himself to thoughts of Fedya and his mother, and he had completely forgotten about his father. If this was true, did they not sense him either or think of him?

"Why did you leave the theater?" the Professor now

inquired. "You don't like gypsy songs?"

"I don't. I had to leave for a second. Why, did you like them?" he countered with his own question, but the Professor remained silent.

They walked home in silence, each thinking his own thoughts. The light was on in Dasha's room, spilling its warm, enticing yellowness into the hallway from under the door. Just as Sanya thought of her, Dasha heard footsteps, opened the door, and appeared on the doorstep with a question:

"Where have you been walking so late? Sanya, come in for tea," she invited unexpectedly. He came in without much prompting and asked her what happened.

"Alexei got drunk and threw a fit," the girl sighed. "Smashed the mirrors in the makeup room; they calmed him down a little, but I had to leave. And you, where have you been?" she smiled with that ingratiating, childlike smile.

"We took a walk through Petersburg. And where's the tea you promised?"

Dasha began to set up the table, bringing hot water, a teapot, and some sugar from the kitchen, while Sanya allowed himself to sit down in the rocking chair and relax a little, looking all around. The tulips he had given her were standing next to the lamp in a glass milk bottle. The picture of Dasha he had drawn over three years ago hung over the couch.

"Would you like to reproduce it in oil? I can pose," the girl said, intercepting his glance.

"Why not," he said sincerely.

"Tell me about yourself," Dasha asked, sitting on the floor in front of him and gingerly handing him a large mug of hot tea.

"What would you like to know?"

"Everything, everything..." she insisted.

"I don't know everything, everything myself."

"Well then tell me what you do know," the girl pleaded.

He listened to her, marveling at how simply and laconically she could express herself, whereas he had to spend weeks just to admit something to himself. Dasha put aside her cup of tea, drew closer, and leaned on his knees.

"If you don't want to talk, then kiss me."

Making an incredible effort not to snatch her up and hold her without letting go in a fit of sudden passion, he leaned down and kissed her on the cheek.

"That's a little brother's kiss, you have to kiss me for real," she grumbled in displeasure.

"I don't know how," he admitted with a laugh.

"Want me to teach you?" And, without waiting for a response, Dasha kissed him.

"Why are you acting like this?" he asked, taking her by the shoulders and pushing her away.

"Because I love you. I've loved you for a long time," she whispered sorrowfully, lowering her head.

"Now there's an admission! There's a turnabout. She said 'I love you!' Some evening! There she is, unpredictable and insane, and what should I do now?" he thought, glancing at the creaky couch like in a bad movie.

"What is it, you don't like me? Tell me the truth," she pleaded.

"Let's talk tomorrow," he said, heading towards the door. Turning around, he saw her sitting on the floor and weeping like a child.

"Don't cry," he whispered, coming back and lifting her up. "You must be lonely, so you decided you were in love with me. Let's go to the Summer Garden tomorrow and have a talk there." Dasha began smiling and nodded in agreement, seeing him to the door.

He returned to find the Professor reclining on the bed with a thick book in his hands.

"Did the conversation take place?" he asked without looking up from his reading.

"How do you know about this?" Sanya asked excitedly.

"Everyone knows about it, even the neighboring apartment. Don't worry; no one here has any secrets before anyone else. We are a family here, and 'the family is the basic cell of the state,'" the Professor joked and continued to quote Mayakovsky: "'One is zero. One is nonsense. One man, for all his glories, can't raise a twenty-foot log, much less a house of five stories.'" The Professor stopped reciting and burst out in laughter: "Only why lift it, this five-story house?" He was not drunk, but he acted like his nerves were on edge. Sanya had never seen him like this.

"My respect," the Professor said, shutting his book and placing it on the floor. "You acted like a true gentleman."

In the morning, little Katya bumped into Sanya and said in a businesslike fashion: "My mom and I are going to be in the Summer Garden all day today. Mom says there will be a play, 'Romeo and Juliet,' but she doesn't know what time. Come with us, we'll have fun."

"No, Katyusha, I have other plans...," he said, frowning.

"Too bad," the girl said as she left.

At three o'clock, he met Dasha in the archway, where they altered their plans, deciding simply to take a walk through the city, assuming that all the curious neighbors would be gathered in the Summer Garden within the hour. Without noticing it, he took Dasha's hand and walked down the street, clutching it firmly, while she followed him obediently, quiet and happy. Soon, they were walking on the old cobblestones of the Peter and Paul Fortress, trying to explain their emotions. Dasha begged him to tell her how he felt about her.

"I really enjoy walking and talking with you..." he said awkwardly. "Looking at you..."

The girl's face lit up with joy.

"I'm going to the countryside on Sunday. My friend gave me the keys to her *dacha*. Let's go together?"

"Just you and me?" he asked.

"Just you and me," she continued hopefully. "Don't worry I won't push your buttons."

Sanya looked at her, thinking of how she constantly pushed all his buttons without realizing it herself. He stopped, hugged her, and gave her a kiss. They walked holding hands the entire time, and Dasha talked incessantly about the history of the city, gladly serving as his personal tour guide. They saw the military dungeon in the fortress, as well as the jail where the city founder's son, the Prince Alexei Petrovich, had been imprisoned.

"Silly man – by which, I mean Alexei," Dasha commented. "I don't understand why he had to rebel, having such a prominent and influential father."

"Our city is relatively young," she continued in a serious tone. "It will only turn three hundred in twenty years."

"We'll be old in twenty years," Sanya said suddenly.

"Old?" she looked at him to see if he was joking. "In twenty years, we'll be in our prime. You'll be a famous artist, and I'll be a famous theater and movie actress." She paused to think, searching for additional arguments, and then continued just as naturally:

---

* A seasonal or year-round Russian second home often located on exurbs of cities

"Look at Peter the Great, for example. He was easily over forty. Look how much he managed to do. He built this wonderful city, this fortress, the palaces, the churches, the canals. Imagine: had he not done this, almost three hundred years ago, we would never have met, and I love him all the more for it. And I love you," she said, hugging him and showering him with kisses.

"And now," the girl continued passionately, pulling him by the hand, "let's go to the Peter and Paul Cathedral and thank him personally."

"Dasha, he's long since dead, who are you going to...?" he began, but she did not let him finish and said seriously:

"A man is alive for as long as someone remembers him. You and I remember him, and that means he is alive." Once again Dasha astounded him with the novel way she perceived things, bordering on superstition. She believed, for example, that it was no coincidence for their first walk to be through the Peter and Paul Fortress, saying that the fortress served as the origin of the city. She searched for meaning in everything, even in places that seemed to lack all meaning. Sanya fell more and more in love, no longer resisting or fighting his emotions.

They entered the Imperial Tomb quietly and stood for a long time by the gravestone of the founder of the city, thinking their own thoughts. Having fallen under Dasha's influence, Sanya also thanked Peter the Great, contemplating that, were it not for this man, he would have never been born because his grandpa Clement and grandma Claudia would have never met here, in the city on the Neva. Afterwards, they sat for a long time on a bench in an alley, and Dasha kept talking about her home city of Volgograd, about her parents and her younger sisters, who were still there, about books and music. Sanya closed his eyes as he listened to her, trying to visualize what she was describing, while she enticed and attracted him with her openness and even straightforwardness. They returned home, deciding not to spend time together until Sunday, minding their own business.

On Sunday, they took the subway and then the commuter train to Dasha's friend's *dacha*. A brick house with two columns in the entryway, fairly spacious for a *dacha*, appeared before them. Wearing blue jeans and a loose shirt, Dasha bustled around, opening the doors and windows and letting the summer scents into the house. Apple trees bloomed all around and numerous field flowers were growing everywhere, mixing into a single, mysterious, intoxicating scent. The day flew by imperceptibly, and twilight approached, spooking the swarms of fireflies flying through the garden, as if underscoring the importance of the approaching moment. The large droplets of evening dew left a pleasant sense of happiness and peace as they splattered on their bare feet. Hugging and kissing Dasha, he forgot about everything else in the world and dissolved in the moment, no longer resisting anything and surrendering to this new and captivating emotion. The fragile Dasha melted in his embrace, merging and weaving together with him, becoming his reflection.

As they returned to the city the next day, the overjoyed Dasha hugged and kissed him the entire way, then said:

"Come live with me if you want."

"We'll see," Sanya said, stroking her hand gently and still having trouble comprehending what happened. His mind kept dashing, now somewhere into the past, where he once again saw the faces of his loved ones and Fedya as a thirteen year old teenager, now into the future, where he dreamed of finishing the academy, getting his mother from the hospital, and bringing her and Grandma Claudia here, to their home city. Then he returned to the present, trying as hard as he could to stay there, focusing on Dasha's dear, beloved face among the surroundings.

Plunging into his work and transferring all his worries and concerns onto his canvases, he passed the summer exams with distinction and received an invitation to travel to the Novgorod region to restore some ancient church frescoes. Dasha begged him to take her with him, but Sanya realized that her presence would distract him from work and become far more important than some frescoes, and so he tried to convince the girl to visit her relatives in Volgograd while he was away. His head would spin at the mere thought of her. He never moved into her room, staying at the Professor's side, where his roots were already planted firmly. His relationship with Dasha progressed, though not as speedily as she would have wanted – it progressed on Sanya's time, calmly and unhurriedly. Every now and then, he heard silly comments from the neighbors about how Dasha, being five years his senior, had managed to rope him in. Simona stopped talking to him, openly expressing her contempt for the lovers.

"Do you see," she would underscore during occasional conversations with the Professor, "how pointlessly your apple has fallen?"

Paying no attention to this and no longer feeling embarrassed, Sanya would sit in Dasha's room until dawn. They would eat breakfast together, and he even allowed her to wash his shirts. Dasha flew through the hallway happily after returning from rehearsals and gladly took on the responsibilities of Sanya and the Professor when it was their turn to tend to the kitchen or the bathroom.

"A very practical friendship," joked the Professor.

In reality, he did not hide the fact that he was very pleased with his protégé's choice. Sanya did not talk about his feelings, realizing that, if Dasha were to disappear from his life, it would be an inexpressible loss. Naturally, feelings of novelty can pass quickly, and relationships can become routine, losing those magnet-like properties, but for now, everything seemed new and special.

"Don't be afraid that you'll grow bored with me," Dasha said, as if reading his mind.

"I'm not," he said, surprised.

"You are," she said stubbornly. She furrowed her brow and continued mysteriously:

"I am a book of thousands upon thousands of pages. Do you know how many you've read?"

"How many?" He found her confidence immensely appealing.

"One tenth of the first page," she laughed, rushing to hug and kiss him reverently.

Soon, Dasha became the leitmotif of his work, posing motionlessly for him and burning him up with her eyes. Driven mad by his feelings, he forced himself to forget about her even for a moment and concentrate on his art. Thoughts of Alya moved to the background, and guilt no longer tormented him. Now he could call Alya a good, genuine friend, and he continued their correspondence, sharing stories from his life. In maintaining this thin thread of a valuable relationship, Sanya saw his reflection in Alya, like a mirror. He saw something comfortable, something that kept him near the source of all his first worries and joys, something that freed him from unnecessary words and explanations about his past. He wished to remain with her forever in that snowed-over city, unmarked on any map: City N.

Right before leaving for his summer practicum, Sanya received an extremely brief letter, practically a note, from Grandma Claudia, wherein she asked him to go to the Smolensky Cemetery and find the place where Uncle Alexander had been buried. The envelope also contained a postcard with a view of the Mamayev Kurgan in Volgograd, which he first took for a message from Dasha's family. The postcard showed the statue of the heroic Motherland with an enormous sword in her hand, calling on the people to defend their land from the German invaders. Unknown handwriting on the card read:

"Hello Claudia and Alexander. It was difficult for me to compose myself and write to you after so many years. I know that I will never earn your forgiveness, and it's not necessary."

"Father!" Sanya exclaimed, putting the card aside and trying to catch his breath. It was so unusual, so cold and distant, to have his father call him "Alexander".

"I do not ask for forgiveness, but I wanted to tell you I am alive. I have a new family and two children. I have tried to forget all that happened, and I suggest you do the same. Respectfully, Ivan Vetkin."

Sanya finished reading and did not even try to restrain his tears.

"Traitor... traitor..." he whispered, only now beginning to understand what happened. For many years, he kept the memory of his father and thought of him as an innocent victim, forgiving him and not realizing that he had chosen the easiest path. He simply left, transferring the burden to Claudia's and his, Sanya's, shoulders. He quickly started a new family and left his mother when she needed his help so much.

"Forget all that happened." This would mean forgetting

the very fiber of his being: the pain, the loss, and the suffering. Forgetting Fedya, even though, he had not lost hope of finding him. Forget! This would mean crossing out the past, ceasing to exist. This would mean... this would mean he could no longer dream of getting his mother from the hospital and bringing her and grandma here, giving them a chance to feel love and care even one more time in their lives. He had learned long ago that hope was an extremely important word if one did not take it lightly.

Sanya lay with his face in his pillow until dark, when Dasha knocked on the door and walked in without waiting.

"Sanya, I heard you were back, and you didn't even stop by?" she said in a puzzled voice. Her question hung in the darkness, and the next moment she turned on the light and saw him lying on the couch.

"Are you drunk or something?" she exclaimed indignantly.

"Don't worry, I'm not. Though, maybe I should be."

"Sanya, Sanechka, what's wrong? Tell me, my love, don't torture me," she said worriedly upon seeing his face. She sat down on the edge of the couch and placed his head on her knees, caressing him and pleading:

"My darling, my precious. My love, please tell me what happened?"

"Nothing much," he whispered. "I... I was crying about the past."

"What's this past, now, if someone as strong as you is crying about it? Sanechka, perhaps I can help you somehow?" Dasha whispered, pressing him to her cheek.

"You can't. Nobody can," he replied, rising and sitting next to her. "I'm an artist, Dasha. And an artist has to suffer, is that not so?"

"It's not," she said and immediately corrected herself:

"Of course, we actors think this way as well. But I, person-ally, do not agree, I think it's an antiquated notion. You are already talented, Sanya, and no one can take that away from you. They've written about you in many newspapers and magazines, and they all praise you. Why suffer? You must live and be happy. To transfer the happiness you experience onto the canvas."

"Everything is so simple with you, Dasha, like a book. You must have a very easy life."

"Life is not easy for anyone. Look at your Professor, for instance. No one knows what sort of man he is. He has no family, no relatives, no children, and yet he hangs on and even laughs and jokes on occasion. Of course, he's changed a lot since you appeared. Become more social, perhaps. See?" Dasha said, leaning back, "even in our daily troubles, we can strive to be happy."

He listened silently to Dasha's philosophizing, having noticed long ago that her presence had a dizzying, relaxing effect on him.

Upon returning home, the Professor found them sitting quietly on the couch. Seeing Sanya's eyes, red from tears, he was somewhat surprised.

Dasha greeted him and pulled Sanya by the arm, invit-ing him to her room, and he followed obediently. They left, leaving the Professor in utter confusion. He looked round and noticed a postcard on the floor bearing the image of the Motherland with a giant sword in her hand. He picked it up and read it.

Appearing in his room early in the morning, Sanya began to question the Professor about Smolensky Cemetery as if nothing had happened.

"Dasha doesn't know how to get there, she's not from around here," he explained.

"Why go to Smolensky?" the Professor asked in a testing voice. "You couldn't find anything else to draw? If that's the case, then go at least to the Nevsky Lavra, it has more interesting monuments."

"I'm not going there to create art. I'm going to carry out a request."

"Whose request?" the Professor kept repeating, his voice guarded for some reason, awaiting a response.

"My grandma's. Her relative is buried there."

The mere thought of the cemetery pierced Sanya with coldness as he recalled the noisy funerals in his home City N. Hundreds; perhaps thousands of departed had been carried past the orphanage windows on their last journey. But he would not show his weakness in front of Dasha, holding her hand firmly and following her as they switched from bus to bus.

"Who are you going to visit?" the girl asked suddenly, breaking the silence.

"Visit?" he asked in astonishment. Her question sounded as if they were going over to his classmates for tea and were still deciding whom to see first.

"It's not a visit, I'm going to carry out a request," he said seriously.

"Whose request?"

"My grandma Claudia's. Her son is buried here, and he was named Alexander, just like me."

"How did he end up here? Weren't you born in Siberia?" she asked in surprise.

"I'm the one who ended up in Siberia, but their home is here, in Piter," he said quietly. "Sometimes I walk through the streets and try to imagine where they lived, what they did," he opened up all of a sudden.

"Simona keeps calling you a 'temp.' You're the last

person, who should be called a 'temp,'" Dasha laughed.

"I don't care what she calls me."

Preoccupied with their conversation, they stepped onto the grounds of Smolensky Cemetery without noticing it and headed towards a low building that looked like an office. Taking his grandma's note, folded in four, out of his pocket, Sanya handed it to the worker. Wiping sweat repeatedly from his brow with a handkerchief, the latter opened and closed five thick, densely written notebooks, and said finally:

"Here, it looks like I've found him. Poor guy's been waiting for relatives for a while," the worker joked hopelessly, handing them a map to find the grave.

Steadying his breath with difficulty, he followed Dasha.

"I want to show you something as well. It's so good we came here! It's a miracle! A real miracle!" she exclaimed rapturously, stopping. "I dreamed of coming here for a long time. Do you know who is buried here? Xenia of Petersburg! She fulfills all your wishes, you just have to write a note and leave it in the chapel. Do you have a pen?" she asked with inspiration.

Sanya stared into her eyes just in case, to see if she was playing a joke on him.

"Do you really believe that someone who died over a hundred years ago can understand your problems and fulfill your wishes? It's absurd."

Paying no attention to his question, Dasha continued just as rapturously:

"See, she was a very wealthy, beautiful, and influential woman who was madly in love with her husband. But it happened so that he died. Unable to bear this tragedy, Xenia gave all her possessions to the poor and, putting on her husband's clothes, traveled the world as a beggar. It was then that she was visited by divine grace. She began to heal the sick and help people with their problems. Even after her death, many people come to ask her for help. You don't believe me?" Dasha asked offended all of a sudden. She had told her story with such faith and passion that for Sanya to reject it would have been like a slap in the face.

"It's not that I don't believe you," he said tactfully. "I've just never heard of this before."

He had assumed that Dasha was a little superstitious, but nonetheless an atheist, and yet here was a hidden religious soul – how else would one call this?

They entered the chapel. Dasha furrowed her brow, closed her eyes, and thought about something intently. She looked very touching at that moment, and Sanya stood there fidgeting and watching her every move lovingly. He caught himself thinking that he no longer felt fear and despair from being in such an impossible place. He had lived his life in fear of even thinking about a cemetery, and everything here turned out to be quiet and routine. There were crosses and monuments here, painted mostly blue, a symbol of the sky, with photographs of the departed when they were young and happy.

He found the place where his uncle Alexander was buried and stood in front of the leaning wooden monument with a tin star on it, feeling no emotion. There were no artificial flowers or photographs here, unlike the other monuments.

"Let's go," he said decisively after standing there a while. He took Dasha by the hand and they headed towards the exit. After they returned home, Dasha broke the silence and asked:

"Your uncle was only fourteen? How did it happen?"

"He fell ill and died," he said dryly.

In the evening, Sanya wrote to Grandma Claudia, in as much detail as possible, about his trip to locate the grave.

"So? Did you carry out your grandma's request?" the Professor inquired and immediately encountered Sanya's reluctance to discuss the topic.

"Have you ever been to the chapel of Xenia of Petersburg?" came the counter-question.

"I have," the Professor said calmly.

"You have?" Sanya asked suspiciously. "And?"

"And nothing," the Professor replied just as calmly. "Why, what do you mean?"

"Do you believe in this... stuff, like Dasha?"

"Do not mock others," the Professor said sternly.

Indeed, Sanya did not understand much at all. Back at home, Grandma Claudia prayed incessantly to some man on a cross, calling him God; she prayed daily, only he did not save Fedya. But here? Even a mind as enlightened as the Professor's had fallen under this dark influence. In a country where religion was forbidden? It was just like the situation with kielbasa – even if you couldn't buy any, people would always find a way to obtain some.

Grandma Claudia's response came surprisingly quickly. In her letter, she expressed outrage at the tin star on her son's grave, and also related some incredible news. After yet another petition, Vitek had received the permission to return to his home country and was due to pass through Moscow in several days. Claudia asked her grandson to go meet him and see him to the Warsaw-bound train. Sanya's heart fluttered at the mere thought of meeting his dear friend. He could still see him in the slanted barbershop on the riverbank, frozen in the barber's chair. At one point, he thought that nothing existed on earth besides City N, while now he thought that his home city was only a dream, a hallucination. And if it weren't for Grandma Claudia's letters, he would have even begun to doubt its existence. And now, suddenly, uncle Vitek was coming, and they could meet so easily.

Dasha had been planning to visit her parents in Volgograd during her time off, and Sanya suggested that she travel with him to Moscow, meet Vitek, and then board the train to Volgograd. She accepted Sanya's invitation with pleasure and began to prepare for the journey. The Professor, once again kept mostly in the dark, glanced at his protégé over his glasses, surprised at the change in the behavior of the latter.

"It's this extraordinary man," Sanya defined, overcome with joy at the impending meeting. "He... he's just a barber, but back in the day he became one of my closest friends."

The Professor took out a map of Moscow from somewhere, invited Sanya to sit down, and asked him to study the map carefully, sketching out his entire route in pencil.

"Your train arrives at this station. Then, you have to get here. After you meet, you'll have to go here," he explained, concentrating. "And why is he going to Warsaw?"

"He's going to see his homeland... it's a very long story," Sanya said, glowing with happiness for Vitek. "He used to live in that country, and he has wanted to return there very much, and now it can finally happen."

"Look carefully and remember," the Professor continued, as if reading a lecture. "Dasha departs from this station and then, to come back home, you have to go here."

"To come back home," Sanya repeated in his mind, thinking of Grandma Claudia, who would remain completely alone after Vitek's departure.

Remembering his old backpack, which had lain unused for almost four years, Sanya got it from the top of the wardrobe and brushed off the dust, deciding to take it with him on the two-day journey, completely forgetting what lay inside. And what lay inside was this: Alya's letters, his father's raincoat, and the watch he had completely forgotten about.

Sanya was about to show the watch to the Professor, but something stopped him. "The Professor is such an odd man. He is not a materialist and would probably not appreciate this," Sanya thought, hiding the watch in his pocket.

Reaching Moscow and arriving at the correct train station an hour before Vitek's train was due to arrive, Sanya sat waiting on the platform with his dear companion, Dasha. He still had trouble comprehending that he was about to meet Vitek, his friend from the past.

The train stopped with inordinate screeching, and joyous shouts could be heard all around. Sanya walked past several cars, peering into the faces of the disembarking passengers. The platform was emptying quickly; the conductors, having picked up their personal belongings, were heading to the city and locking up the train cars. Sanya was looking tensely from side to side, painting various scenarios in his imagination as to what could have happened, when suddenly... A large man walked out of practically the last car, looked round, and headed for the exit.

"Dasha, it's him," Sanya whispered, unable to move.

"Wave to him," she said and began doing just that without waiting for a response.

Vitek looked behind him, unsure as to whom she was waving, and, seeing no one there, waved back. Passing by them, he paused and exclaimed in surprise:

"Sanya! My dear friend, you came after all!"

The very next moment, they were locked in a firm embrace, not moving.

"And what about me? Why is no one hugging me?" Dasha said, interrupting the joyous reunion.

Moving away from Sanya and looking over the girl, Vitek gave her a warm hug as well.

Having some time to spare, they sat down in a train station cafe and ordered dumplings, sharing their thoughts and feelings and not embarrassed to express their joy at the meeting.

"Are you leaving for good, or just visiting?" Sanya inquired.

"I don't know it myself, my friend. We'll see how my homeland receives me. Claudia is all alone, too," he said quietly, taking a small gift she had given him out of the side pocket of his enormous suitcase.

The dumplings arrived, along with hot tea. Vitek questioned Sanya about everything to the last detail, having already been informed about many things by Claudia.

Dasha watched them silently and, seeing her beloved's sincere joy, could not stop admiring him as he expressed himself so openly, without fear, reassuring her that Sanya was not just a "quiet type" but a refined soul.

The friends shared laughs and sorrow as they recalled various moments from their past.

"Uncle Vitek, promise me you'll come to my first solo exhibition."

"I definitely will," he promised. "When will that happen, my friend?"

"I don't know yet. Sometime in the future, but will you come?"

Everything moved quickly in Sanya's conscience. He did not even want to think that he would never see Vitek again. Now, a new, completely alien dimension called Poland had appeared, about to swallow his close friend.

"It's not far, Sanya. Only a border away," Vitek reassured him, sensing his young friend's anxiety.

"It's time," Sanya said, taking the watch out of his pocket and handing it to Vitek.

"Yes. It's time," the latter replied, taking the watch from Sanya's hands and placing it on his palm.

"You've kept it after all," he said proudly and returned the watch to its owner.

Finding the right station according to the Professor's directions, Sanya and Dasha waited for Sanya's friend by the doors of the train. After dragging his suitcase inside the compartment, Vitek returned to the platform.

"Take good care of him, Dasha, don't hurt him. And you, Sanya, take good care of her as well," Vitek said warmly all of a sudden, and his words sounded like a blessing. Just as mothers and fathers bless their children as they leave for army service, as they fly far, far away from their homes, so did he bless them in parting amid the train station commotion, making it an unforgettable, significant moment.

The train had already vanished from view, and they were still standing on the platform holding hands, having become much closer and achieving a better understanding of each other. An ordinary barber from a distant past had returned unexpectedly to Sanya's life, giving him this incredible moment and linking him and Dasha forever. Making her someone he could trust absolutely while being himself. Three hours later, he saw Dasha off to Volgograd with the sensation that he had finally found the missing link of the chain and closed the circle. Dasha, having witnessed his emotions, had become a participant of his private life, closed to everyone else.

The Return

Returning to home, Sanya found the Professor deep in thought. He changed his clothes and placed the watch once again in his backpack, then tossed the backpack in its former place. For some reason, he felt silly using the watch in front of the Professor. His mentor's most expensive possessions were the stacks of his favorite books, most of them related to the subject he taught.

Thoughts of Grandma Claudia would not leave him. He never stopped thinking of her or missing her, but now, after seeing Vitek, these feelings intensified again. It had been many years now that he kept promising her he'd visit, but he could not manage to do so. After Vitek's departure, he received an express letter from her wherein she asked her grandson insistently to go to the proper office with a request to remove the absurd star from her son's grave.

Ready to carry out any request from her within a day, Sanya started preparing for another trip to Smolensky Cemetery. Inquiring where Sanya was headed, the Professor began to fuss around all of a sudden and, five minutes later, declared:

"Well, let's go then."

"Are you going to see that Saint Xenia or something?" Sanya asked, quite pleased, he would not be going alone.

"That's right, Xenia," the Professor said firmly.

They were sitting on opposite sides of the aisle in the half-empty streetcar, deep in thought and looking through the window at the houses, people, and trees flickering past. Every now and again, Sanya would turn his head and study the Professor's silhouette, contemplating the latter's very pleasant appearance. Even Simona, stingy on compliments, had once joked: "Oh Professor, if it weren't for your strange tendency towards loneliness, I would have proposed to you."

Creaking, the streetcar crawled slowly through the surprisingly quiet June day in the big city, plunging Sanya into memories of Fedya. He could not remember a single day that he didn't think about his brother. It had been almost six years since the day he last saw him. He had often heard various expressions about time, from others and from famous literature, to the effect that it healed all wounds. Only, for some reason, time did not have the requisite effect on him. How nice it would be to wake up someday without feeling, in his very core, that constant pain and fear for his brother.

The companions were silent as they walked up to the cemetery gates and entered the grounds. The Professor stopped suddenly. It looked like he didn't know which way to go.

"I know where she is buried and can show you, just wait a bit while I visit the office."

"I need to visit the office as well," the Professor said without much emotion, following Sanya into the small yellow building.

"Do you remember me?" Sanya asked reluctantly of the familiar worker, glancing sidelong at the Professor, who was standing next to him.

"What, you need to find someone else?" the man said, ready to pick up numerous notebooks from the shelf at any moment and locate the right name.

"No, thank you, I'm not looking for anyone. I wanted to ask if you have a saw."

The man stepped back and shook his head, unsure of what was being requested of him.

"I understand notebooks, but a saw? That's not my department," he grumbled, pulling a handkerchief out of his pocket.

The Professor, standing next to Sanya, also took a step back and looked at him in confusion.

"Don't worry," Sanya tried to explain, suddenly realizing the full absurdity of the situation. "I just need to saw something off really quickly."

"Saw something off? Here? Do you realize this cemetery has long been declared an architectural monument?" the worker said indignantly. "As if anyone can come in and start sawing things. Do you know that, even during the war, during the blockade, the people here did not dare take a single piece of wood from the cemetery to warm themselves? If they had, we wouldn't have any idea where anyone is buried. And here you come with your saw."

The room was so stuffy it was hard to breathe. Upset at the rude visitor, the worker walked over to the tightly sealed window and tried to open it. The Professor covered his face with the palm of his hand, and Sanya thought he saw an awkward smile.

"You see, my grandmother is very upset. There is a star on the grave of her son, Alexander Voronov, and he was never even in the Komsomol," Sanya said finally, handing the worker a letter folded in four.

The door banged, and Sanya turned to find the Professor gone. He regretted not going alone, given how awkward everything had turned out. He found the Professor in an alley, sitting on a bench and clutching his downcast head in his hands. Sanya became even more upset.

"Please forgive me," he said, hurrying towards the Professor. "I made arrangements and they promised to help me, no need to saw anything off."

The Professor continued to sit motionlessly, disorienting Sanya even further.

"You keep mentioning your grandma," the Professor said suddenly. "And what of your grandpa... what happened to him? What was his name?"

"Grandpa Clement, he fell ill and died... Let me show you to the chapel."

Hearing the response, the Professor got up abruptly and began to walk away with the words: "Wait here for me." Sanya sat waiting, not knowing how to explain his friend's behavior and thinking up various reasons. When the latter returned, his somewhat puffy eyes were shining with joy. "He must have prayed to that Xenia," Sanya thought. "What do I know; it seems she really helped him." Walking up to Sanya, the Professor hugged him harder than ever, even scaring him a little.

"Follow me," he ordered, and an hour later they were standing in a long line at the train station.

"Are you going somewhere?" Sanya asked in confusion.

"Yes, Alexander, we are going somewhere," the Professor said in a serious, official tone. "We are going to Siberia. I have always dreamed of going there and now... At last, this is possible. Two tickets to City N, please, for today," the Professor spoke decisively, stunning Sanya completely with his answer. The purchase of the tickets was followed by the purchase of a real travel suitcase for Sanya, leaving his backpacking life behind once and for all atop the Professor's wardrobe, with all its contents from the past. Then speedy preparations came, which left no time for talk or explanations. All his earlier plans were crumbling, although Sanya did not regret it. The only important consideration at that moment was Grandma Claudia, who had no idea of the impending surprise. They did not have time to send her word they were coming, and it was only on the train, sitting in the two-person compartment, that Sanya truly realized how insanely happy he was, and that, were it not for the Professor's crazy decision to see Siberia, it would probably have taken Sanya several more years to plan a trip there.

They spent the first half of the journey discussing the Renaissance, carefully dissecting all of the famous artists of the period. They spoke of changing forms in indigenous art, and of course about such innovators as Kandinsky and Malevich, who contributed to these changes.

"Art is completely driven by love, only a feeling of love is capable of giving birth to beautiful forms," the Professor spoke confidently.

"And what of the forms in art that leave one shuddering, are they inspired by love as well?"

"Imagine, yes! As he creates these forms, the artist suffers immensely, and he shares them with his audience, cautioning it against these things, because he is driven by love. The same tendencies are found in literature. True literature is only born when the author is driven by love: for life, for people, for his heroes. There are numerous forms of love and they all lead to the same result."

"So this means that, whenever I start a new piece, I should ask myself: 'Am I driven by love?'" Sanya asked, trying to fully understand what the Professor was saying.

"Please understand that, if you start a piece with this question or seek a confirmation of your feelings, it means it's all over. It means that the brush strokes placed on the canvas or the words written on the page are meaningless and empty. You experience that unimaginable feeling of sharing long before your hand touches the brush. You simply cannot help doing it, and if it happens, then you are driven by love, and your creation will definitely be seen and heard."

Contained in the narrow space of the train car, mixing up days and nights, discovering one another anew through their conversations, interspersed with long pauses, they did not even notice how, on Sunday, they reached City N. Shaving and dressing elegantly, as if preparing for an important exam, the Professor walked out on the platform first, put down his suitcase, and froze, gazing at the plain concrete building of the train station and the passengers strolling around as they waited.

"It's not Piter, of course, but there are more interesting places to be seen here," Sanya said, fighting a wave of excitement.

Soon they were walking on the wooden sidewalks towards Third Proletarian, like two extraterrestrials, their clothing and behavior attracting the attention of passersby, leaving questioning expressions on people's faces. And when he was already near the house and feeling his own heart beating, Sanya forgot completely about the Professor, who was somewhere nearby, and dashed towards the wooden gates leading to the yard. He pulled impatiently on the rope, opening the gates, ran up onto the porch, and stopped before the locked door. Turning around, he saw his friend standing motionlessly in the open gates and watching him with interest.

"We should wait here, Grandma probably went to church," Sanya said, sitting down on the porch.

"Take me to the church," the Professor asked insistently, dragging both his and Sanya's abandoned suitcase into the yard in a businesslike fashion. Frankly speaking, Sanya did not want to wait either; he wanted to hug Grandma Claudia as soon as possible, sit down over tea, and tell her about the years spent apart.

The open gates of the small wooden church, painted a tender blue color, gave a warm welcome to the two visitors, who had seemingly appeared out of nowhere. Entering the cool of the well-kept church courtyard, they both sat down on a bench, as if on cue, to catch their breath, not sure of what to do further.

"I… I'm going to go in, I must go in…" the Professor announced decisively, heading for the church door. The scent of frankincense, peace, and grace blanketed his lonely soul once again, as in childhood. He wanted to see the elderly woman that he had journeyed so far to see as soon as possible. Walking further into the church, he leaned against a column and looked at the numerous praying people. Peering into their faces, he tried to sense something very important to him, fighting insane excitement. When all the people around him fell to their knees, he remained standing, not knowing the rites of prayer and thereby attracting the attention of others. The service ended, but the congregation was in no hurry to leave the building, discussing the strange visitor.

"Must be some party worker blown our way again, to see what we do here," they commented. While the interest concerning the Professor spread among the congregation, he was overcome with a conflagration of emotion. Approaching the icon of the Madonna, he got on his knees suddenly and began to pray, further confusing the faithful. Clustering in groups, they whispered to each other, trying not to miss such an incredible event: a praying party worker wearing foreign clothes.

The unsuspecting Professor, believing that he was in a sacred place where anyone could pray without embarrassment, got up from his knees and suddenly found himself the central focus of attention, like on a movie set. He looked in surprise at the people crowding around him, while they were scrutinizing him from head to toe.

"Are you here with an inspection, Comrade, or what?" someone asked.

"Forgive me, what inspection?" the Professor said, confused.

"Someone came once, just like you, all elegant. They nearly closed the church after he left," said someone's concerned voice.

"Only that one admitted right away why he was here, while here you are pretending to be a believer, as if we can't tell you from our own."

Appearing in the doors, Sanya looked from side to side in search of Grandma Claudia. Seeing his friend surrounded by the crowd and drawing nearer, Sanya heard him whisper:

"Alexander, they took me for some sort of party worker. Save me before they give me a beating!"

"This is Grigoriy Petrovich, my friend," Sanya said, trying to dispel concern. "He's no party worker, he's a real professor."

An incredible rumble ensued. The word "professor" was

even more powerful. Here, in this town, they had never met anyone who could claim to be a real professor.

"You're not lying, kid? Is he, seriously, a real professor?"

"One hundred percent real, from Leningrad," Sanya said proudly, glancing at the embarrassed Grigoriy Petrovich.

"And who might you be?"

"You mean you didn't recognize me? I'm Sanya, Alexander Vetkin."

Rapturous voices repeated the same things from all directions: "How you've grown! How you've changed! How handsome you've become! Claudia!" someone shouted. "Your grandson is here! He finally came!"

Grigoriy Petrovich was happy that attention had finally switched to Sanya and waited impatiently for the woman walking towards them through the parting crowd. But his happiness was short-lived. People lined up to meet him and make acquaintance. When would they get another opportunity to shake a real professor's hand?

"You came, my darling!" Claudia whispered, dashing towards Sanya, who could barely restrain tears of joy.

"This is that same Grigoriy Petrovich that I wrote so much about," he said, pointing at the group of church members taking turns greeting the Professor.

Grandma Claudia had not changed much, and despite her advanced age, remained young in spirit, independent, and self-sufficient. When the three of them were finally left alone, a shaken and embarrassed Grigoriy Petrovich bowed his head and introduced himself.

"Claudia Voronova," she said, shaking his hand warmly.

That day the church members went home with the

incredible news that they had witnessed such an unforget-table reunion and, once in their lives, seen a real professor.

Entering his home, Sanya first went to the room that used to belong to him and Fedya, where everything had remained the same. Sitting on the edge of the bed, he tilted his head back and kept shutting and opening his eyes, not believing that he was really here.

He heard Claudia fussing around in the kitchen, while Grigoriy Petrovich entered and froze in front of a heavy picture frame with numerous photographs hanging above the dinner table. He gazed at the familiar faces as if re-calling a forgotten dream. Unable to handle the flood of memories, he hurried outside and sat on the porch in an effort to calm down.

Noise came from behind the fence.

"Hey, buddy, got a cigarette?" a hoarse voice said.

"I... I don't smoke," Grigoriy Petrovich said perplexedly and got up, trying to look over the fence.

"Don't move!" came the response. "Stay where you are. This is a secret, if my wife sees us, she'll kill me."

Grigoriy Petrovich leaned closer to a hole in the fence and saw the face of his neighbor, who was lying on the ground surrounded by young potato tubers.

"My wife's a beast. Won't let me smoke, or drink."

A window flung open just then, revealing Grusha, who summoned him back home for dinner in a commander's voice.

"By God, I was better off in prison," the neighbor whined, rising from the ground. "I wonder what I could pull off to go back there. Hey, buddy," he said pleadingly as he walked away, "buy me a pack of cigarettes tomorrow and toss it over the fence."

Claudia walked out on the porch, heading to the nearby

shed with an aluminum bucket in her hand. Taking the bucket from her, Grigoriy Petrovich hurried after her and, putting on the large mitten lying on a pile of black coal, he began to load the coal into the bucket.

"Thank you for Alexander, for helping him. How long will you be staying?" she said.

"I don't know," he said in embarrassment.

"You don't know? Does this mean you'll stay in my house?"

"We'll stay, we'll definitely stay," he muttered in response, and, picking up the heavy bucket of coal, walked first out of the shed.

Fish cake, compote, and fresh green salad appeared on the table. No longer shy in Grigoriy Petrovich's presence, Sanya told Grandma Claudia about their life in Leningrad, about Dasha, about his studies, and about anything else he could remember at that moment. Grigoriy Petrovich listened to him with detachment, immersed in his own thoughts and not daring to begin the conversation about that most important thing that had haunted him for many years.

"Will you tell us about yourself?" Claudia turned to him all of a sudden.

"I don't even know where to begin," Grigoriy Petrovich said, at a loss.

Sanya fell silent immediately. The usually quiet man's newfound willingness to speak seemed strange to him.

"Do you have relatives, a family?" Sanya's grandma continued.

"Yes, I have a family, although I did not know it for a long time," he replied, tilting his head with interest and gazing at Claudia's face with a concealed sort of smile as she sat across from him. He wanted to get on his knees before her, as if in confession, and impart to her his terrible secret, freeing himself forever.

"I was born on Vasilevsky Island," he continued quietly.

"On Vasilevsky," she echoed him, also quietly. "It sounds so familiar."

"We lived there, the four of us: me, my parents, and... my younger sister, Anna."

Opening wide his eyes, Sanya listened and thought about the deep influence of Siberia, which had changed even this previously taciturn man. Leaning back, Claudia gave a start, studying her guest intently.

"I... I remember the last Christmas evening," Grigoriy Petrovich continued. "My sister, how happy she was – she got a violin as a gift." Rising, Claudia retreated to her room, lit the icon lamp, and got down on her knees before it.

Twilight approached, and Sanya went into the garden to close the window shutters for the night. Walking back, he saw, in an overgrown corner of the garden, the very same ball that Fedya had tossed. Or rather, all that was left of it. Deflated, cracked from the frost, lying here all this time. "Even this inanimate ball is still here, and Fedya is not," he thought sadly.

"Tomorrow, I will show you the city," Sanya said promisingly, finding Grigoriy Petrovich sitting motion-lessly in the same spot.

Grandma Claudia returned to the living room. Sitting across from the visitor and not taking her eyes off him, she asked suddenly:

"And you? What did you get for that Christmas?"

"And I... I got a pocket watch."

And if words could describe the true state of blessing, it was precisely what descended that moment on Grandma

Claudia's wounded soul. She sat there, clutching her own shoulders with her hands, and her face lit up suddenly with incredible surprise. Her eyes gazed at Grigoriy Petrovich with remarkable happiness and bewilderment as he sat across from her, and his face also changed abruptly. The next moment, their hands met, and tears began to pour down their cheeks. Everything happened in a fraction of a second. It happened simply and piercingly. Trying to comprehend and accept what had taken place in his presence, Sanya realized suddenly that hundreds of brilliant canvases and talented books describing human emotion could not relay even a small part of what had happened in that narrow room, in a plain wooden house on Third Proletarian Street, in the insignificant City N.

Epilogue

In the spring of 1986, after yet another petition, Anna Clementievna Vetkina was permitted to leave the Restricted Access Regional Psychiatric Hospital, where she had spent nine years. She was met by Claudia along with two Alexanders: brother and son.

In the fall of 1992, soon after the fall of the Soviet Union, Clement Voronov was acquitted and posthumously rehabilitated. The family, now living in St. Petersburg, received an official letter revealing the place of his burial.

A year later, the first solo exhibit of the work of Sanya – Alexander Vetkin – dedicated to his brother Fyodor, opened with great success in the exhibition hall of the House of Artists in St. Petersburg. Many of the great and powerful took note of him and extended their condescension to congratulate the new genius. The exhibition was followed by numerous offers, including trips abroad, which he categorically refused.

In a short time, Sanya and his wife Dasha traveled to many large and small cities and settlements in Russia, presenting his original and unique art to the people.

His artistic colleagues teased him, saying that he was squandering his talent on trifles when he could be making a great career for himself. They said that he was casting pearls before swine. Yes, the Biblical books opened with the collapse of the regime, allowing the people to include their many meaningful expressions in the lexicon.

But Sanya, he thought otherwise. He thought that the heart of the great nation that nursed him lived in its people. And that the understanding of important subjects lived in them as well. And also the everyday relationships called love.

During each exhibition, he greeted the visitors personally at the door, looking closely into their faces. Then, pacing through the halls unhurriedly, he watched their reactions, especially if any young people stopped to see his early drawings.

In the drawings, nothing had changed. In the drawings, City N was still swept over with snow, and somewhere at the end of his home street, Third Proletarian, a youth ran, hurrying towards warmth and comfort. He was holding on to his hat with earflaps with one hand, hiding the other hand under his arm to stay warm. He ran, stepping awkwardly in tall *valenki* up to his knees. The lower button of his bluish gray coat was torn off. The scarf, almost slipping off his neck, fluttered behind his back, now rising, now falling low to the ground, brushing the clean white snow.